A SEA OF BUTTERFLIES

John M. Hooks

ISBN: 9781521063019
Cover design by: Art Painter
Library of Congress Control Number: 2018675309
Printed in the United States of America

For M'Day and Bud, who gave me life, and kept me safe.

For my family's veterans: Beena, Junior, Luke, Odis, Charles, and Marshall; all who died on the trash heap of victory.

For Black women everywhere, the true source of our strength

A SEA OF BUTTERFLIES

John M. Hooks

"WERE YOU THERE WHEN THEY CRUCIFIED MY LORD?"

-OLD NEGRO SPIRITUAL-

CHAPTER ONE

*T*HE TRIP TO PITTSBURGH HAD STARTED the night before just after midnight when the telephone rang. Dean had answered the phone angrily, thinking it was a wrong number. The voice on the other end was soft and apologetic.

"I'm sorry for calling so late, but I think you might be a relative of a Charlie Campbell. I apologize if I've made a mistake." It was a male voice, and he paused, as if waiting for a response.

The voice was almost soothing Dean thought as he struggled awake, sighing deeply.

"Just a minute." Shaking Nell roughly, he handed her the phone.

"Honey, honey, somebody calling about Charlie Campbell. Could be about your Uncle Charlie. Honey! Here, take the phone." Nell stirred, exhaling deeply.

"Damn. At this time of night, what time is it anyway?" Dean didn't respond, but lay the phone on the pillow next to her head as he slid from the bed. She sat up, her heart and breathing reacting to Dean's words. His feet padded softly across the hardwood floor toward the bathroom down the hall. She glanced at the clock next to the bed, hesitating before picking up the phone. She felt tense. A call in the middle of the night was probably bad news.

"Aw fuck, not again," she thought about the soiled letter she had received from her Uncle Charlie several months ago. It had stirred old, long forgotten memories of him. The return address printed on the envelope was from a homeless shelter in Pittsburgh, and the writing had the unmistakable trait of someone struggling to control the pencil. Nell's heart sank when she sensed that Uncle Charlie, more than being homeless, was possibly on the alcohol again, and emotionally unstable. His printing of her address covered the entire front of the envelope. The words were shakily drawn, and of different sizes. And as always, he simply asked for money, promising he would pay her back once he got back on his feet. That evening at dinner, she shared the note with Dean, who remembered her Uncle Charlie well. When they were children, Dean had believed, for a long while, that Charlie was Nell's older brother.

"We should take a weekend soon and check on him, Nell. He probably needs your help again," Dean said in response to reading Charlie's letter. "I'll wire him some money tomorrow," he said returning the letter to her. She remembered the silence that had settled in the house the remainder of that evening.

"You will tell Mae about the letter tomorrow, won't you," Dean finally said after dinner.

Nell shared the news by phone the next day with Mae, her mother who received the news with resigned acceptance.

"He's probably doing the best he can...I guess! I'm sure Bella's probably left him," Mae said softly. "You know she was really the real anchor for him. Just knew something was wrong though. I just felt it...Charlie never did write, but he would send a card every now and then. He even stopped sending Christmas cards a coupl'a years ago. I guess he just lost touch. Every now and then I would write him at his old address. He never wrote back, and, my last two letters came back last year marked with 'No Forwarding Address."

Nell remembered how she sensed her mother's tension that day as they talked. Mae sighed deeply several times throughout the conversation, and Nell visualized her, then in her late eighties, sitting in her old chair rubbing her hand over her face -- as is still her custom when she is distressed. Charlie had been close to Mae, closer than he was to her husband, his brother Grady. Around Grady, he was quiet and withdrawn, as if he believed his older brother was judging him. With Mae, he was different. Their quiet conversations would cease whenever she or Grady came into the room. To Nell it was like Charlie replaced the son, Mae had lost soon after birth. It was obvious, even to a young Nell, they had developed a special bond over the years, and throughout the time Charlie moved in with her family.

He also related well to Nell, when she was younger.

Nell thought fleetingly of the last time she had seen Uncle Charlie. It was the day they buried her father. It was over thirteen years ago, but she remembered the day clearly. Uncle Charlie was hurried and, except for a brief moment, he was more of a shadow that day than anything else. His bus was delayed leaving Pittsburgh, and he was late to the service. He hurriedly elbowed his way through the small group of mourners to slide a hand softly unto Mae's shoulder. She turned at his touch.

"Charlie," his name escaped as she looked up, and they both smiled quietly at each other. His other arm embraced Nell standing close by. His hands felt hard and calloused, she thought. He looked strained and tired. There was a hunch to his shoulders, and the dark bags under his bloodshot eyes dominated his face.

"Uncle Charlie," Nell embraced him briefly.

"Charlie...I'm so glad you're here. I wasn't sure you even got the telegram," Mae said as she held his hand.

"You know I'd be here, caught the first bus after leaving work this morning. I can't stay long, but I had to come see Grady. He's the only brother I got." He looked beyond her at the casket sitting at the front of the sanctuary, before continuing.

"I was so shocked to hear about the stroke comin' on just like that. He was always the healthiest one in the family."

"At least he didn't suffer Charlie."

"How'd it happen?"

"Oh Charlie! Grady'd been complaining about headaches most last week...even went to bed early that day. I found him when I went up to bed that night." Her voice broke as she shuddered at the thought, she sat down in the pew, sobbing and wiping at her eyes.

Feeling the need to comfort her, he squeezed her shoulder warmly.

"It'll be all right Mae," he whispered. Nell instinctively sat next to her mother, drawing her close rocking her gently in her arms.

"We'll be alright mother, God knows best," Nell said softly to her mother, watching her Uncle Charlie curiously as he leaned over and embraced her mother again. The strong odor of mouthwash on his breath washed over her face as he spoke.

"Excuse me," he whispered moving away from them toward the casket. Nell thought he seemed to be nervous as if affected by the contact with them again. She wondered if he felt it too. There was nothing more he could do here with them. He had come to honor his brother. It was time to do that, she thought, he 'll leave before there could be more discussion about how, or what he has been doing.

"Where's Bella?" Mae asked behind him. He turned and smiled briefly, but didn't answer. He continued on down the aisle to acknowledge Dean who was standing off to the front of the church. They didn't speak, but shook hands. Dean followed him to the casket. They stood silently together for a long time, each caught up in separate, but reverent thoughts.

Nell watched as Uncle Charlie, standing by the casket stroked her father's folded hands. She was keenly aware of her uncle's presence, appraising him across the rows of the church. Even in grief, her mind noted the qualities that gave hints of his past life. He stood rigid like a toy soldier. Hair cut close to his skull, he was clean-shaven. His black shoes, though scuffed, were highly polished and reflected the light. He was dressed in a stylish blue serge suit, but the metallic odor of the steel mills in his perspiration mingled with the cologne he was wearing. The mixture of the odors hovered loosely around him. She looked away when he sobbed briefly glancing up at the ceiling. With a clean, neatly folded white handkerchief he dabbed lightly at the tears forming in his eyes, and the perspiration on his forehead.

Whatever happened to him rattled in her mind? We were once so close. At least he looks healthy again. Daddy would be happy about that I'm sure, she thought. She appraised him again, before he glanced her way. She looked down avoiding eye contact, but she was pleased to see the confidence and strength he carried within himself. It was unmistakable. She had felt it in his embrace, and she watched him again as he sniffled softly, walking back up the isle to where she and Mae sat. He bent down momentarily taking Mae's hand.

"I have to go Mae, I'm sorry...I wish I could stay longer, but I got to get back for the midnight shift."

"I know Charlie. Thank you so much for coming. You

look real good Charlie. Pittsburgh was a good move for you. I'm sure Grady would be pleased."

"Thank you Mae, for everything you did over the years. Remember, you need anything... anything at all, let me know. I'll be there for you and for Nell too. Grady taught me about the importance of family more than anything. I love y'all. I only wish I could have been here for Grady, if I had only known." Nell responded to his words by breathing deeply, and looking away, afraid the doubt she felt for his words might show on her face.

When he turned toward her, she looked down at the floor continuing to avoid his eyes. He rubbed the back of her shoulder lightly before he turned and continued down the aisle toward the door. She didn't look up again until Dean returned to his seat; by then Charlie had passed back, through their collective grief back into the sunshine. He was gone without ceremony. Dressed in his dark suit, he reminded Nell of her father. They had the same walk, the same piercing black eyes, and they stood the same way leaning forward when they talked.

"Charlie looks good," Mae said into the silence, just before the preacher took the podium.

"Praise God," he said loudly. "Let us celebrate the home-going of Brother Grady Campbell." Those were really the last words, and images Nell remembered from her father's funeral. She was affected by the words of the preacher, and the music. She cried, and was overcome with emotion, but the service remained a blur and buried in her memory until Dean offered her the telephone.

ON EDGE NOW, Nell considered what type of news waited at the other end of the phone. Before answering, her thoughts shifted to the last time Charlie and her father were together. She had watched them walking off the back porch of the tenement house, where they lived. For the first time in years it seemed Uncle Charlie was a different person. He wore fresh clothes Mae had washed, starched and ironed for him the night before. In his right hand, he carried a small leather valise. It was scarred, and torn from too much use. In his left hand, held slightly away from his side, he carried a large Alga syrup bucket. The bucket held some of Mae's fried chicken and half a loaf of day-old sliced bread. The odor of the food hung to the outside of the bucket, and one or two flies landed on the lid when Charlie stopped momentarily to say good-bye to Dean who was waiting for Nell in the backyard.

Charlie and Grady walked through the yard, past the open gate and slowly down the alley in the direction of the downtown Greyhound bus station, when the back door creaked open on its rusty hinges. It slammed shut when Mae rushed out on the porch followed by Nell. Mae smelled like fried chicken and she fanned a dishrag at several flies attempting to investigate the smell.

"Goin' to Pittsburgh...Uncle Charlie's going to Pittsburgh," she said softly shaking her head as in disbelief. "He's going to get a job and a new start there in the steel mills." She paused, flicking the rag more furiously at the flies.

"Bella's supposed to be going with him," she continued. "Charlie say they gon'a get married...I just pray they takes the Good Lord with them." Squinting her eyes against the setting sun, she looked lovingly at the receding figure of her husband of the last twenty years and his younger brother. They were fading into the distance. She smiled broadly when she noticed the thin figure of a young woman, also in the distance pacing about near the back fence of Mrs. Meade's house. An old suitcase sat on the ground near her as she waited impatiently for Charlie, and Grady.

"This will be good for Bella too," Mae said as to herself.

Nell pushed past her mother and bounded from the porch laughing, following them briefly down the alley. In one hand she held the small Kodak Brownie camera Charlie had bought for her last year from the second-hand store. The camera still worked, and she yelled at Charlie and Grady. When they turned around she encouraged them to stand still while she snapped several pictures. After which, giggling loudly, she runs back to the yard, excitedly gives the camera to Mae and throws a clump of hard dirt at Dean. Excited, she backs away from him toward the gate, giggling and squealing when he playfully threw it back at her.

Mae watching, suspected Nell was shyly attracted to the young man, and determined it was time to have a serious talk with her. Dean grabbed Nell before she could get another clump of dirt, and, although she was tall and gangly for her age, he held her firm blowing wet air bubbles into her cheek. She giggled frightfully and Mae could smell the Juicy Fruit gum she was chewing when she opened her mouth. Some of her braids were coming loose, and her long skinny black legs kicked in the wind trying to get away from him. She screamed for her mother who simply said, "Stop y'all! Wave good-bye to Uncle Charlie now! They're almost at Mrs. Meade's house."

Nell quit squirming as Dean released her. They stood watching the back of Charlie as he followed his brother. When the two of them moved slowly past the back fence surrounding Mrs. Meade's house and backyard, Bella Collins joined them. A warm smile crossed her face, and looking back she waved excitedly at Nell, Dean, and Mae before taking Charlie's arm. Mae waved the dishrag back at her.

"May the Lord bless and keep them," she said to the children. But they had returned to their play, lost in each other. They didn't hear a word she had said. Charlie's gone, she thought looking back one last time before she momentarily took the handle of the screen door. She watched as they finally disappeared from sight across the vacant lot on the other side of the fence lines. Charlie had looked back briefly, but he didn't wave. Mae wondered if his thoughts were crowded with the presence of Bella and the promise of finding a new life in Pittsburgh.

NELL MANAGED A CAUTIOUS HELLO into the phone, and the voice quickly refocused her thoughts of Uncle Charlie. The voice told Nell his name, and said he worked for the VA hospital in Pittsburgh. He had been the counselor for a man named Charlie Campbell who had recently entered the hospital, and he was calling-- hoping to get in touch with a relative of Charlie.

"Charlie told me several times he had a niece by the name of Nell Campbell who lived in the Detroit area. He always spoke highly of her...said she worked as a photographer for a news service. I couldn't find an address or phone number in his file, but I did find your address on a letter you sent him awhile back at the homeless shelter where he lived."

Nell's heart stopped as she listened to him. She held her breath. She remembered the letter. She had sent it right after Charlie had sent the note asking for money. Dean had also sent him some money in a separate letter, and with some misgivings about not telling Dean, she also sent a note inviting Charlie to come and stay with them for a while. She was quietly relieved when he never responded to her letter.

"That's what led me to you," he said tentatively.

A silence settled on the phone. He anticipated Nell's response. But she remained silent; barely breathing, she knew the voice was speaking about *her Uncle Charlie*. She dreaded the thought of Charlie coming into her life again. If he's in trouble again, I don't know if we can handle him again, she thought, especially Mae.

"If I have the wrong number..." His apologetic voice sounded as if he was about to end the conversation. It irritated her.

"No, no, please don't apologize," she exhaled loudly. "You have the right number. I'm Nell Campbell. You're probably talking about my Uncle Charlie."

"I'm so happy to have found you Ms. Campbell," he sighed. "Charlie said he had no family when he first came to the hospital, always joked about a full bottle or a stiff shot was the only family he needed. He never even talked about Detroit...talked mostly about a place called Eden. Never will forget the way he talked about that place. Kind 'a made it sound like a combination of the Garden of Eden, and Hell...someplace right out of the Bible, here on earth."

"It's OK," she cut him off, hoping he did not hear the exasperation in her voice.

"How can I help you, what's going on with Uncle Charlie. Is he drinking again, how's he doing?"

"I'm sorry to have to tell you like this--over the phone," the voice said solemnly, "but your Uncle Charlie, he died last week--throat cancer and alcoholism. "

Nell's heart sank as the words; 'he died' resonated in her mind. They were hard to accept. She suspected when she received his last letter things were not going well for him. The shock of the news forced her to sit up on the side of the bed. She was fully awake now, her heart beating again in her throat. Dean sensing her discomfort sat next to her on the bed. His eyes searched her face questioningly. The voice paused momentarily before continuing.

"I was supposed to be his counselor, but he was extremely focused those last days. Sometimes I think he helped me more than I did him. Even with the drinking there was an unexplained balance in his outlook on life. But that's not why I'm calling. I'm calling; because, they--the hospital will dispose of his body this coming Wednesday. If his body is not claimed by the family no later than tomorrow evening, the Veteran's Administration will bury him in one of the government cemeteries for veterans," he hesitated. "It would be an honorable service, but that's not what Charlie wanted. Before he passed, he made me promise to find someone in his family." He hesitated again, letting the words sink into Nell's consciousness.

"Yes. Yes, of course he's got family," Nell protested! "We'll come tomorrow. We can bring his body back home. My Daddy, rest his soul, would want us to do that," She blurted into the phone.
Silence came from the other end of the line.

"No," she continued. "We want him here with his family!"

"I'm so glad because it's what Charlie wanted." The voice sounded relieved. He continued. "He knew he was dying, and after we took him off the alcohol, his mind was perfectly clear. He didn't have much, a few books and things, he left it all for you...made me swear on the Bible to find you and tell you what he wanted done with his body. Charlie was something else. He even made me write it down."

The words, 'done with his body' nagged at the recesses of Nell's mind, but she didn't say anything, or question the caller further. An uneasy silence settled over the phone again, as the voice hesitated, trying to remember if he needed to tell Nell anything else.

"Uncle Charlie's dead," Nell told Dean mournfully

during the silence. Her words pierced him through the chest. He caught his breath, and quickly said "oh no!" Putting his arm around her, he laid her head on his shoulder gently rubbing the back of her neck as she sat rigidly silent, glued to the phone. When the voice started to speak again it was with a heavy sigh of relief. He repeated his joy at having found Nell.

"You just don't know how glad I am to have found you." He said again. "I promised Charlie I wouldn't stop until I spoke directly to you about his last wishes. He said he wants his body cremated...said to scatter some of his ashes along the fence line at the old tenement house where the Morning Glories grow, and take the rest to Eden...put them in the red dirt and the creek down there where he was happiest." He paused. "Do you know what he was talking about?"

"No, I don't know anything about Eden, never heard of it. Did he say where it was?" Nell asked.

"Never did say...only said that he hoped the waters from the spring that feeds the creek would cleanse his soul, so he could meet the Lord. I'm not sure..."

"Cremation?" Nell interrupted him. Where he was happiest? What's he talking about?" Suddenly Nell's mind swirled with the request Charlie had fostered upon her. The questions continued to churn as she mulled the notion of his request. Mae was too old to go back south again, and she couldn't ask Dean.

"Shit!" She exhaled silently under her breath. How could he burden her that way? She fought the rising anger. It's true we were family, she thought, but she hadn't really been close to him since she was a youngster. "God! Why cremation," she questioned his motive.

She didn't say anything over the phone but cremation would be so final, she thought. It reduces a person to a container of ashes, capable of being accidentally spilled, maybe disappearing in a gusty windstorm, or simply being lost without ceremony. They, the family, and especially Mae, would be robbed of a chance to celebrate Charlie's humanity at a funeral, to put flowers, or a blanket on his gravesite over the years. We need to be able to do that, for Mae to be able to mourn properly she thought. She was uncomfortable about cremation, and even more so about taking his ashes to a place called Eden. She needed to talk to Dean and Mae about Uncle Charlie's request.

Nell collected the information, and assured the voice they would arrive in Pittsburgh the next day to claim Uncle Charlie's body.

"I'll leave a note for the hospital social worker that I finally got a hold of you," he said. "She'll get it first thing in the morning and will be expecting you at the hospital sometime tomorrow. You'll probably need his discharge papers or some proof you're related," the voice said before hanging up the phone.

NELL'S MIND FLASHED TO HILL, the bureau chief at her old wire service. To stay busy, since her retirement, she had taken an occasional assignment as a freelance photo-journalist. Hill, her old boss and longtime friend had retained her to do an upcoming photo-shoot and a story-line on the impact of crack cocaine on children, and grandchildren in the families of females addicted to crack cocaine. The shoot was scheduled to take place in New Orleans during the coming week.

Hill had arranged for her to interview and take photographs of the living conditions of young women who had used, or was still using crack in the area of the French Quarter. She was supposed to meet Hill for lunch before the end of the week to exchange ideas for the story line. She glanced at the open folder on her night-stand. It contained her notes on the assignment, collected articles on digital photography and a series of old photographic prints she had been studying for ideas about available light photography. Part of the file had been created when she first started working full-time at the wire service. After the assassination of Dr. King, she had ventured into the heart of the City, and shot a series of rare photographs using only available light. The urban centers around the country were filled with violence, and it was not wise to use flash photography in the midst of urban snipers, and the National Guard carrying live ammunition. While many of the more established photo-journalists refused to go into the inner city, Nell worked free-lance practically nonstop throughout the unrest. Assisted by Dean, who drove the car, she concentrated on human-interest stories inside the violence. Undaunted by the curfew and other restrictions, she interviewed the subjects and wrote graphic stories about the impact of the carnage, the fires, and the looting on their lives. Once her photographs and stories hit the local papers, the news services bought her photographs and stories immediately syndicating them across the country. After that, she was widely sought after, hired full-time by Hill, and the wire services continued to give her assignments dealing with the issues of race, drugs, civil rights, and urban conflict.

Pursuing these types of stories had become an obsession for her over the years. She thrived on them -- creating a reputation for being a sensitive, yet hard-nosed photo-journalist. She suspected it was the reason Hill had selected her for the shoot in New Orleans. When he had called last week, she had asked him...'why me, and why New Orleans?' Hill was always direct, his response was typical.

"This story, in particular, needs a woman's perspective, and I like the idea of doing it in a modern Sodom and Gomorrah, like place. The French Quarter is not the only place that qualifies, but right now, I don't have time to think of a better place. It's a gastronomic, sexual anything goes, nasty feeling pink cloud, dirty drinking and puking kind of place. Put a female spin on addiction, and family life in that kind of environment, and you got something special. It won't work as well anyplace else, and I think you're the best woman for this job. Don't give me such a hard time Nell! You want this job, or not? Just get it done. It pays your usual rate and expenses. Just do it Nell! I need to know by Wednesday," he growled.

Without answering, she laughed loudly into his ear, hanging up the phone. She was hooked, and he knew it. It sounded like the challenge she needed to arouse her creative and adventurous spirit again. Hell yes! Her mind swirled; she was excited. I want the job, she thought to herself. I'm tired of shooting commercial advertising photography in studios. Dean broke into her thoughts.

"What about your lunch with Hill tomorrow? Are you going to be able to do the assignment for him?"

"We have to go get Uncle Charlie first. Hill can wait! I probably wouldn't even know Hill if it hadn't been for Uncle Charlie. He gave me my first camera. You remember that old Kodak Brownie?"

She paused, but didn't hear Dean's response, as the weight of the phone conversation settled into her mind. Her eyes slowly filled with tears. "Uncle Charlie's dead," she said again in disbelief.

"How do you think Mae will take this?" Dean asked handing her a tissue.

"I don't know...not good, probably bad. We need to tell her in person. We'll tell her in person tomorrow," she emphasized curling up on the bed.

"You're right," he said getting back in the bed. "Think you'll be able to sleep?"

"I'll be OK," she sighed, slipping under the bed covers. Dean switched off the light and cuddled her in his arms. She stared into the darkness. Later that night, unable to sleep, Nell listened to the quiet breathing of her husband, and watched the passing car lights reflect off the ceiling. Her troubled mind sifted through the memories of her Uncle Charlie trying to make sense of his life as it interfaced with hers over the years.

She was three years old when Charlie first came to live with them. He was a teenager right out of the cotton fields of Alabama. She remembered her childish jealousy from the very start. Even as a child, she knew he and Mae were close, and she disliked having to share her mother. Mae had said often he was a big help with Nell during the early years. There were times when he was like a child himself, and played with her and her young friend Jacob in the back yard. It was a pleasant time, but over the years, there were times too when he was almost unapproachable.

Many nights after dinner he and Mae would sit in the large room by the heater talking quietly while sharing a pot of tea and lemon. Her father, Grady, rarely joined them, but always sat nearby reading the newspaper while listening to the radio. Nell remembered how she would seek the comfort of her mother's lap sometimes, or lie on the floor close as possible playing with her dolls trying to listen to their muffled conversation. Whenever Mae became aware of her interest she would send her off to bed.

Over time her most dominant memory was of Charlie sitting alone after dinner on the steps of the front stoop. Simply sitting there for what seemed like hours with his head in his hands staring into space. She would watch him cautiously from a distance. Mae always said to leave him alone at those times. Sometimes Grady would go out, closing the front door behind him, and the two of them would talk quietly into the late evening. Nell would watch them through the side window as they sat close, Grady gesturing pointedly as he talked to his brother. Sometimes the mood would change and their muffled laughter could be heard late into the evening.

Dean mumbled and turned in his sleep pulling the bed covers with him. Nell, still wide eyed, readjusted them to cover the chill on her back, and struggled to remember when Charlie was drafted into the army. Nothing about the event stood out for her, except for the small banner with the lone star Mae hung in the front window of the tenement house. There was also marked excitement in the house whenever she and Grady received one of his short letters from overseas.

When he was discharged from the army, and came home, the excitement in the tenement house was electric, and contagious as other men in the neighborhood also returned from the war. Other families continued with their celebrations, but it was not long before the mood in the tenement house changed.

Charlie had started smoking and drinking while in the service. It seemed most weekends he would sit alone on the stoop, a wine bottle between his legs drinking and muttering to himself. The drinking got progressively worse, and finally Grady, urged by Mae, approached him about his drinking.

It was a warm summer night, and Grady had sat on the back porch in the dark waiting up until Charlie came home. His voice startled Charlie as he stumbled up the back steps.

"Charlie! Look at you! What are you doin'! Why can't you just stay away from Joe's beer garden? You killin' yourself! Drinkin' like this all the time. Man, you cain't keep doin' this to yourself. I don't like it, Charlie...don't like this, what you doin' to yourself." Grady approached his younger brother, the concern showing on his face. He reached out to help him up the steps.

"Whatever is bothering you Charlie, drinkin' ain't gonna' help non!" The words were angry and cold. They broke through Charlie's warm feeling like a hand striking him in the face. He recoiled away from the intrusive voice, before reacting to the meaning of the words.

"What the' hell!" He backed away, while balancing himself against the porch railing. "Grady, what the hell you talkin' about! Just leave me alone." His words were slurred. Rolling his red eyes angrily at his brother, he said loudly "What the hell do you know? You never been hurt...did the things I did. I'd give anything to have a life like yours. Sure! I may drink too much sometimes, but drinkin' the only thing I got to give me some peace...and I don't care what you say, I ain't givin' it up!" He glared at his brother.

Grady did not back down. He was in Charlie's face now blocking his entrance into the house. His anger showed through the intensity of his words.

"I don't care Charlie if you drink yourself to death no more. I just want to help you...that all. But we just cain't have you drinkin' over Mae and Nell like this anymore! You got to stop...we cain't have this no more." Charlie turned away. His face stung from Grady's words about Nell and Mae. He stiffened up struggling with his remorse,

"Why? Did Mae say something...she think badly of me?" Suddenly there was a heavy silence between them. Grady was aware of his seething anger, and the concern he felt for his brother. While Charlie was aware of his awkward shame, consumed with what Mae and Nell had been thinking of him. Charlie sighed deeply breaking the tension between them.

"I don't want to hurt Mae and Nell. I'll try to do better, I promise," he finally whispered brushing past his brother into the house.

Grady suddenly tired from the tension he had been

carrying sat on the back steps wondering what he could do to get his brother to understand all he wanted was the best for him. Later he heard Charlie snoring loudly on the old couch in the big room by the heater when he returned to join Mae in the bedroom. She was still awake.

"Is Charlie all right? I'm really worried about him Grady," she said as she pulled the quilt back for him and moved over in the bed.

"No, he's not alright," he said, "the aftermath of war, I guess." He kissed her forehead. "Try to get some sleep."

Mae lay awake. She knew it was not just the war Charlie was dealing with. She remembered when he first came to live with them as a young boy. He had a recurring dream that left him crying aloud and viciously fighting with his bed covers in the middle of the night. It was at a time when Grady was working midnights. The episodes didn't last long, and he always managed to settle himself down, when she would awaken him. She never betrayed his condition to Grady. Not just the terror of war, she concluded, turning on her side to stare out the bedroom window.

Charlie and Grady never talked about his drinking again. Charlie did stop going to the beer garden, but he did not stop drinking. He only started hiding the alcohol. Daily, after work he would hide a half-pint of Four Roses whiskey in his pants pocket, and sneak it into the house. Most evenings, over Mae's objections,he would take his dinner to the stoop and eat alone. Later after Grady and Nell were in bed, Mae would awake Charlie from his drunken sleep. He always denied his drinking, sometimes even with a half empty bottle nearby. She would hide the empty bottles at the bottom of the trash. If the bottles were not empty, she would pour the contents into the toilet, flushing it with bleach afterwards to hide the smell of the alcohol.

Grady finally confronted her about covering for

Charlie, and eventually found a room for him in one of the neighborhood rooming houses when he continued to deny his drinking. Grady knew it had taken over his life, because his personality changed when he was drinking. He would get moody, loud, and disruptive whenever he was approached. Worst of all, Grady knew Nell was now afraid of him.

◆ ◆ ◆

EARLY THE NEXT MORNING BEFORE DAWN, Nell called Hill's voice mail, and then, as had been her habit since her father passed away, she called Mae. As she expected, Mae questioned the early time of the call

"Morning Nell. You're mighty early this morning. It's not even six o'clock yet! Everything alright?" The concern showed in her voice.

"Yes Mother. Everything is alright." She lied, hoping Mae did not notice the heaviness in her voice. "I'll be over later this morning...just wanted to make sure you would be home," she said before hanging up the phone. She knew, in order to claim Charlie's body, they would need some legal documents to prove they were related to him. She hoped they would find what they needed in a small footlocker he had stored with Mae when he came back from the war.

The sun was just starting to rise in the eastern sky when Nell and Dean pulled into Mae's driveway. The colors in the sky, slits of orange and purple-hued clouds were splashed against an awakening field of quiet blue. The scene was striking, Nell thought as she got out of the car. The dark clouds permeated with shafts of light seeming radiated up from the earth. Momentarily she wished she had a camera. The thought passed quickly though as she pulled the collar of the jacket closer around her neck. The smell and feel of winter was in the air, and she shivered briefly after stepping from the warmth of the car.

"Charlie's dead!" Her mother took the news of Charlie's death badly. "How could it be," she cried struggling to catch her breath. "No. Not Charlie!" Nell could feel her body react to the flood of Mae's emotions. She intuitively reached out drawing her mother to her. The sound of Mae's grief sent a chill through her, and she struggled to hold back her own tears. Dean sat silently at the dinning room table feeling helpless. He had seen this scene over the years before, and always preferred to keep his distance from grief.

"He's been on my mind a lot lately. Felt something was wrong, but I thought maybe Bella had left him. How'd you find out, Bella called you? Mae said moving away.

"No mother, someone called from the VA hospital in Pittsburgh."

"Poor Charlie. She probably did leave him! I heard your daddy movin' around in the house all night long, last night." She paused, releasing her pent-up breath before crying aloud again. Finally, after settling down she said over and over, "Charlie's gone. I just don't believe Charlie's gone." She spoke randomly, as talking to herself. A long silence followed before she asked in a more controlled manner, "I wonder. Will they ship his body home?"

"We'll take care of it Mother...we're on our way to Pittsburgh soon as we leave here," Nell said. "The counselor from the hospital said Charlie asked to be cremated Mother. I don't feel too good about that. You feel OK about that Mother?" Nell was surprised by her mother's response. Mae rebuffed her. A shadow crossed Mae's face, but with acceptance, she spoke softly.

"Lots of people getting cremated nowadays. I don't

think it's the right thing to do...but the Lord will help us Nell. We just have to pray about it," she said, wiping the tears away from her eyes.

THE OLD FOOTLOCKER seemed heavy for Mae, but she insisted only she could dig it out from the bottom of her closet. She wiped away the dust before bringing it to the dining room table. Inside, on top of his neatly folded Army uniform, they found his dog tags, and discharge papers; old check stubs, various collectible baseball cards, several fading old newspapers with headlines on the end of World War II, and a worn, and tattered Bible. As Nell picked it up, the pages parted exposing three old faded photographs. They were neatly placed on top of three yellowed letters. A brittle rubber band held them all together.

Curious, Nell sat down, putting the letters aside; she removed the photographs to examine them. They were old faded sepia prints.

In one photograph, a young boy, looking like Charlie stared out of the picture. He was probably twelve or thirteen years old. He stood rigidly straight dressed in coveralls too short for his lanky frame. His hair was like a bushy cap on his head and he was wearing scuffed work shoes without socks. A thin young girl with long, light-colored stringy hair had her arms wrapped lovingly around his waist. She had wide-set eyes, and a small pale face that grinned intently into the camera. The photograph showed them standing in front of a small wooden shack. It stood in the midst of what looked like a partially cleared cotton field. Off in the distance, standing high above the cotton stalks, amidst a series of smaller shacks stood a larger rickety cabin. Nell struggled to make out the fading sign over the door,
                    "*Sangster's School House,*
Nappy and me, Jan 12, 1934, Coon's Cove in Eden, was in-

scribed on the back of the photograph. In one of the other faded photographs, Nell could make out Charlie and the young girl with a group of other black children. There were eight in all, probably ranging in age from seven to eleven or twelve, she thought. Most had wooden smiles on their faces, and were standing in front of the school-house. Nell passed the photographs to Dean and to Mae, who looked intently at the group photograph. She concentrated on the last one passed to her. It was of the young girl with the stringy hair. She was looking very stern into the camera while holding the hand of a small toddler who stood close by. They were standing in front of one of the small shacks near the school. Mae's eyes scanned the back of the picture. The notation was also fading, but, with help from Dean, she finally made out the words:

"We miss you Nappy - Angel and Louise -1939"

It was crudely written on the back, and the inscription struck a chord of peaked interest in the room, and Nell instinctively knew they had intruded into a part of her Uncle Charlie's past life he had carefully guarded. Intrigued she took the rubber band off the letters and opened the first one. The remains of a small bouquet of dried flowers, crumbled in the seams fell out when she carefully opened the old drying paper. The letter was addressed to her Uncle Charlie at the old tenement house. Nell briefly remembered the mood changes Charlie had suffered right after he moved in with the family from the south. She briefly wondered if these letters had some impact on Charlie's behavior. She blocked the thought and opened the letter. It was a single page and the script, drawn with small block letters, spoke briefly of the closing of the schoolhouse in Eden.

Nell opened the other letters. They were all from Louise, written in the late summer of consecutive years just before Charlie was drafted into the war. The contents were similar except for the last one in which Louise expresses her longing, and her need for Charlie. She accepts he would not be coming back, but professes her love for him, and the baby, Angel. This letter, more than the others, stirred a sense of sorrow in Nell. In Louise's simple phrases she found the depth of her feelings for Charlie, and a sense of the future she, and the child faced without him.

Nell passed the letters to Mae who, without reading them passed them quickly on to Dean, who noticed on the back of the last envelope, among other faded scribbling, written in neat block letters the date of his discharge and the note:

"...When my death comes, please purify my body by fire --Not buried. And my ashes, scatter some in the
flower bed outside the tenement house where the morning glories grow...take the rest to the Cove...pray for my forgiveness and sprinkle my remains in the creek, and in the red dirt in Eden... Places I always wanted to be back at... in my mind."

Under the note he had placed, *September 22, 1945*, and signed his name, *"Charles Campbell."*

Nell read the note aloud. Mae took a deep breath, and momentarily turned away from them. her chest was still. Charlie's intentions settled around them like dust drifting through the shafts of sunlight in a still room. Mae and Dean each took turns reading the note silently. Mae had a stricken look on her face as she stared at the letter. With a sense of finality, she dropped it and the other letters back into the open footlocker before finally sitting down at the table. They seemed to float in slow motion -- settling in with the rest of Charlie's life traced on the documents and other things in the footlocker. After a prolonged period of awkward silence in the room, she reached over, extracting the photographs again. She examined them closely, slowly sifting them back and forth. Although Nell didn't say anything, she knew the note from Charlie had impacted her mother. She also knew and accepted, it would be wrong to bring his body home and intern it in the family plot at Elmwood Cemetery.

"He doesn't leave any doubt about what he wants," she said into the room looking at Mae who continued to sit silently at the table.

"No, not at all," Dean responded awkwardly. Mae remained detached from their conversation. But the tenement house and the flower garden are long gone, Nell mused. Perhaps, Eden is in Alabama; he mentioned the creek, and the Cove...Where the hell is the Cove? I'll have to think about it later. She sat down across from Mae who finally placed the photograph of the children at the school-house back in the Bible, but she continued to finger the photographs of Charlie and the young girl.

"Pictures faded really bad," she said. "But surely does look like Charlie," she said squinting her eyes. Her glasses sat on the bridge of her nose and they moved when she spoke. The behavior made her skin wrinkle around her eyes and down her nose. Mae, even in her nineties still had regal bearing. Her thinning white hair was always pulled back into a respectable bun behind her neck. She now walked with a slight stoop, and used a cane for balance, but was fiercely independent, preferring to continue living alone in the old house after Grady's death. Nell looked deep into her wide set eyes measuring her mother's silence.

"I know Mother. *IT IS* Uncle Charlie...but what's he doing in this place called Eden? I thought the Campbell family came from Mobile, Alabama. I didn't think, know that Uncle Charlie went to school. I thought he could barely read and write."

"The Campbell's did come from Mobile," Mae insisted defensively. "We had schools back then. Weren't much... Only had schooling two months out of the year. But children whose parents could afford the weekly ten cents went to school... had to work the rest of the time chopping and picking cotton. They were mainly one-room places, with one McGuffey reader, when the teachers could get one. Mainly we just copied words and numbers from the board, and took turns reading aloud from the few books we had." She smiled nervously at the memory.

"When the teacher would come back in the evenings, a few of us went to school then, after we finished workin' the fields. I'll never forget how my Mama would switch me good whenever I couldn't do my spelling. We'd all, sometimes as many as twelve us kids, would all be in the same one room with one teacher. Your Daddy, and me we both finished the sixth grade," she said looking off in the distance. "Not too many schools for the coloreds went beyond the sixth grade in them days."

"Some of them must have been integrated then," Nell replied. "I'd swear on Daddy's grave, that's a white girl in that picture." Mae responded with a heavy sigh and laid the photographs back in the footlocker. Nell looked at her mother expectantly. Dean impatiently shuffled his feet. Slowly Mae placed the letters back on the table, shuffling in her chair.

"Leave it alone Nell," she said resigned, shaking her head from side to side.

"But Mother," Nell protested, "a white girl, and uncle Charlie?" Her voice trailed off as Mae silenced her by raising her hand, shaking her head harder.

"Leave it be, Nell," Mae was adamant. Nell was shocked by the tone, and knew Mae was agitated. The ensuing silence in the room was deafening, and it hung over them for what seemed like an eternity before Mae spoke again.

"For many years, your Daddy and Charlie, since he turned eight years old, went to Eden every spring. They would stay through the fall helping their grandparents who lived there. Just before the winter months came, they would go back to Mobile. Charlie was too young but your Daddy would work the shrimp boats in the winter."

Nell and Dean looked at each other, both realizing how little they knew about the family's history. The question about relatives rarely extended beyond the old photographs adorning the walls of the tenement house. Growing up Nell had assumed they were all dead and never asked questions about the family's past.

"Well...Charlie, he kept going to Eden, even after your Daddy quit going when we moved up here," Mae continued. "Miss Annie B, Grady's Mama--she kept sending Charlie to Eden every spring to help his grandparents in the fields til Grady finally brought him up here to live with us. They say he was a big help to Big Poppa and Shugababy." She paused as if she remembered something important.

"Well Shugababy wasn't Charlie's real Grandma. She was Big Poppa's second wife, a lot younger than him too. They say he was too much man for most women his age." Her words settled into the curiosity surrounding Nell. Dean, intrigued by the tension between the two women, sat silently sighing in the background. Mae chuckled to herself.

"But...I didn't know much about her and that part of the family; they weren't Campbell's. They were the Robinsons. But, Miss Annie B, she sent Charlie every year until he was about fourteen or fifteen. Heard he was a real good worker, choppin' and pickin' cotton...you know plowin' with the mules and such." Nell noticed she had frowned emphasizing the words 'he was sent' as she looked away.

"Why did you and Grady bring him north?" Dean was finally intrigued, but Mae ignored his question.

"One of them times," she continued, "is probably when them pictures was made. You can see they' be really old." She sighed while picking up the stack of letters again. She fingered them as if she wanted to open them, but didn't. Finally, she leaned back in the old chair still holding the letters; it creaked complaining of her shifting weight.

"You know...well maybe you wouldn't know, but in those days family members would help each other out whenever it was needed. Charlie would always go 'cause his grandparents sharecropped on this big old plantation with a lot of other poor, scufflin' families, like a lot of us colored's did back then. Times were real hard back then, took all of them to bring in enough to pay for their advances and things. I heard Big Poppa and Shugababy worked from 'can see to cain't see in them fields. Would'na made it some years without Charlie. He was a big help." Nell, intrigued turned in her seat.

"Mother, did Uncle Charlie ever go back there after the war?" Nell's question broke the train of Mae's thoughts.

"No, not that I know of. That was a long time ago Nell." Her voice trailed off as she looked off in the distance. She thought deeply trying to remember. An uneasy quietness settled around them again as Nell realized how little she knew about what her family had gone through before she was born. She sensed the conversation had opened doors for Mae about times, and things she would rather have left undisturbed.

Dean also sensed the awkwardness of the silence. He signaled to Nell it was time to go, but she was preoccupied with the reaction of her mother who raised the letters to her nose while running the tip of her fingers over them.

"Still got just a faint odor of wild lilacs," she said. "In the picture be that white girl Louise he took up wit...she helped learn him to read, what little bit he could. These dried flowers they must be from her!" Nell felt Mae's words sink into her like a weight, but refused to acknowledge her uneasiness aloud. Rather she looked at Dean, and changed the conversation.

"Mother any of the family members still living in Eden...do you know?"

"Why? Why Nell?" Mae's tone had changed as if she had been rudely awakened from a deep sleep. "What you want to know for? I know what you're thinking, but you can't take Charlie's ashes down there Nell. I don't want you going down there! Besides you'd never find the place. It was mostly swamp down there, even back in the old days. All them folks all dead by now and those old shacks probably all rotted down to the ground." She stared defiantly at Nell, but softened her tone as she continued.

"Eden, it was just a little green place. Mostly black folks that grew up around the mill on the Coosa river. I spec it's all gone by now."

"I just want to know Mother. There's no particular reason, but, if we can, we should at least try to carry out Uncle Charlie's wishes, that's all...especially if that's all he wants." Nell defended her thoughts, waving her hands as she spoke.

"No! No Nell," Mae was adamant again. "Your Daddy wouldn't want that, I just know he wouldn't. Eden ain't no place for somebody like you. You ain't spent no time in the real south. Eden, and the Cove is country... real country. Not a place like Atlanta, or Birmingham. It's dangerous. Just bring Charlie's ashes home. I'll scatter some in the flowerbed in the backyard, and the rest... you and Dean take down to the river; down where old Hobo Junction used to be, next to the cement factories sitting on the banks." Mae was insistent. She turned away, and her voice indicated she was through with the conversation, but Nell challenged her.

"Dangerous? What are you talking about Mother? What could happen?" Nell was not through with the conversation.

"Things, Nell."

"What things?" Mae finally glared at her. Her jawline hardened, and Nell knew the conversation was over.

"OK! OK Mother." Nell accepted it would be useless to argue with her mother. But the thought of going to Eden had crossed her mind right after she read Charlie's note. The old photograph of Louise and the little girl drove her curiosity. She could take a few extra days, and drive there from New Orleans after she completes the photo-shoot for Hill next week. It would be an easy drive to Eden from New Orleans. She could stay for a few days, complete the story line for Hill while she was there, and follow Charlie's wishes. She further rationalized if some of the family members were still living down there, the trip would be even more special.

"I wonder if Eva is still living down there," she asked Mae, who assumed things were settled between them.

"Maybe...I think she is a Prad now if she's still alive. Yeah, I think she is a survivor. Cain't be sure but I think she could'a been one them Robinsons most of them lived into their nineties." The chair creaked as Mae shuffled her weight, pondering deeply trying to remember distant people from a distant time.

At the sound of the name Dean frowned, sensing another conversation was about to start. He sighed, shuffled in his seat, and motioned impatiently to Nell they needed to be going. She nodded, standing up she reached over to close the footlocker, but hesitated.

"We better get on our way Mother. The weather looks threatening. Maybe we can beat the snow. We'll call you later." Now lost in past-memories of Eden, Mae ignored her.

"Shugababy just ate sweets all the time, that's what I heard. That's how she got the name...so Charlie said." Mae continued speaking while staring into the depth of the room. "That was a long time ago, you know. In those times a lot of people had children...you know, in and out of marriage. Sometimes the man gave them his name sometimes he didn't. Sometimes different people raised other peoples' children too...seemed like something bad was always happening back then."

She had lost connection with Nell and Dean.

Nell fingered through the footlocker again. She had been right about what it contained. All the contents seemed to trace bits and pieces of the life of her Uncle Charlie. In addition to his old uniform, and his discharge papers, there were a variety of colorful medals and ribbons he had won while in the service. At the bottom of the locker, she found several old silver dollar coins, old pennies, and a small stack of one dollar-silver certificates. An old jewelry box wedged tightly into the corner of the locker caught her eye. Dean had dislodged it earlier when he picked up Charlie's cap to the uniform. Nell opened the box.

"A Purple Heart!" She whispered. "Uncle Charlie got a Purple Heart," she said louder looking at her Mother.

"He never mentioned it," Mae said as Nell took the medal out of the box holding it at a distance while focusing her eyes for a clearer look.

"Nell...we really need to be going," Dean insisted.

"Uncle Charlie was really something," Nell said proudly. Dean finally got up. He placed the discharge papers, and the photographs in a brown envelope, before replacing the Purple Heart and the other things back into the footlocker. Picking it up he returned it to the safety of its place in the closet.

"Nell, we really have to go," he insisted, handing her the brown envelope. We've got a long drive to Pittsburgh,"

Mae watched through the window, parting the old

lace curtains as Dean backed the car slowly into the street. The mood Nell had created with her questions about Charlie, and the Cove still lingered around her.

She finally sat in the old rocking chair by the window in the living room. It was where she read her Bible, or talked daily on the telephone with Nell. It was the spot she could always depend upon to give her peace, or relieve her tensions. She was aware; the uncomfortable tension brought into the room when Nell opened the photographs was still there. She sat quietly absorbing it, rocking back and forth in her old rocking chair. The questions still lay in the room, and she sensed in herself a sharper edge of anger towards Charlie, and the contents of the footlocker. She wondered what Grady would do if he were alive. Would he take Charlie's ashes back to the Cove, or would he simply bury Charlie's body here in Elmwood? A grave at Elmwood would be respectable. Lots of respectable colored folks buried there. She rocked harder, thinking of the colored regiment that fought in the Civil War buried there. Her chair creaked loudly, and for the first time since his death, her anger settled on Grady.

As if he felt her discomfort, a sudden warmth settled around her. It was as if he stood over her looking over her shoulder. She sensed his presence, his arm circling her shoulder.

"You shouldn't left me to do this all alone Sweetheart...things always came out better when we did them together...you always knew that better than me!" Looking up she spoke to the image in her mind.

Charged by the old photographs, and the questions about Charlie, she opened the Bible to the Twenty Third Psalm, and tried to read to quiet her mind.

"Were you there when they crucified my Lord?

CHAPTER TWO

*T*HEY ALL SAT CLUSTERED IN THE SMALL LOBBY. Some looked lost, while others acted as if they were quietly, pleased to be sitting there. A few chatted with animation across the rows of waiting seats. These seemed too alive and well to be in this place. Too many faces smiled. While most of the others simply sat in the odor of their lives, stoic, quietly staring into the space of memories, unaware of the movement around them. Occasionally laughter wafted above the crowd. It seemed out of place in such a dark, serious place.

Outside of the place it was a blustery day. The atmosphere was dark and gray. And at times a gust of wind had a cutting edge to it. Damp snow showers were starting to coat the ground, and murky clouds of a threatening storm swirled overhead. Small groups of men stood against the cold wind. They stood, smoking in random clusters, waiting for a ride back home or they simply stood stomping their feet against the cold patiently aiting for the parking attendant to deliver their cars.

The revolving door to the VA hospital, a huge garish-looking old building on the west side of Pittsburgh, constantly hummed as many unshaven men bundled against the cold wind and snow passed into the huge structure. They sighed with relief to be safely inside when they came through the heavy doors. Large numbers of them came to this place every day. Many of them came in old clothes, some of them unwashed and appearing with broken spirits.

All came seeking sanctuary in their common instincts. Like butterflies with tattered wings they could not fly anymore, and this place vainly tried to feed their needs like a poverty-stricken mother trying to care for her hungry children.

When Nell and Dean arrived at the hospital, close to a hundred men sat in the dim light of the lobby. They were a mixture of races, and represented a variety of ages. Beyond their common masculinity, they were quiet simply linked together because they were all veterans of some past war, or other government sponsored conflict. Other men, leaders of governments-- both foreign and domestic, had prescribed the time and the conditions of their armed service, without considering the impact of their decision beyond the immediate need. Most of these men, Nell thought, had responded proudly, and they clustered in groups represented by the conflict in which they had served.

"It's easy", Nell whispered, as she glanced around the room, "to distinguish the Vietnam veterans from the Korean veterans, and the World War II veterans from the Desert Storm veterans. Beyond age there is a distinctive look to each group." Dean agreed as they stopped momentarily surveying the room.

"Lots of untold stories here," she said softly as they made their way toward the reception desk.

"I can feel it," he responded, leading her as they threaded their way through the crowded room. They had seen men and women like these, younger-- but seemingly just as eager and patriotic, on CNN recently in Afghanistan. As a professional photo-journalist, Nell had taken photographs of, and written about their families just before she retired from the news service last year. She had been close-up to men like these, and their families, when she covered the return of a National Guard unit from Desert Storm in the fall of 1991.

She remembered trying to capture in her photographs the knowing weariness etched in many of the faces of that returning Guard unit. Like these men, they had also served well, but the dim light in some of their eyes betrayed growing inner battles for their futures. Nell could sense it in some even as they embraced their loved ones on that happy day. She knew past wars, battles, sacrifices, and old memories would always be talked about across the chairs in this room. She felt the mood in the large room. The nervous laughter, and chatter she heard hung like an attitude in the space. And she knew it only belonged there--- as an aura of respect and knowing pain. Nell had felt its presence when they first walked into the place. It humbled her as if they had stumbled onto a private altar reserved only for the tested survivors of sanctioned armed conflict. It was that sense that finally made her realize they were intruders in this special space. The knowledge of past battles--the shared experience of looking the horror of war in the face and living through it, bound these men into an inextricable brotherhood that neither she nor Dean would ever fully understand or share. They look worn, she thought. Several of them blatantly stared at her with questions in their eyes as she walked past them. She noticed their interest and took hold of Dean's arm, inching closer to him to quiet her discomfort with the stares.

'You OK?" He asked looking back at her. Small beads of perspiration had started to form on the bridge of her nose, and he sensed her discomfort.

"Yeah, I'm OK," she lied. "But...we really don't belong here though."They deserve better, she thought---better than this."

"Why? It's just a hospital. You think it's not good enough?"

She gripped his arm firmer, before speaking again.

"No Dean, this is not like Walter Reed! It shouldn't just be another hospital! Sure. It's a place for the physically wounded, but I sense the emotional damage in this place." She remembered the quality of the care for the paraplegics she had observed at Walter Reed.

"Could be," Dean responded. "Maybe." He was surprised that the stares bothered her. Men had stared at her most of her adult life. She was a tall woman with flawless black skin, direct brown eyes, a ready smile, and a rich head of graying shoulder length hair. Age had been kind to her. Her eyes were always alert and her face was practically without wrinkles. She was physically active, and maintained her weight well. As a seasoned photo-journalist, for many years he had watched her engage many difficult situations with self-assurance, and seemingly without flinching. Sometimes against his wishes, she would take on the most heart-wrenching assignments. Some were dangerously violent and trauma producing for her, yet she always seemed to prevail. And her stories and work with the camera belied an internal strength uncommonly displayed by most women.

Concerned, he stared back at her. Although a camera was not around her neck, she was dressed, as for work wearing a worn pair of Levis, her down jacket, and a pair of lightweight scuffled boots. Dean took her hand pulling her closer as they approached the reception desk.

The ceiling in the lobby area was very high. It was a dimly lit place with a series of old naked overhead fluorescent fixtures. A few of which blinked off and on occasionally, and some were dark, and needed replacing. Fortunately sharp bright daylight flowed through two large windows directly across from the revolving doors. Large eerie shadows crossed the highly-polished floor each time someone passed in front of the windows. The abstractions formed by the merging shadows as people passed each other in the faded light were intriguing to Nell as they stood waiting at the reception desk.

The clerk speaking with animation into her phone, acknowledged their presence by indicating they should sign in. Directly behind her desk a general office area was filled with several other clerks at computers, open bulging file cabinets, and telephones that rang incessantly.

Off to the right of the reception desk, a security guard sat near a door leading into the general office area. Beyond that door ran a long hallway ending suddenly at another waiting area, where another security guard sat at a desk. Examining rooms were on either side of the hallway. The ceiling in that section was lower, brightly lit, and filled with activity. There were two nurses' stations, one on each side of the hallway and periodically, a sporadic trail of men made their way down the hallway as their names were called.

After signing in at the reception desk Dean found a place for Nell to sit near the door to the office area. He stood nearby silently waiting for the social worker. He was anxious to be at the end of this fateful journey.

Nell had slept fitfully during the trip to Pittsburgh, and in the uneven light of the VA lobby, her eyes started to falter. She leaned back in the chair, closing her eyes to block out the flickering lights and the movement around her. Her mind slowly drifted as she thought about her uncle Charlie, and sleep quietly overtook her.

❖ ❖ ❖

SHE AND MAE WERE in the kitchen at the old tenement house. Mae had just put the last large handful of turnip and mustard greens into a pot of hot water seasoned with a piece of salt pork. She stirred the pot, not looking at Nell who stood in the kitchen door leading to the back porch. Jacob, Nell's best friend, sat anxiously in the shade on the backporch steps. He closed his ears against Mae's warning about him and Nell sneaking off to Hobo Junction.

"It ain't a safe place for you two young'uns." Mae spoke with loud irritation in her voice. "Most them men down there at the Junction they be war veterans," Mae said. "And a lot of them ain't right, and they may never be...again. That's why we don't want you and Jacob going down there, Nell." She looked directly at both children sternly.

"You hear me Jacob?"

"Yes Mam, I do," Jacob responded.

"I do feel sorry for them though. Except for the Sisters at the Mission on the Hill, most folks just wish they'd go away." Nell felt her stomach sink at the harshness of her mother's words. She turned to look at Jacob, who acknowledged her glance by turning his eyes toward the unmistakable sound of his father's car horn from the front of the house. He became animated.

"Bye Nell, bye Mrs. Campbell. My Daddy's here."

Mae had talked about Hobo Junction like it was a painful subject she didn't want to talk about. But after Jacob left, she continued, wanting Nell to have a full understanding of her concerns about the Junction.

"Most them veterans from the wars...they cain't get no jobs, the condition they're in. Most arn't right either," she said pointing to her head. "They just ride the freight trains all over the place, not sure what they lookin' for. Your father says they like the butterflies. They come back every year to stay down there by the river every summer. Just before the weather turns --- those that can, jump a freight train back south somewhere, maybe Florida, or Georgia." She stopped momentarily looking at Nell who she knew was measuring her words carefully.

"Those who cain't figure out how to leave, for one reason or another build makeshift shelters against the coming cold. They spend most their days keeping those fires burning in those large metal drums you see turned over in the summertime. They never let those fires go out. It's how they keep from freezin' in the winter."

Nell, still silent, shifted her weight in the doorway, and wondered about the impact of Mae's words on Jacob. She was sure they had no impact, as it seemed Jacob always did what he wanted to do. Mae mixed the biscuits in one of the large bowls. She had already greased a sheet pan for the biscuits, and was heating the belly of the old stove.

She looked at Nell as she shaped the biscuits on the sheet pan. Nell stared blankly back at her as she scraped the dough from her fingers expertly making twelve crudely shaped biscuits.

"We can have some of these for breakfast tomorrow," her mother said. But Nell was wondering what it would be like for Charlie to be riding on a freight train in his condition, as Mae put the biscuits in the stove.

"Grady should be home soon," she said while taking Nell by the hand. They went into the big room and sat in the overstuffed chair behind the heater.

"Carver Collins and your Uncle, they keep those fires going. I hear Charlie still works at Ms. Meade's though. Bella, one of the girls living there, looks out for him, and makes sure he and Carver get something to eat." Mae adjusted herself so they both could fit comfortably into the chair.

"He saw so much destruction and death, I imagine... fighting in the war, he just stays drunk most the time now. Charlie was a gunner, you know--on one of the few Colored Sherman Tank Units...said, he and Carver was both gunners...sittin' just above the driver in one of them bubble lookin' things comin' out the top of the tank. They both fought in France and North Africa, just before the Germans gave up."

Silence settled around them until Mae got up to check on the greens.

"Charlie really lost it though after Carver Collins got hurt and was sent home. He never really had another close friend during the war, and he was never the same again after that. That's all he would write about. I believe it's what started him drinking...you know to being like he is now. We tried to help him after he was discharged. Your Daddy even got him on at the packinghouse, but Charlie just wouldn't come to work on time, or he would show up sweaty and unwashed, smelling like stale alcohol. They finally let him go. Grady offered to let him stay with us, if he would stop drinking, but Charlie couldn't be caged in. He would die like them butterflies you kids keep in them jars."

She put her arms around Nell drawing her closer. Her eyes were soft and Nell thought, at that moment, Mae was the prettiest woman in the world.

"Charlie's just needs to be free Nell, that's all!" Sighing, she got up and went back into the kitchen to check on the cornbread, and the greens cooking on the stove.

"Your daddy gives him a little money whenever we can afford it," she said from the kitchen, "but that's the most we can do." Nestling deeper into the chair, feeling its warmth cushion her, Nell closed her eyes and vowed she would share her allowance with Uncle Charlie so he could buy cigarettes the next time she saw him.

Suddenly she was snatched back to the uneven lights of the VA when laughter from one of the veterans nearby invaded her space, scattering her thoughts.

SHE OPENED HER EYES BRIEFLY, and quickly closed them again, against the noise and the glare of the room. Sinking quickly back into herself, she tried to recapture the comforting images of Mae from her past. But they had been replaced as the noise and the smells of the VA flooded her mind, and she sensed the presence of Uncle Charlie hovering over her. Suddenly, he kissed her cheek, his arms circling her shoulders before whispering.

"Remember the butterflies, Nell? From the Junction, you remember the butterflies, don't you?" As he hovered he raised his finger to his lips, whispering.

"This is where the butterflies come to die Nell." His voice was soothing, and reassuring. But suddenly, moving swiftly he flitted away from her toward the men waiting in the VA lobby.

"It must be," his voice yelled back at her, "look at them, Nell. You can see right through to the misery they carry." He nodded knowingly, twirling again towards her. "It's where I came...I came...I came here too, because it's all they gave us...and it's the only place most of us have left." The image waved its hand indicating the men sitting in the room."Nothing---but each other Ms. Campbell!" He sounded angry, flitting past her, he brushed her hair.

"Ms. Campbell!" the words seemingly vibrated around her. She flinched, quickly opening her eyes and closing them again against the jarring light, as the intrusion of another closer voice seemed to reach out, touching her face.

"Nell." It was Dean. He was stroking her hair to awaken her. The other voice became clearer and clearer as the sound of her name came over the loud speaker on the wall near the office door where a young woman was walking toward her, smiling.

"MS. CAMPBELL I'M SO GLAD YOU COULD COME," the voice intruded more aggressively, breaking into Nell's confusion. She opened her eyes to see the social worker standing at her side. She was a small woman with skin the color of dark chocolate. She was dressed in a long skirt and had a friendly smile. It was the warmest smile I have seen in a long time, Nell thought. Her face seemed to light up when she spoke. Nell introduced Dean, as she ushered them into a small office of the lobby.

The social worker opened the file on Uncle Charlie after she closed the door.

"If you had not contacted us today...later, we would have buried your Uncle in one of the VA cemeteries. We would have provided a headstone because he is a veteran...a simple white cross. And there would have been a service...more a simple internment." She looked at Nell as she spoke, hardly acknowledging Dean's presence in the room.

She looked at the documents and verifying Nell as a relative of Charlie. She had her sign the release documents before contacting one of the attendants in the hospital. Within a few minutes the attendant brought in a large clear plastic bag. A steel cable was threaded through thick loops around the top of the bag, that was secured by a combination lock.

"These are the personal effects your Uncle Charlie had when he checked into the hospital." She removed the lock from the bag, placing it on the table.

"You can use this room to look through the things. Take whatever you want...usually when the veterans are homeless though there isn't much to take. What you don't want, simply sign the forms in the bag indicating you want the VA to dispose of the remaining items. We'll take care of them for you." She stood up, moving the phone closer to Nell.

"There is only one other thing we have to do before we are through here," she said. "We can only release the body to a licensed funeral home, so you'll have to make arrangements with one of the local places. If you plan to take the body back out state, they can make all the arrangements for you. If you want, I can call one for you before I go, but..." She hesitated. "I have been dealing with these places for a long time, and they all insist on payment before they come for the body."

"Of course, we understand," Nell, responded.

"Since he was a veteran," the social worker continued, "we provide some support for the funeral arrangements...and of course there will be a flag for you as the next of kin."

"Thank you."

"The funeral home will know how to get these services for you. We can call one for you that will take a credit card...Visa or Master card, I think."

Squinting her eyes, she looked up at the clock on the wall behind Dean.

"And they're pretty reputable." She hesitated, her hand on the phone waiting for Nell's response. Overwhelmed by the weight of what was facing her Nell was silent. The social worker finally looked from Nell to Dean.

Dean said, "Yes please. We would appreciate that, but we need a place that does cremations." He turned to look at Nell.

"Honey...I been thinking...the tenement house is gone, but there is this beautiful bay jutting out from Lake Erie on the way home. We could stop on the bridge there and scatter most of Charlie's ashes in the lake. I know it's not this place he talked about, the Cove, but I think it would be a fitting place. Besides we don't even know if such a place exists any more. The rest Mae could put in her flower garden. I'm sure she would be satisfied we had done right by Charlie." Nell didn't answer.

Concerned for her silence, he reached out taking her hands as he looked deep into her eyes measuring her response. After thinking about it briefly, she nodded in agreement.

"I know the place, and it is a beautiful spot," she finally said, "we can scatter most of the ashes there, or take them to Mae's. But I think I'll take some of them with me next week. When I finish up in New Orleans I'll take a few days and try to find Eden. It's got to be somewhere in Alabama down around the Gulf, or the Florida Pan Handle...can't be too far from Mobile. "

"What about Mae?" He was concerned.

"We just won't tell her," she said standing up. "She really doesn't have to know. It's the least I can do for Uncle Charlie. Any way I can charge my time off to the wire service. Hill won't care as long as he gets the assignment on time." She coyly smiled at him, "otherwise you'd have to take time off to go to this little hick town in the south with me," she pouted, "you wouldn't want to do that?" She questioned him smiling. Dean smiled back. He knew it was pointless to argue with her.

The social worker dialed the crematorium, and handed the phone to Dean. She touched Nell's shoulder as she left the room.

IT WAS AFTER THREE O'CLOCK the next day when they picked up the neatly folded American flag and the simple urn containing Charlie's ashes. They headed back on the interstate hoping to get outside the city before the rush hour traffic began. The roads were slightly coated with the light snow from the day before and the wind had picked up again. Nell was thankful Dean had insisted on driving. She felt tired. She settled back into the soft leather of the warm car staring absently through the window.

It was not long before her mind wandered, melting into the landscape as it flowed rapidly by. Soon images, long forgotten crowded her mind. She watched herself, as from a distance, interacting with the people she loved. She could hear the voice of her Mother yelling at her Uncle Charlie as he tossed her in the air when she was a child. Those were the days she would giggle with excitement when he took her for long rides in the old wagon, and bought lemon cones at the Italian ice cream parlor. There was the laughter of her friends Jacob, Dean, and Rose Ann. She could smell the greens, seasoned with bacon grease cooking on the stove in the tenement house.

She settled into her thoughts, exploring the visits into her life by death and how it alternated with prolonged periods of happiness. Both had impacted the various phases of her life, she mused. To her it seemed like death and happiness were colored ribbons, wrapped together, but constantly unfolding. They had intertwined around her throughout the span of her life, and happiness was always cut short when the ribbon of death would suddenly run out without warning creating a painful empty space. She closed her eyes against the rushing landscape, and was transported to the time when the ribbon of death marked with Jacob's name, suddenly and without warning rolled out, and collected around his ankles. Shocked, she moaned aloud.

"You OK?" Dean asked.

The car was warm. The ride was smooth. She heard

Dean as if he was far away. She tried to answer him, but could not form the words, easily fading back into the cocoon of her memories. Other than her parents, and Charlie, Jacob was the only other person important in her early life. In his own strange way, he managed to help her identify those years as happy. He was the bridge that helped her discover the magic of Hobo Junction; discover confidence in herself, and helped her to discover the importance of friendship. He was the one that, in his own careless way, took her back to Uncle Charlie when, as a child, she thought her parents had denied him to her forever.

"...Were you there when they crucified my Lord?"

CHAPTER THREE

DETROIT, MICHIGAN: THE YEARS 1937 - 1950

*T*HE DAYS IMMEDIATELY after Jacob's death were the worst of Nell's young life. Although Mae tried to comfort her, she secretly blamed her Uncle Charlie. It was several days before the shock wore off, and she wanted to talk about how important Jacob was to her. She could hear Dean in the backyard bouncing a tennis ball off the walls of the tenement. She wished he would come inside so she could explain the anger she was feeling toward Uncle Charlie. But the dark was breaking, and she knew he had to soon find his way home. She needed to talk to someone other than her Mother. She knew Dean would understand and know what to do to make her feel better. Mae would simply try to explain Uncle Charlie's actions away, and she did not want any of that. Her thoughts were soon rudely interrupted by an insistent knock on her bedroom door.

"Nell...you in there?"

Mae opened the door of her room, approaching her from the rear of the bed. Her strong hands lifted Nell's limp body cradling her in them as she strained to lift the resisting child.

"No Mama, I can walk!"

Cautiously Mae put Nell back to the floor and led her to the large room across the hall near the kitchen. She sat Nell in the large over stuffed rocking chair behind the heater, and squeezed in beside her. Warmth radiated from the glowing red belly chasing the chill from the room. Mae put her arm around Nell, nestled her head against her breast, and soon both were peacefully asleep.

For that brief, moment, in the care ot her mother's arms, Nell forgot the recent tragedy of her young life. but, later that night when Charlie stood at the door to her room to say good night, she called him in. She wanted to apologize for being so angry with him, and urged him to sit on the side of the bed near her. He sensed it was important for her. He sat on the floor at the side of her bed. She peeked over the covers at him as the sound of a fall rainstorm pelted the room's only window.

She talked to him about losing her friend, Jacob propping herself up in the bed so she could look over at him. She wanted to make sure he remained awake and late into the evening she told him of the good times she had with Jacob until sleep finally overtook her.

Charlie had listened intently until sleep started to drain him, and he nodded in and out. Somehow, he knew talking was therapeutic for her, and he was relieved she was no longer angry with him. He stayed with her until she quit talking and was deep in sleep.

He quietly slipped from the room and retreated to the warmth of the couch where he slept in the big room. Mae and Grady were still awake, and Charlie kept them up late into the night talking about the promise and concerns he had for starting a new life with Bella in Pittsburgh.

WHEN NELL FIRST MET JACOB, she was close to four years old. They met at a small storefront church where his Father was the minister. It was a small church, with barely thirty members. Poorly constructed benches served as pews, and the place was always dimly lit. But the service was always joyous, filled with loud singing, shouting people, and, as Mae always said, the Spirit of the Holy Ghost. After the conclusion of the service one night, following the tradition in Baptist churches, the minister "...opened the doors of the church," to take in new members. Mae dragging Nell behind her proceeded to the front and accepted the Lord Jesus Christ as her Savior amidst a chorus of "Thank You Lord," many shouts of "Amen" and other acclamations from the small membership. Later, after the service was over, while Mae talked with the minister, Nell busied herself while waiting. She used her hands to slide along one of the hard pews near the door. Jacob watched her with interest as he and his Mother stood at the front door of the church waiting patiently for his Father. He stood partially behind his Mother, bashfully holding onto her hand. Finally, she led him by the hand from behind her. Now he stood shyly in front of her. His thumb immediately went to his mouth, and his eyes looked at the floor when Nell faced him. She stood watching him from the safety of the other side of the church. Cautiously he raised his eyes and smiled at her. Curious, she shyly approached him as his Mother urged him forward to meet her. Nell noticed he waddled when he walked. She also noticed his short-cropped hair, and his blue-black skin except in the areas where he carried scars. In those areas along the side of his small face and down the front of his neck and extending down, and under his shirt, the skin had taken on a slick blacken copper look. A metal brace encased his left leg from the knee down to his shoe. This was the foot he kicked as he walked. It gave her the impression he was waddling like a duck.

She wondered what had happened to him. After their fourth visit to the church, Mae explained his condition, and had even scolded her about staring openly at him.

Still she wondered if it would be out of line to ask him about his brace. He always smiled when she saw him. Was it fun wearing a brace? Nell knew her Mother would have not approved. Suddenly she smiled back. Soon they were both laughing loudly and sliding along different pews in the small church. His Mother, Mrs. Turner finally came and took them both by the hand. They followed her in-tow back to stand patiently by the door for Mae and the minister. Jacob was two years older than Nell, but he was as receptive to her as she was to him. Tall and skinny for his age, he seemed to hover above her when they stood together.

◆ ◆ ◆

"THAT WAS HOW OUR FRIENDSHIP began," she told Charlie the next evening. "He was really my best friend for such a long time," she continued. She sat on the couch next to him, as Mae washed the dishes in the small kitchen; she listened quietly to their conversation.

Grady sat reading the newspaper across from them in the old rocker behind the heater.

"Better than Rose Ann?" Charlie asked thinking of the little Irish girl who had recently moved into the neighborhood and befriended Nell. They were the same age, and every evening at dusk in the summertime they would sit on the back porch playing with paper dolls, and talking with Mae about things that mostly interested girls. She took a deep breath yawning widely.

"It was a different kind of friendship, than with Rose Ann. She's too scared of bugs and things. She can't even catch a grasshopper! Plus, she's no good at marbles. Jacob, and me we just did lots of things together...always" Nell said sounding wiser than her age. She yawned again, and he could feel her body relax against him.

"Jacob was special Uncle Charlie. Didn't you think so?" She asked sleepily. Charlie didn't really know how to answer, and an awkward silence followed. Charlie could hear, and feel her heavy breathing against his side. She didn't respond when Mae called her name, and they knew she was finally asleep.

"She's been staying up too late," Mae said into the void. "Charlie, wake her up so she can go to bed," Mae's voice drifted over the cracking of the fire in the large heater. Grady put down his paper, picked Nell up and carried her to her room, dropping her on the bed. She partially woke up and crawled silently under the bed covers with her clothes on. Before leaving, Grady looked at the little clock on the dresser near the bed. It was just after ten o'clock in the evening. Mae came in and helped Nell get into her pajamas before joining Grady in the front bedroom.

It was Sunday night and their small radio broadcast the services of a church softly into the big room when she opened the door.

"Nell's pretty tired," she said. "Do you think she blames Charlie?"

"She's probably still dealing with the shock of losing someone so close to her as Jacob. They were friends only for a short time, but he was significant in her young life," Grady said quietly.

In the big room, Charlie quietly stretched out on the couch near the kitchen, listening to the sounds of the coming winter as the rising winds rattled the windows in the old tenement. He wrapped himself in the heavy quilt looking at reflections from the large red heater. He closed his eyes hoping to welcome sleep, but images of Jacob had been planted in his mind, and as in a parade they stayed with him well into the night. Charlie had never really thought much about the closeness of Jacob and Nell, but he was aware of Jacob's influence on her.

Charlie had been a teenager when he moved into the tenement house, and beyond his own troubled times, he watched Nell grow up a quiet, withdrawn, and bashful child. Seemingly afraid of the speed of the other children's play. She always stood on the outer circle watching, as the other children played in the neighborhood. Sometimes she would silently watch them from the safety of the back porch when they played in the street. When she tired of watching, she would catch some of the many small insects in the backyard, store them in a Mason jar with leaves and call them her children. Charlie noticed her change when Jacob came into her life -- slowly at first, but steadily from that point on. Jacob helped her to become more assertive, increasing her confidence in herself.

He could not run and play with the other children either and they immediately took to each other. Mostly they both chose to stand at the outer circle of the group, slightly afraid of getting too deep into the mix of the running and jumping children. After they started talking, Mae became more involved with the small church, and Jacob's Father, on his way to work, soon began dropping him of at the tenement once or twice a week to play marbles in the backyard. Jacob made those times special for Nell by bringing his prettiest marbles for her to play with. It was clear although they argued sometimes; he was Nell's best friend at the earliest stages of her young life. And unknowingly, it was his sense of adventure that helped her to move beyond the secure bounds of family and into the rest of the world with a growing confidence.

Although Charlie did notice Jacob's foot brace and how he walked with a struggle, placing one foot carefully in front of the other, waddling from side to sid; his eyes always were drawn to where Jacob's skin was burned. The scar was patchy-smooth on most of the right side of his face from the hairline down to his chin. Charlie, always fascinated by the look of the burned skin, wanted to touch it. He wondered how it would feel. It looked like it would feel like skin carved by a knife or cut by the lash of a bullwhip. He kept his thoughts to himself, and he did not want Nell to catch him staring rudely at her friend. He was self-conscious whenever he was caught staring, and he was sure it made Jacob uncomfortable too. But his eyes were always drawn to the scars. As he thought back on it he was more uncomfortable with the scar than Jacob was with his staring. One day while Charlie was sitting on the back-porch steps, Nell and Jacob were playing marbles, and Charlie was unconsciously staring at the scar again. Jacob quietly got up from the ground, dropping a small handful of marbles. He walked over and took Charlie's hand, and put it to his cheek so Charlie could feel the hardness of the scar. Nell sat on the ground patiently watching them, as if she knew, and understood in advance what Jacob was going to do.

The hardness of the skin was a shock to Charlie. The skin was smooth except for the ridges. They stood up hard against his hand. Jacob didn't say anything, but stood silently until Charlie removed his hand. Later Charlie and Nell learned about Jacob's scars from Mae.

"Their house caught on fire one night while Mrs. Turner was cooking. Grease spilled on the hot stove, some of it caught fire spattering on the curtains and the crib where Jacob was sleeping. Mrs. Turner got burned all up her right arm trying to put out the covers on the crib, but Jacob was burned real bad. Mr. Turner was at work that night, and Mrs. Turner blames herself for what happened to Jacob. She, his mother," Mae continued. "She goes way out of her way now to try to make up to him for the accident...They never deny that child anything," she said shaking her head before continuing. "But...I'd probably do the same thing...if I could--too," she reflected.

It is true Charlie thought, Jacob, as an only child, seemed to have every toy imaginable as he was growing up. The most exciting of which was a bright red miniature car. It was large enough so two children could sit in it at the same time. It moved when they both pushed the revolving pedals near the floor; and the driver could steer the car.

Mae was fully involved in the little church. She was, as most black women, proud of her pastor and his ministry. Mr. Turner was an imposing figure. He had one of the only cars in the neighborhood, and cut an impressive figure in his clothes. He always dressed in suits and wore a gold chain across his belly. At the end of the chain was a shiny gold watch he kept in his vest pocket. Most of the people in the neighborhood, including some of the Greeks and Italians, scattered throughout the area looked up to him. Mae said people respected him so much because he was a man of God. However, she could never encourage Grady to join her in the church. She approved of the friendship between Jacob and Nell. Occasionally, after Sunday school, Nell, and the other young children from the church were invited to go by Jacob's house between church services. Mrs. Turner always served homemade ice cream, or some other homemade treat. The children played for a while with Jacob and his toys, especially the red car. And as with most young children, the friendship between Nell and Jacob grew progressively over the next several years.

On those rare times when Mae did not go to church, Charlie would go with Nell to Sunday school, and, although he was older, after service he would also go along with the children to the Turner house. He enjoyed visiting Jacob's house. The red car intrigued him, and the house was located close to the river, where he loved to walk by himself. In the summer the river was where many people and their children from the neighborhood gathered on hot days. Some sat underneath shade trees fishing from the banks for hours while their children caught crayfish and minnows along the water's edge and watched with an undying curiosity the big tankers and their colorful flags as they cruised by.

This was the city's "Black Bottom." Where even beyond its reputation for hard-working people, racial conflict, and old cobblestone streets, the river was a magnet for everyone. A majestic lady, she flowed from the crystal lakes of the eastern suburbs, bringing sleek white sloops with her, and the colors of dotted sails on sunny days.

Her waters always ran blue and cold. They were deep and treacherous, but to walk there by her banks always brought a settling peace to Charlie.

Right after the war the smoke stack industries, foundries, and tool shops, crowding the river banks were slowly giving way for the creation of new high rise housing complete with marinas and small private parks. It was clear the city's politicians and the developers did not plan to accommodate the needs of poor people in future developments along the riverbanks. New developments were planned for every inch of space along the riverfront. Everyone in the neighborhood knew the area would soon be off-limits as the new river front developments were designed for more affluent families, and Charlie knew his walks along the riverbank would soon be over. He also knew he would miss the blaze of color from the wildflowers growing in the vacant lots along the river's edge. He knew the life the river gave to the people of the "Bottom" somehow would never be the same again in a few years.

It saddened him, as the river had also become a magnet for veterans from the war who were forced to live on the street. In the late summer afternoons, these men, as by an unknown instinct, would gather at this one spot on the river bank. Most of them had come to the area riding the freight trains looking for work in the car plants. A few, too old or too disabled to be hired would stay begging on the streets for a while. Some were transients, and would only stay while the weather remained warm. Others made the spot their home, and the place soon became known in the neighborhood as the 'Hobo Junction'. On cool evenings and throughout the winter months the men would build roaring fires in several of the large empty metal drums to keep warm. These large fires would burn off and on most evenings and nights, and throughout the year.

The fires could be seen in-land from the bottom road following the curve of the river, and mothers in the neighborhood, concerned about the motives of the homeless men cautioned their children about venturing into Hobo Junction. Over the fires the men, seemingly always, cooked a collective chowder of foods they had either stolen from neighborhood victory gardens, or salvaged from the excess and spoiling foods thrown away by farmers at the open-air market on the lower east side of the city.

Jacob's house was across the street from, and closes by the cement factories sitting on the riverbank. The house was also not far from Hobo Junction, and the railroad tracks of the switching yard where the neighborhood curiosity, Po'ke Chop Jones lived in an abandoned boxcar.

Po'ke Chop, always clean-shaven weighted close to four hundred pounds. He wore a bowler hat, and worked the docks unloading the ships at the port close to the railroad tracks. The tracks ran north and south to, and from the cement factories.

ONE DAY NELL OVERHEARD her father, Grady tell Mae about

the times he would see Charlie at the Junction with his friend Carver Collins. It was one of the few times she had heard her parents disagree about anything. She was awakening by their conversation, and at first she thought she was dreaming. She had never heard them confront each other before. It was unsettling.

"I'm sorry Mae, but I don't like it. He's always stopping there…I'm sure he's drinking. I cain't figure out what to do to get him to understand."

"Understand? Understand what Grady…he's just a young man trying to adjust after the war. There are other veterans besides him and Carver down there. He's probably trying to make friends."

"Come on Mae…you know he's drinking again. You even helped him by hiding the empty bottles." Grady sounded angry as he continued, "You're not helping him Mae!"

"At least I'm not driving him away…like you are!" She had turned away to walk toward the kitchen when Grady took her arm roughly, turning her to face him.

"Baby…he's a man now. I know you helped raise him; since he came here like he was your child…but he cain't replace the baby. Luke died a long time ago, and you got to let it go baby."
He was pleading, hoping she would understand they needed to stick together and confront Charlie in-order to help him. She stared through him, and her eyes told him she was in a different place.

"Please…don't ever bring up Luke again!" the words wanted to escape her throat, but were stuck there. Finally, she said, "You through?" She was more controlled.

"Yeah…I guess." He was more accepting.

"Turn me loose then…if you don't mind." It was a nasty rebuff. The words were like an assault in Nell's mind, and their confrontation frightened her. Questions about the stability of their relationship, and what was happening with Uncle Charlie disturbed her, and she stayed awake late into the night.

The next day, she sneaked off to the bottom road, and from a distance, sat for a while on the curb watching the activity in Hobo Junction. Charlie had stopped there, as usual, on his way home from his job at the laundry. He, Carver Collins, and the other men stood near a fire, drinking from several bottles. Many of them still wore their frayed army uniforms, and heavy combat boots. Charlie seemed comfortable there, Nell thought, as the men laughed loudly, seemingly happy to be together. She wondered if drinking from the bottle was a big part of the ritual binding the group together. She knew her parents would never approve of her going there, but she was fascinated by the mysterious life in the place.

She shared her observations with Jacob, and together, over Charlie's objections, they constantly pressured him to take them to the Junction. He finally relented and, soon every Saturday when the weather was hot, the three of them would sneak off to the Junction seeking relief from the stifling heat. There, even on the hottest days a cool invigorating breeze always blew in from the river. On those days, while Charlie dozed in the sparse shade of the stunted trees, Nell and Jacob, their skin darkening in the hot sun, would spend their time catching grasshoppers, butterflies, and other insects. They would put them among a few leaves in one of the large Mason jars they had taken from Mae's cupboard.

The Junction, overgrown with brush, wild grapes, weeds, wildflowers, a few stunted trees and discarded wine bottles, and other trash became a favorite place for the children. It ran several city blocks along the banks of the river just south of the railroad tracks. At a time in the past when the river levels were higher, it was part of a beach and the dirt in the Junction still had a high sand content. Dirt-sand mounds were scattered close to the water's edge, and if Nell they stood on the highest dune looking west, they could see Po'ke Chop's boxcar off in the distance. Sometimes they would see him sitting in the switching yard talking with one of the women from the neighborhood.

At the end of the Junction, jutting into the river, there was a half sunken old wooden dock. It extended out beyond the shallows into the deep water. The old folks in the neighborhood had laid claim to the dock as the one used by the Purple Gang in the twenties to sneak bootleg whiskey from Canada into the country. It had partially fallen into the water many years ago, and was rotting from disrepair. The humid summers, and the cold snowy winters had twisted and cracked the old wood. The platform was splintered and leaning to its side into the water. Noisy sea gulls were an ever-present part of the life around the dock. Sometimes, while Nell and Jacob caught grasshoppers and sat eating the wild grapes from the straggly vines, Charlie would carefully pick his way through the droppings of the sea gulls onto the dock. Sitting on the rotting cross beams he would dangle his feet in the cold water. He never got in the water, but sometimes would take his homemade fishing pole, occasionally catching a bluegill, or small catfish. But those times were rare.

Other times the three of them would lie next to each other on the hot sand enjoying the cool breezes mixing with the heat of a strong sun. It was at those times when Nell and Jacob would fantasize about growing up, indicating the names of the people they would marry, the kind of cars they would drive, and the types of homes they would live in as grown-ups.

These were the times when Charlie would leave the children, wandering off to the group of men deeper in the Junction. He would look for his friend from the war Carver Collins. Carver mostly walked the streets begging for coins from people on corners. Other times, Carver and one or two of the other men could be found at the Catholic Mission's kitchen up on the hill. Whenever Charlie found Carver at the Junction, he always shared his pack of cigarettes with him, and sometimes they would share a drink from the half-pint bottle Charlie always seemed to carry in his pocket.

After Grady found out Charlie was taking the children to the Junction, he quietly confronted him. They were in the back yard away from the house when Nell overheard their conversation.

"You cain't stay here no more Charlie. I cain't stand by and let you take my daughter and that little cripple boy down there to the Junction with those men." Grady's eyes flashed with his anger, "...and you won't get any help for that drinking."

"I know," Charlie responded; "I should' a left a long time ago" He was surprisingly agreeable. "I'll move back to the rooming house over on Congress Street tomorrow after work." They both were relieved by his decision.

"What do you want me to tell Mae, and Nell?" Grady soften.
"Nothing. I think Mae'll know what happened, and Nell, she'll be all right. She'll still have Jacob," Charlie said.She watched him walk out the backyard gate toward the bottom road and Hobo Junction. Just before he reached the hill, he stopped briefly at the front of the mission to look back at the tenement house.

Grady, his brother remained in the back yard watching him walk away, as Nell fought back her tears.

"...Oh, oh sometimes it causes me to tremble"

CHAPTER FOUR

J IM'S DINER WAS AT THE END of the tenement house where Nell lived. The building was a two-story brick row house. There were eight units in all, with four on the lower level and four on the upper. Each set of units had their own entrances from the street, and small separate basements. Jim, a big Irishman owned the Diner on the corner and lived upstairs over the restaurant.

Although there were large plate glass windows on either side of the front door to the Diner, the place always looked dark from the outside. Single bulbs dangled from the old tin ceiling casting a pale light over most of the interior, and the three metal tables sitting in the middle of the scarred floor. The little daylight managing to get through the windows was also dim. It was filtered by the incessant humidity running down, and clouding the windows. The tall steamy windows were partially covered by several large green plants sitting in huge buckets on the floor close to them. The place had a rectangular shape, about thirty by twenty feet. There was a small counter with four tall stools facing directly into the small kitchen area. In the winter, a large heater provided heat from one side of the room opposite the kitchen area. Jim wore a reddish complexion, and had an easy smile whenever he saw Nell and Jacob together. He was always dressed in a stained white apron over clean white pants, and a white undershirt. It covered a mass of graying, wiry, black hair that covered his chest and back. He also wore what looked like a white paper cap on his balding head.

It seemed Jim was always in the Diner. No matter what hour of the day, he was there.

Sometimes he would ask Jacob and Nell to run errands for him to the neighborhood store up the street. He knew they could always be depended on to take the shopping list to his cousin Lena, who owned the grocery store. She would carefully pack several pounds of pork chops, chicken feet, bacon, ground meat, bread, spices, and occasionally coffee, eggs, and milk in large brown paper sacks. After placing them in Jim's small rusty wagon, she helped the children maneuver it through the front door and onto the sidewalk.

One of the front wheels wobbled, and the wagon squeaked when it moved, but Nell and Jacob alternately pushed and pulled until they got it back to the Diner. Jim waited for them, pacing outside, by the large window; he would have one of his ritualistic cigarettes, watching as they maneuvered the wagon across the street. These were the only times they ventured openly into the Diner, but it was always an adventure for them. They were excited when Jim placed a shiny quarter into each of their outstretched hands. Nell also got to sit at the counter while Jacob stood close by as they stuffed their mouths with one of the day-old glazed donuts Jim kept in a greasy box on the counter. Sometimes if he didn't have customers in the Diner they would hang around long enough to watch him prepare food for the evening blue plate special. Nell knew she would never forget the first time she saw him cook for Po'ke Chop.

"For Po'ke Chop Jones," he would say in his heavy Irish brogue, sliding six of the fresh pork chops into the sizzling grease.

"All them?" Jacob's face looked puzzled. "He eats all them? At one time?"

"You've seen Po'ke Chop? He's a big man," Jim answered, covering the skillet with a heavy iron top.

"Yeah...but my whole family cain't eat that many, and my Uncle Charlie can really eat!" Nell snickered.

"Yeah," Jacob chimed in.

Jim took the wagon, and pulled it to the rear of the small kitchen.

"Nell, help me put the rest of the groceries away." He stood on a chair, and as they handed him the various packages he placed them high on a shelf on the side of the stove. He stepped down after placing the basket of eggs on the shelf.

"You best get along home now," he said leading the children to the door. "Po'ke Chop be coming any time soon, it's near three o'clock."

"Cain't we stay to see Po'ke Chop?"

"Maybe next time." Jim said, "Too much other stuff to do right now."

The children eventually did get to see Po'ke Chop at the Diner. He was there for his afternoon meal when they brought the groceries back from Lena's one day. An extraordinarily large man he would always eat a plate of beans, at least two pounds of pork chops, and half a loaf of bread, washing it all down with several large cups of coffee. It was a regular ritual with him. He always ate the same heavy meal in the afternoon before he went to work at the dock, unloading the freighters.

One evening, Nell described for her friend Rose Ann, with animation, how Po'ke Chop never used a fork with the meat.

"He simply picks the chops up with his hands, stuffing the food in his mouth. He closes his eyes when he chews. Me and Jacob, we watched him eat in awe," she said, explaining, "...he would stuff the food into a pouch on one side of his mouth. It would sit here," she touched her right cheek, "his cheek bulging outward as he chewed on the other side, savoring every bite of food as he swallowed it. Every so often he would stop to lick the grease as it ran down his huge fingers, and take a large drink of water or coffee. Rose Ann, he's got to be the biggest man in the whole wide world," she said one day, using her out-stretched arms to emphasize his girth.

Certainly, he was the largest man in the neighborhood, and when he was not eating, he was chewing on a short fat cigar stuck between his full lips. Most people in the area found him to be a welcomed curiosity, as his big voice and friendly manners always seemed to brighten any place he happened to be.

NELL HAD OVERHEARD most of the conversation in the tenement house about Po'ke Chop. Charlie had whispered to Mae that he had a quick eye for the ladies, and was always taking some woman down to the abandoned box-car where he lived. And that sometimes when he, and Carver walked to the Junction, they would see Po'ke Chop walking with his latest conquest. The woman, he said, looking around apprehensively, would follow Po'ke Chop at a distance along the railroad tracks running east and west out of the switching yard. They would walk de-liberately toward, and enter the old boxcar where Po'ke Chop lived.

One spur of tracks running along the river just south of the river road and into the silos at the cement fac-tories near Hobo Junction was always littered with coal that had accidentally fallen from the trains. After work, sometimes Grady said, Po'ke Chop would walk the mile along the railroad tracks to the dock where he worked, and pick up the coal scattered along the tracks.

He told Mae he heard Po'ke Chop traded the coal for sex with some of the willing women in the neighbor-hood. When he was not unloading the freighters at the dock. It seemed he was always dressed up, walking the streets of the neighborhood.

The day Nell and Jacob met him at the Diner he wore creased gabardine pants with cuffs breaking just right over his large black shiny shoes. A black bowler hat was on his head and a striped vest was stretched over his ample stomach. On his vest, he wore what looked like a million buttons advertising everything imaginable. He wore buttons advertising Coca-Cola, hot chocolate, Saltine Crackers, Bulldog sardines, and lots of other products few people in the neighborhood recognized. Many of the buttons wore the faces of politicians and other prominent people in the city. Others simply had writing on them--meaningless to the casual observer. Before leaving the Diner that day he took two of the buttons from his vest and pinned them on the front of the children's shirts. Several months later he was arrested for living in the boxcar.

"He knew he was trespassing all the time. What, with all the building going on down there at the river, he should have known they would catch him sooner or later...too bad." Mae said coldly when she heard the news from Grady.

By then Po'ke Chop had given Nell 12 brightly colored buttons. She kept them, and all the change she had earned at the Diner under her bed in an old cigar box Jim had given her.

Most of Jim's customers were single men who lived in the rooming houses peppering the neighborhood. When the place was filled with customers, a smoky haze, and tempting smells filled the air from their cigarettes and the steaming plates of food he served. The oilcloth tablecloths always felt slick from the grease in the air in place. It was known around the neighborhood Jim's was a place where a man could get a free meal when he was down on his luck and didn't have any money. Carver Collins found the atmosphere around the Diner attractive. Most days, when he was not with Charlie or sleeping in the Junction, he stood outside the Diner on the corner sporadically talking and cussing loudly to some unseen foe or friend. The rest of the time he begged for cigarettes and money from people passing by. Whenever he gestured wildly at the air, as if fighting an unseen foe, or cussed threateningly at the customers, Jim would come outside, give him a few cigarettes and urge him to move on.

Every day early in the morning, and in the evening just before closing, Raymond, the dishwasher, a razor thin black man would be in the Diner with Jim. People in the tenement house always knew when it was time for the Diner to open or close. Raymond would show up around the same time each day. He was a solitary figure, almost a stick man who never talked, and because of his shuffling walk could be easily recognized from a distance. He would walk from his rooming house on Congress Street with his head down until he got to the end of the tenement house. There he would cut through Nell's backyard and down through the alley to the back door of the Diner, and let himself in with his key. Sometimes, in the evening, when Jim needed space in the ice box, and Carver was close-by, Jim would call him inside so he could help Raymond pack the rusty wagon with food leftover from the previous week. On his way home Raymond would walk out of his way followed by a cussing Carver across the bottom road. They would pull the wagon down along the riverbank to feed the homeless men living among the brush and weeds in the Junction. Carver would help Raymond distribute the food at a respectable pace sometimes offering sandwiches to the impulses in his head.

Before the war, Carver Collins and his family had lived by the Diner on Fort Street. At that time most every weekend he and Charlie would share a quart of beer and listen to the baseball broadcasts in his back-yard. He was the father of three young girls, and because he worked at the packinghouse, could get fresh meat cheaply. Everybody in the neighborhood knew him to be an expert butcher, and sooner or later would approach him about getting them a cheap ham or pork roast. He was a happy man and always jokingly told his friends Bella, his oldest daughter, was really his son. When she was a young child, he took her everywhere with him and, against her objections, encouraged her to excel at sports in school.

After he came home from the war the voices in his head wouldn't let him hold his job anymore. His wife asked the state for support for her and the children but the worker insisted Carver had to move out of the house. Within weeks after being put out of the house, he was found in the middle of winter walking partially naked through the downtown streets. As he walked, he removed, and dropped his clothes, piece by piece, mark-ing a trail in the snow behind him. The police were called and, finally four of them were able to overcome, and transport Carver to the Crisis Center at the City hos-pital. After an initial evaluation, City transferred him to the VA hospital. They treated his hallucinations with a course of strong drugs before releasing him.

His children were ashamed of his condition, and eventually the two younger girls denied him as their father. Bella was conflicted, but she never denied him or turned her back on him.

On days when his mind was clearer, Charlie helped him scrounge the alleys. They collected rags, paper, and scrap iron, rubber -- anything they could sell at the scrap dealer. In the evenings, Charlie drank wine with the rest of the men in the Junction, while Carver sat by him near the old dock enjoying a quiet smoke.

◆ ◆ ◆

FROM THE FIRST-TIME NELL asked her Mother about doing the errands for Jim with Jacob, Mae cautioned her about eating in the place. She believed the place was not sanitary, and a haven for cockroaches, mice, and probably rats. But she did admit she had been intrigued by the smells of the food coming from the place for a long time. They came from Jim's blue-plate specials of pig ears, navy beans, plates of sauerkraut and sausages, or barbecued pig feet. The Diner was also popular for greasy hamburgers, and heaping bowls of chicken and rice soup. Nell brought some of the chicken and rice soup home one day, offering her Mother a sample as she opened the hot container. Mae warily tasted the soup.

"Oh! Is this good," she proclaimed.

"Can't be that good!" Grady teased her. "You always said the place was too dirty for you. What happened?" She took another spoonful of the soup, nodding her head at Nell who smiled knowingly.

"It's really good Grady!" She finally acknowledged. "Jim's really a better cook than I would ever have thought," she said. This soup flavor could only come from simmering chicken feet, backs, gizzards and chicken livers. He probably cooks them overnight to make the soup stock this good." Grady grunted agreement, and Nell smiled, looking at a picture of Uncle Charlie that sat on his footlocker by the couch.

"Mother, you seen Uncle Charlie lately? I used to see him every now and then down by the Junction...but I haven't seen him lately." Mae ignored the question, but Grady responded sharply.

"Down by the Junction? Nell, what are you doing down there? You stay away from that place! You hear?"

"Yes sir." She begrudgingly answered, confiding to herself to be more careful and to never mention the Junction again in the presence of her parents.

The time that Nell, and Jacob spent helping Jim in the Diner fed their friendship with other worldly knowledge, and pleasant memories for a long time. It expanded their growth by providing a vision of life beyond the world of the child's life. But it was also a place where they would soon learn a valuable lesson about the dark side of the small world in which they lived.

"...Tremble, tremble, tremble"

CHAPTER FIVE

*I*T SEEMED TO NELL, JACOB always complained about the years passing too slowly when they were young. Each winter, except for taking the bus to school, he was primarily house bound. Whenever there was a big snowstorm, it was difficult for him to walk outside. During those times, he was always talking to his Mother about his impatience in waiting for the winters to end, and summer to begin so he could spend more time with Nell catching spiders and butterflies.

As it turned out, every summer, unknown to their parents, he and Nell would frequently walk along the edge of the Junction hoping to see Uncle Charlie. They hoped he would invite them in to join him again in the cool breezes on the river's edge. Occasionally they would see him there with his friend Carver Collins. The two of them, and Carver's daughter Bella, would be walking quietly along the river, or sitting near the old dock talking. Generally, he ignored the calls from Nell and Jacob, but sometimes he would angrily wave them away.

Months passed, and the winters continued to blend into summers. Charlie's drinking worsened. He lost his full-time job at the laundry, but continued to work at part-time jobs as they became available to him. He passed out handbills for the merchants in the neighborhood, and he helped the iceman deliver ice to the local markets and homes in the area.

As a result, they soon saw less and less of Uncle Charlie in the neighborhood, or even when they would sneak off to walk along the bottom road along the edge of the Junction. Sometimes Jacob would pressure her, and they would visit the old dock at the waters edge.

One Summer Jacob's Mother while tending to one of the Church's sick members who lived off the bottom road, observed that Nell and Jacob were frequent visitors to the Junction. She did not tell Mae, but she confronted the children insisting they never go there again. She knew the place had peaked their interest after they heard Charlie spent a lot of time there. She knew the place had a strange beauty about it, and a pull on them like a magnet, but she was concerned for their safety, especially with the strange men staying in the place.

Nell would have never disobeyed her, and gone there again, except for this one special butterfly. It was on a warm afternoon close to Jacob's ninth birthday. His Mother had fed them cupcakes, and ice cream to celebrate the occasion. Later they went outside to catch spiders and grasshoppers in the side yard next to the house. Then they saw her.

She flitted and danced through the air landing on a colorful patch of Phlox planted near the wire fence around the yard. Her wings moved slowly with the breeze when she settled momentarily over one of the sweet buds, and her beauty stunned Jacob and Nell. She was large for a butterfly, and was colored purplish-black with yellow spots on the edge of her wings, and there were large orange crescents in the center of each wing.

"Catch her Nell...boy is she, wow lets just catch her!"

Jacob stumbled over to the fence yelling to Nell, just as the butterfly lifted unconcerned to the crown of a near by Morning Glory. He quickly dumped their catch of grasshoppers from the Mason jar they were using and timidly approached the butterfly. Just as he raised the jar, she lifted and danced through the air. She caught a slight breeze and headed in the direction of the few blocks leading toward the Junction. Without thinking, Jacob followed her in his own special way of running; he chased behind her while yelling excitedly at the top of his voice to Nell.

"C'mon...c'mon Nell, she's getting away!"

Yelling back, Nell took the Mason jar as she ran past him. Before too long, they had forgotten their commitment and were chasing the butterfly past the old dock, through the wildflowers, and into the depts. Of the Junction. While Jacob struggled to catch up, Nell followed it plowing through the sand drifts and the bushes until she found herself in the heart of the Junction. Jacob following Nell at a slower pace crashed into her laughing as she came to an abrupt stop. She was stopped cold by what lay before her. In front of her stretched out, and sitting in various positions in the sand were a group of men. Three of them were black, the rest were what Mae called, poor whites and Mexicans. Most were heavily bearded and dressed in stained, shabby military uniforms. Those who were not drunk or sleeping turned their attention to this new intrusion into their sacred space. Jacob and Nell knew they were like Charlie, veterans from the war.

Nell knew her parents had whispered about these men all the times. And especially at those times when, these men walked the alleys around the neighborhood looking through the garbage cans, and or were seen on street corners begging.

She stood in the Junction appraising their surroundings as Jacob, gasping for air pulled her arm from the rear. She rudely shook him off, as her gaze rested on one of the men that looked like her Uncle Charlie. Instinctively she felt in her pocket for the quarter from her cigar box. She had carried it for the last month to give to Uncle Charlie if she ever ran into him on the street. It was the first of many quarters she would give to him over the next several months. The man she was looking at sat facing the river talking quietly in a small group. When he turned to look at her and Jacob, his eyes gave no indication he recognized her, but she walked boldly up to the group and held out the quarter for him.

"For cigarettes," she said softly, dropping the Mason jar. To her disappointment, he gave no sign of recognizing her, but took the money with a pleased look in his eyes. Quickly she brushed her disappointment aside, took a deep breath, satisfied she had accomplished her goal, she slowly walked away into the wealth of wildflowers and butterflies surrounding them in the heart of the Junction.

There was literally a sea of butterflies flitting among the wildflowers, she thought. It was like she was sucked into a living work of art, a moving abstract rainbow. She danced happily with them as they flitted around her against a stunning blue sky and the rippling blueness of the river. Suddenly she realized she had lost track of the beautiful butterfly they had followed wildly into the Junction. The butterfly had simply merged into the large group of butterflies, and although Nell had glanced upward hoping to find her again among the dancing shapes she had lost her.

Damn...we lost her, Nell thought to herself.

But Jacob was still after her with the Mason jar, and when she heard his excited voice, she glanced in his direction. Jacob held the jar out in front of him as he waddled toward her, a broad grin on his face. He had managed to catch the butterfly, and he held the prize high above his head in the old Mason jar.

"I got her Nell, I got her!" He was excited until he became aware of the relentless stares of the men sitting near them.

"Come on Nell, come on...let's go!" He took her arm, whispering softly. When she resisted, Jacob pulled harder at her arm.

"Nell!" He pleaded.

Finally, he released her and backed awkwardly away from the group. Looking at each of the men, he noted how similar they all looked --like Uncle Charlie, he thought dirty and unwashed.

"Hey! You kids get the hell out'a here! What you want? Ain't no kids' s'pposed to be here...go'wan home!" The voice was slurred. It was the man closest to them. He had been asleep when they stumbled into their midst. He sat up eyeing them angrily, picking up a stick, and brandishing it as if he would attack them.

"Y'all go'wan now." Nell turned to face him.

"My Uncle Charlie lives here," she yelled back at him defiantly. I came to see Charlie Campbell...He's my Uncle," she stammered softly as speaking to herself.

The man grumbled under his breath turning his back to her. Shocked by her own bravery, she looked over her shoulder for Jacob. He had dropped the Mason jar, retreating to a spot near the old dock. When he caught her eye, he beckoned for her to join him. She ignored him, stooped to pick up the Mason jar and admired the beautiful butterfly flitting frantically inside.

"I KNOW YOU...why, you're Charlie's niece."

Nell reacted to the sound, dropping the Mason jar when she turned in the direction of the voice. The voice was soft and melodious. Initially it was difficult to determine the direction of the voice, but Nell caught the scent of the young woman just as she came into view, approaching partially hidden by the scrub growing along that part of the Junction. She smelled like the lilac bushes near Jacob's house when they bloomed in the spring, and Nell temporarily forgot about Jacob and the men around them when she heard the rustle of the young woman's satin dress.

The young woman was close enough now to touch her, and Nell looked up just as she felt the young woman's thin arm encircle her shoulder hugging her briefly. Nell was shocked. She was the same young woman she had once seen walking with Charlie and Carver Collins in the Junction. Nell was surprised when her heart started beating at a faster rate. Up close, she instantly knew from the way the young woman dressed, looked, and walked she probably worked at Mrs. Meade's house on Congress Street.

Her skin was smooth, and the color of a lemon that had stayed in the sun too long, and a large happy smile creased her face. Her shoulder length hair, straight and soft, blew in the slight breeze. Nell's eyes were immediately drawn to the small gold cross glinting in the sun around her neck, and the large grease stained brown bag she carried with her left hand. Nell's heart jumped, but sank again as soon as she realized the woman knew her. Concern that she might tell Grady, or Mae of seeing her at the Junction made Nell's legs weak. But her touch was warm and soothing and Nell quickly relaxed, appraising the woman more closely. Almost instantly, Nell thought this was the prettiest young woman she had ever seen. She had a young-looking face with full lips and high cheekbones, but the carriage of a mature woman. When she walked, her hips moved rhythmically under her skirt, and her breasts jiggled freely under her top. But it was her eyes that drew Nell to her. They were quiet and stable, peering solemnly from behind long lashes that seemed to be growing haphazardly out of a dark circle of makeup circling them. They were brooding and sad, and made Nell want to ask her why she was not happy. Her rich lips were painted a bright red to make them look smaller than they were.

She smiled hesitantly; and Nell could see a smear of lipstick had stained one of her perfectly shaped teeth.

They were the whitest teeth Nell had ever seen, and the smell of her breath was like fresh flowers...like Mae's smelled whenever she went to church.

"Hi. I'm Bella...what's your name?" Her eyes danced when she spoke, and the warm smile creased her face again.

She picked up the Mason jar, and walked with Nell back into the center of the group of men. The men started to gather around them.

Bella beckoned for Jacob to join them. Frightened he remained by the dock and called out.

"Nell, come on...We should leave now! Come on!"

Nell sensed his fear, and she knew he was right. They should leave, but she was intrigued by the presence of Bella. She beckoned to Jacob to join them, and as the men sat down around Bella, she also sat down with them. Bella sat on the edge of the group, and opened the bag. She first took a folded newspaper from it and spread it on the sandy ground. Reaching again inside the bag she produced a variety of poorly wrapped sandwiches, slices of caramel cake, and several pieces of fruit.

Over that summer, it became obvious to Nell, that Bella had adopted the men at the Junction. Taking care of them became a mission in her young life. She came every Saturday afternoon into the center of the group of men. They quietly gathered around her and Nell. Waiting patiently, they anticipated the treats she brought in the greasy bag from Jim's Diner on Fort Street. She always showed up at the same time, having arranged the time off with Mrs. Meade. But she never stayed longer than a few minutes, as she had to be back at the house before the Saturday night clients began arriving after dusk.

She beckoned again for Jacob to join them, but he kept his distance.

After she passed out the food, the men left the circle, moving silently away to various parts of the Junction to eat. She placed a few of the leftover sandwiches and cake back in the greasy bag, and quietly picked up the Mason jar again, holding it to the sky. Jacob who had watched from a distance finally, cautiously waddled over to join them. Bella motioned for him to sit down.

"She is beautiful...Look at her color and size. I think she is the most beautiful butterfly of them all. They call her a Swallowtail," Bella said. "I saw a picture of one in a book once. See the spots on the wings with the different colors? That's how you tell."

She paused, handing one of the sandwiches to each of them. They were simple watercress lettuce and butter sandwiches on wheat bread wrapped in torn pieces of wax paper. Nell ate hers with relish. It was the first time she had eaten wheat bread. She thought it was the best sandwich she had ever eaten in her young life.

"We have to let her go, you know." Bella's voice had a pleading tone. She looked first at Jacob, and then at Nell. "She is too beautiful to die in a Mason jar...and luckily she's not broken yet. That's the best part! You didn't touch her wings, so they are still intact. I read in the book.... The wings are made up of all these beautiful scales...you know, just like a fish. That's what the wings are made of." Pausing, she bit into her sandwich.

"You mean like the scales my mom scrapes off a fish before she cooks it?" Jacob's eyes were wide with disbelief.

"Yeah, just like a fish.... except butterfly scales break real easy. They're delicate...like powder, and rub off on your fingers when you touch them."

She used her hands drawing circles in the air to describe the scales.

"If we touch the butterfly when we catch her, we break the scales with our hands...some of them come off, you know they look powdery on the fingers. Then the butterfly is broken, really crippled." She looked at them intently. "We don't want that...do we?"

They were taken by her open friendliness. Nell shook her head from side to side responding to her question. Bella looked at Jacob, who was pondering her question. He was reluctant to give up his beautiful prize. When Nell also looked at him questioningly, he slowly nodded his head in agreement.

"Yeah, I know," he said as Bella quickly removed the top from the Mason jar. She held it upside down and released the butterfly. It flitted away into the blueness of the sky. Jacob, watching it blinked his eyes, shielding them from the sun as the delicate creature disappeared into the sunlight.

Bella gave him the Mason jar and said, "The men here are like broken butterflies, only the cycle is reversed for them." She nodded in the direction of some of the men sitting by the river.

"Did you know butterflies are ugly little things for awhile after they are caterpillars?" She didn't wait for them to answer. "Most people, if they see them while they're in their cocoons probably kill them." She looked again in the direction of the men. "Too many people treat these men like they are ugly creatures that deserve to die, "she said. Moisture started to form in her eyes, and she turned away to dab at her eyes with the tips of her fingers, careful not to disturb her makeup. Turning back, she cleared her throat and continued.

"It said in the book, butterflies are one of the few creatures this big thing happens to...it's kind of like a big change that happens while the caterpillars sleep in their cocoons. And when they find their way out of the cocoons, they're these beautiful creatures we call butterflies. They live for a while spreading their beauty along their journey, fall in love, mate, and the process starts all over again. It's really a beautiful life cycle." She picked up some of the sand, letting it fall through her fingers. Jacob, uncomfortable with his sitting position struggled to stand, and moved closer to Nell. Bella watched him with interest as he adjusted, to stand more comfortably on his crippled leg, before she spoke again.

"Have you noticed, its just like they come out of nowhere. You look up, and suddenly there is one flitting along a flower, or in the sky. I've often wondered where they go at night. When they are captured by people, they become broken and die a slow death...much like these men here in the Junction." She sighed deeply looking blankly at Nell who still sat by her side.

"They too have gone through their own special changes." She nodded in the direction of some of the men. "All you have to do is look at the different colored ribbons and the medals on their uniforms. We can only imagine what they have seen or done to stay alive." She looked down wiping at her nose.

A strange silence settled over them when she stopped talking. After awhile it felt uncomfortable for Jacob and Nell. Jacob wanted to break the silence by saying something as worldly as the things Bella had said. But he couldn't find the words. They simply stayed as they were--connected in space, but lost in their individual thoughts. Finally, Bella broke the silence.

"Nell, the man by the grape vine sitting at the big sand dune down by the river is your Uncle Charlie. The man sitting next to him is Carver Collins...he's my father."

She spoke directly to Nell, but looked away across the Junction toward the spot where her Father and Uncle Charlie sat. Nell looked at the side of her face, steadily studying the young woman. Had she heard Bella's words correctly? Her mind raced. Could it be true, someone else had a family member that looked and acted like Uncle Charlie? She was surprised at Bella's revelation, while at the same time she was happy too. She was not the only one personally affected by the life the men in the Junction were forced to live. Immediately she felt a strong kinship with Bella, and she looked more intently at the man Bella had said was her father. Jacob squirmed uncomfortably by her side, as Bella followed her gaze.

"They are very close to each other, having served in the same unit overseas...and all. They love, and under-stand each other. I guess I'm lucky, cause your Uncle Charlie looks out for Carver.
I appreciate that." She took a deep breath.

Jacob was now leaning on Nell to support his weight, and he watched Bella intently quietly peering down her neckline staring at the fullness of her breasts under the sheerness of her top.

"Their humanity has been taken away from them though, both-of-them," she said, "As are the rest of these men!" She waved her arm. "All of them...they were in the war, did things, saw things...unspeakable things." Her voice broke momentarily. "All of them...every one of them came home hurting and broken in their minds. No-body escaped."

She looked at Jacob who struggled to sit down again next to Nell. He squirmed to get more comfortable.

"Most of them," Bella continued, "they only remem-ber the Junction as a part of the happier days when they played as children in an area like this. That's why they come here. Some of the other men leave when it gets cold, but not Daddy and your Uncle. They stay huddled together in that makeshift shelter they put up every fall, and it usually lasts all winter."

She stopped speaking, wondering about the shelter they would put together that fall.

"They probably caught butterflies as kids too," she said wistfully, looking up. They came back from the war like this. It must'a been bad for them over there. You can't even begin to imagine... But maybe worse for the refugees though, in those camps I read about...killed by the millions, and treated bad, for no reason," she said looking in the direction of her father.

"Nell pondered the words 'millions' and 'refugees' briefly. She knew she had heard her parents talk about the killing of Jewish people before. They owned the packinghouse where her daddy worked. She resolved to ask Mae about the meaning of refugees and millions. Bella cut into her thoughts.

"But, my Daddy...he does'nt even know what is happening to him, for that matter what happened to him last week, or the week before that. Your Uncle Charlie's not quite so bad. I believe if he could just quit the drinking, he might have a chance. At least he can still work. Every week now he cuts the grass and cleans the yard at Mrs. Meade's house, you know."

"That's good, right? I didn't know," Nell responded.

A wry smile crossed Bella's face. She's just a child. How could Nell know, she thought, while touching Jacob's outstretched leg. The feeling was electric for him, he told Nell later. He was conflicted when he felt the warmth of her hand. He wanted her to move it. While at the same time he wanted her to keep it there. She massaged his crippled leg as she spoke again.

"Promise me you'll never let them do this to you," she said to Jacob. "Run away if you have to. Wars don't really solve anything. They just kill other people, their children, their mother's, and the men, it destroys their souls. I get so angry when I look at my Father...what a waste of a beautiful man.

"Why do they have wars anyway?" It was Jacob. He seemed more comfortable now and had been listening intently to Bella after she removed her hand. She didn't answer. The question just hung there, as the three of them silently settled into their separate thoughts again.

OF ALL THE WOMEN WORKING at Mrs. Meade's house Bella was the smallest. Nell overheard Charlie tellGrady she was also the youngest, and the prettiest. Lately she seemed to be one of the happiest since Charlie had started working at the house. One day the previous summer Charlie had delivered ice to the house while working for the iceman. Mrs. Meade was sitting on the front porch. As he was leaving she called out to him.

"Hey, you, come here a minute. You wan'a make a coupla' bucks after you get through wit your ice job?" He stopped on his way back to the ice truck pointing at himself as he looked at her.

"Yeah. You," she said pointing back at him. "Come here a minute!"

She was a big brownish, yellow looking woman, with skin the color of a ripe pumpkin. During the summer months she was always on her front porch, sitting on a large wooden recliner pushed back out of the heat of the sun. Her face was dominated by a huge set of lips. They spread across her face, topped by a set of piercing intense eyes. Soft wavy hair hung below her shoulders. She always wore a sundress and a large straw hat. Struggling, she sat up as he approached. And although she smelled the stale alcohol cloaking his presence, she offered him a job.

"You come back later I give you two dollars to cut the grass out front and pick up all that chicken shit in the backyard. I think the kid I had doin' it must'a quit...ain't seen him for two weeks. The place looks and smells like hell!"

Later that evening Charlie returned to cut the grass,

and rake the backyard. An old rooster, who was strutting around out back, immediately charged him. Four clucking hens and several baby chicks scattered under the back porch of the house. Concerned for the charging rooster he slammed the gate and hurried back to the front of the house. Mrs. Meade was still sitting on the porch.

"Hit him wit the rake boy! He just thinks you after them hens," she yelled. "He's old as sin...go'wan back there; he'll leave you alone if you hit him!" She laughed aloud and her belly was the only thing that moved on her.

After that, every Saturday morning Charlie would cut the front grass, rake the backyard, and take out the trash from the house. Bella was happy to see him every Saturday, and as he cut the grass, or raked the chicken droppings in the backyard, she would watch him from the upstairs window. Occasionally several of the other women in the house joined her, sitting by the window they talked to her, but her primary focus was on Charlie. She rarely spoke to Charlie, but she watched him with an increased interest, as she knew he was the only friend her father had at the Junction.

Once a month he worked in the house bringing cases of beer and wine from the basement to restock the large cooler and ice box in the kitchen. Charlie said the house always seemed like a happy place, and full of activity. There always seemed to be music playing, and one or two of the women would be sitting in the parlor in their brightly colored gowns and housecoats. They sat on large couches while talking quietly, and endlessly smoking cigarettes. The furnishings in the house were all antiques. Large expensive oriental rugs covered floors of polished oak, and in the living room, large damask drapes shrouded the tall windows.

All the women working at the house had their own

rooms, and entertained a steady stream of men arriving in large black cars, or by taxi cars starting after dusk each day. Except for the policemen who stopped for a free lunch once a week, most of the men wore suits, drank cognac, and smoked large cigars.

Also, living at the house was a small older man named James. Charlie said he wore brightly colored clothes, and looked, walked, and talked like a woman. He had his own small apartment in the attic of the old house. He cooked most of the meals for the girls, and the clients of the place. James had his own list of clients who came just to see him, and he entertained them freely in his own space. In his free time, like a mother hen, he fussed over the girls, fussed with their hair, and kept the place spotless.

Mrs. Meade was the largest woman in the neighborhood. All the men called her "Baby Doll" because of her weight, the different wigs, and tight dresses she wore. Each one distinctly designed emphasized her large breasts. She wore large diamond rings on each of her fat fingers, and was always cooling herself with several large cardboard fans she carried with her where ever she went.

Everyday in the summertime, she either sat on the front porch, or if it was raining outside, she lay on a day bed placed strategically between two large windows in the parlor of her house. Propped up on two large damask pillows she looked out on the large front porch of the house, and counted the customers coming to the house daily. Sometimes when things were slow she would give instructions about the art of pleasing a man to the girls of the house. She never addressed them as a group, or raised her voice -- rather she would call them into the parlor individually and give out recommendations for their individual dress and behavior.

One of the women in the neighborhood, who had worked at Mrs. Meade's for a short while, expressed to

Mae, her concern for Charlie working at the house. Mae told Grady, according to the woman, Charlie should be careful of Mrs. Meade as she was unstable, and subject to strange behavior. Concerned for the welfare of his younger brother, Grady questioned Mae more intensely.

"What can she do?" He asked anxiously, "what could she do to Charlie. Hell Charlie's not too stable himself," he said.

"This is more than drinking Grady," Mae said, "after the activity dies down for the night at the house, Mrs. Meade spends the rest of the time in her large bedroom."

"So, what's so strange about that?" He laughed.

"Well, according to what I heard, she just perches in front of the large triple mirror on her dresser. She sits on the stool in the middle and adjusts the mirrors so she can see all parts of her face, large back and breasts."

"So!" Grady looked at his wife questioningly. "I still don't see where the concern is...most women look at themselves in the mirror."

"Naked? All night? I don't think so! She simply sits there naked from the waist up trying on different wigs and drinking Remy Martin cognac. She stares at herself, turning this way and that. She appraises her huge face while fondling her large breasts and nipples, rubbing scented oil into them. Sometimes she picks at a pimple on her face, but mainly she just sits there silent, lost in a vision of herself."

"Sounds like she's just in love with herself," Grady said laughing. "If that's All we need to worry about for Charlie, he'll be alright." He turned away looking for the paper.

"You think she's crazy?" He asked over his shoulder. Mae was concerned. Grady had just come home from work, and she took his jacket hanging it in the closet.

"Maybe, I know she's smart though...could be crazy too, but no crazier than Carver Collins. He's the one I'm concerned about. If Charlie hadn't been hanging around with him so much, he'd probably still have his job at the laundry. I heard he was always going down there acting out. You know asking for Charlie, talking to himself and acting crazy." Grady dropped into the big chair behind the heater to remove his shoes.

"Where's Nell?" He asked struggling with the laces.

"She was out back with Rose Ann a minute ago," Mae responded.

The two young girls sat in the shade under the back steps. Nell listened intently to her parents conversation, while Rose Ann tried to get her more interested in the paper dolls, she had brought over.

"Have you seen Charlie lately," Grady asked. "I wonder if he is still drinking as much. You know I was hoping he would move back here with us so he could kind'a get back on his feet." She sat across from her husband on the old couch where Charlie had slept. It still had a faint odor of the soap, and shaving cream he had used.

"No Mae, you know we cain't have him drinkin' like that...not over you and Nell. I'll do what I can to help him, but I'm not going to sacrifice raisin' Nell right!" Mae looked at Charlie's photograph still sitting on his footlocker near the couch.

"I suspect he's sliding Grady, going down...I'm worried about him." She shook her head.

"I know," Grady said solemnly. "But he won't listen to me."

"He's funny though," Mae responded hoping to change the mood. "Last time I saw him going down the alley, he told me he loves Bella...and he thinks she likes him. Maybe she will help to straighten him out," she said crossing her legs, and smiling broadly.

"Then he told me about the time Po'ke Chop visits the house. Cause he's so big all the girls refuse to...you know, take care of him. He said this was the only time he knew of when Mrs. Meade took a customer. Word's out in the neighborhood Po'ke Chop's got a dick the size of a horse," She laughed out loud.

"How do you know?" Questioningly, Grady looked over the paper. Mae laughed even harder.

"Aw Grady...that's just the story in the neighborhood. Don't be so serious...anyway, they say he rode her once so hard, and so long she finally lost control, moaning, and crying his name so loud she could be heard through-out the house. Charlie had me dying laughing. He said after the first three times he did it to Mrs. Meade...she asked him to move into the house with her when he was put out of the boxcar."

"Is that where he stays now?"

"Sure does!"

Grady and Mae were still laughing when Nell and Rose Ann walked in the back door. Nell was unusually quiet as Rose Ann chattered loudly about clothes, makeup and paper dolls.

"...Were you there when they nailed him to the tree?"

CHAPTER SIX

ONE EVENING LATER IN THE MONTH Nell and Jacob were sitting with Rose Ann on the front stoop. Mae had told them to stay in the front of the house while Jacob waited for his father to pick him up after choir rehearsal ended at the church. As they sat there talking bouncing a rubber ball of the steps, they yelled a greeting to the familiar figure of Raymond. He walked slowly past them through the backyard toward the back door of the Diner. He responded to their greeting by throwing up his hand, but, as usual, never looked their way. The streetlights were just flickering on and Rose Ann finally drifted off toward home, after she heard her mother calling her name

Nell also knew it was time for her to be in the house, but asked Mae if she could sit on the stoop with Jacob until his father arrived. At first Mae insisted they wait inside, but reluctantly gave approval when Nell argued it was cooler outside than in the house.

To entertain themselves while they waited, Nell suggested they race each other down the block to the door of Jim's Diner. Jacob was apprehensive, but agreed with conditions.

"You have to give me a head start, Nell...you're faster than me."

"OK, why don't you start down by the street light...is that far enough?"

Jacob, excited, started to waddle down to the streetlight when a loud noise came from the direction of the Diner. It sounded like someone had set off a firecracker. It froze Jacob in his tracks, and startled Nell momentarily, but she ran toward him. Frightened, Jacob wanted to return to the security of the stoop. But curious, Nell took his hand and they ventured forward until they were close to the front door of the Diner. The sound of scuffling and loud voices greeted them the closer they got to the door.

It was open, and in the dim light they saw Jim on the floor sprawled in a pool of blood. He was struggling to get to a small nickel-plated gun lying on the floor several feet in front of him. There was a large creeping bloodstain in the front of his apron. It had crept down his pant legs and had started to stain his white shoes and socks. Raymond was struggling viciously with a gray figure near the counter. The gray figure held one of Jim's large butcher knives high in the air. He was trying to wrest it free as Raymond held onto the arm holding the knife with both hands.

They struggled back and forth, sometimes slipping in the trail of blood Jim had left as he crawled slowly across the floor. The change from the cigar box, and a broken wad of dollar bills were scattered all over the floor.

Jim was now sitting up against the wall. He had the small gun in his hand, but he never raised it. His glassy eyes tried to follow the struggle playing out before him, while his hands tried to stifle the blood pooling around him.

He finally saw Nell and Jacob. They were frozen, standing silent and still -- horrified in the doorway.

"The police!" He urged with a halting breath. "Get the police!"

In the distance, in a hollow space they heard his words, but both were too frightened by the scene unfolding before them to move.

Raymond finally managed to bring his knee sharply into the groin of the gray figure. The man went stiff with the pain and seemed to lose all his resistance. He doubled over from the pain and could barely walk, but somehow managed to hold onto the knife. He balanced himself against the wall near the counter, and swung the knife at Raymond when he tried to take it away from him again. Raymond, breathing hard, finally sat on one of the stools at the other end of the counter. Like prizefighters resting between rounds, they didn't speak, but glared at each other.

Raymond looked at Jim on the floor. He was not moving, and his eyes stared blankly unfocused into space.

"You fuck...aw shit man, why did you have to!" Raymond screamed! Waving his hand at Jim's slumped figure he started to cry, blinking his eyes furiously. A stream of snot leaked from his nostril into the stubby growth on his face, and he whimpered struggling to control his breathing.

"Why? You bastard! Why?" He wiped at his nose.

Still holding the knife, the man started to move away from the wall. He looked over at the door, trying to move in that direction. His pain was still with him as he grimaced. He sucked air in through his mouth, giving off a whistling sound each time he inhaled. Raymond with a deep sigh watched him struggle to get to the door. Finally determined, Raymond turned quickly and reached into the cooking area near the counter picking up the large meat cleaver. Deliberately closing in on the man, he spun him around and chopped him with a glancing blow across the front of the head. The man, reacting automatically, frantically stabbed back at Raymond slashing him through his jacket across the arm. The sound from the second blow of the cleaver splitting the flesh and going into the bone was more than either child could handle. When the blood flooded the man's face, they both screamed and backed out of the doorway stumbling over each other. They ran back down the street, as Nell frantically screaming called "Mama, Mama...Mama!"

Mae was already in the backyard looking for them.

"Oh, my God!" She screamed when they blurted out what they had witnessed. She ushered them into the house, and immediately called Dean from the vacant lot near the tenement where he was out playing catch with his brother. She sent them running down the street to find the policemen who usually walked a beat down on the bottom road.

Soon the sounds of sirens and the screech of tires filled the air down at the Diner. The street came alive with the neighbors. They filled the block, talking and craning their necks to try to see inside the Diner. Those close by watched as Mae admonished Nell and Jacob to stay on the stoop to wait for Jacob's father, Mr. Turner.

Shaken, the children followed her direction. Jacob slowly followed Nell. Crying, he was still reacting to the scene in the Diner.

"Nell...Did Jim get killed. This is bad ain't it? Nell?"

"Yeah Jacob...real bad, I think they're all dead, except maybe Raymond." She was surprised by her circumspection, and, although the scene had disturbed her too, she was more in control of herself. He sat next to her on the stoop, and buried his face in his hands.

"Come on Jacob...come on, it's going to be alright," she said with a motherly tone, while putting her arm around his shoulder.

LATER WHEN NELL OVERHEARD her parents talking about what happened, she learned it was the second blow from the meat cleaver that killed the man attempting to rob Jim. After he crumpled into a heap on the bloody floor, Raymond exhausted and bleeding sat down next to him waiting for the police.

Jim, the big Irishman who had fed the men living at Hobo Junction, and introduced Nell and Jacob to the greasy donuts had died on the floor of his restaurant.

The man who had come to rob him was the homeless man from the Junction who Bella had said was her father. He was the primary reason she took the food to the Junction to feed the men.

Mae found out later, when the VA hospital quit treating Carver for the voices in his head, one of Bella's customers from the house; a medical doctor had been providing him with the medication he needed. Whenever she had them, Bella gave the pills to Charlie every Saturday morning, and he administered one to Carver every day.

The doctor had recently married, quit coming to the house, and providing her with the strong tranquilizers to quiet the voices in Carver's head. Carver had been without the pills for two weeks before he attempted to rob the Diner. During that time, Bella and Charlie hoped alcohol would do the same thing as the medication, but the alcohol had only made his hallucinations and behavior worse

SEVERAL WEEKS AFTER THE INCIDENT, Nell and Mae were in the kitchen. Mae had just put the last large handful of turnip and mustard greens into a pot of hot water seasoned with a piece of salt pork. She stirred the pot, not looking at Nell who stood in the kitchen door leading to the back porch. Jacob sat silently in the shade on the back porch listening to their conversation.

"Most are from the war, they're all over the country

like that," Mae said. "But they're really not home yet; some may never get back. I feel so sorry for them. Nobody helps them much, exceptthe catholic mission on the hill. Most people around here wish they would just simply go away." Nell felt her stomach sink as always when she heard those words.

"How come our church doesn't help out?" She asked glancing briefly at Jacob.

"Our church does, but just for the church members... Daddy says they should come join the church, and pray. He says prayers help with everything."

"Prayer does help," Mae said. "But they need more than prayer right now. They cain't get, and keep jobs...not with the condition they're in. Most just ride the freight trains all over the place looking for a place where they can feel welcome. Grady says they are like the birds. They come here and stay in the Junction every summer, and just before the weather breaks and turns cold, those that can, catch a freight train going south to some place where the weather is warm."

She stopped momentarily, looking at Nell who stood quiet, measuring her mother's words carefully. Nell wasn't satisfied with the answer she got about why their church didn't help the veterans out,
and she suspected her mother dodged the question because Jacob was with them.

Nell, standing silently in the doorway of the kitchen, had closed her mind to the conversation thinking she would have the conversation later with Mae when Jacob was not there. The response about the role of the church from Jacob was unsettling. Somehow it didn't fit with her vision of what churches were supposed to do. Besides Uncle Charlie had gone to the church for several years when he was younger. They should at least look out for him, she thought. Her mind needed a better answer. She shifted her weight watching Mae mix the corn meal in one of the large bowls. Mae had already put a small amount of bacon grease in the black iron skillet. It was heating on the stove. I'll ask Mae later she concluded, putting the issues away.

"Cain't stir too much water in here," Mae said. "It'll be too soupy for bread," looking at Nell. She sensed Nell's preoccupation. Nell simply stared blankly back at her. She was thinking about what it would be like for Uncle Charlie to ride a freight train in his condition. At least he'd be warm, she thought. Mae poured the corn bread mix into the hot skillet and put it back on the stove.

"Dinner won't be long now," she said taking Nell's hand. They went to the large room near the kitchen, as was their habit, to sit in the big chair behind the heater. Jacob followed them, and slouched quietly on the old couch.

"With Carver gone, your Uncle Charlie gonna' be mostly by himself now. I imagine he'll help keep those fires going. I hear he still works for Mrs. Meade's though. Bella looks out for him." Mae settled into the chair making room so Nell could squeeze in beside her.

"I can just imagine losing Carver must be too much for him. They saw so much together during the war. Charlie probably stays drunk all the time now, and who knows what he did in the war, sitting up there as a gunner on one of them big tanks." She started to rock the chair backward and forward by moving her weight.

"You didn't know this Nell, but Charlie and Carver they were part of a colored tank squadron fighting the Nazis in France and Germany," she said proudly.

"Weren't too many colored outfits fighting in the war, though they were capable of fightin', most colored outfits were forced to build roads, air strips, and deliver supplies. Charlie's outfit was different. They saw actual combat," she smiled. "He wrote to Grady about the time they liberated one of the concentration camps...all the people looking like living skeletons. Some could barely walk, but they cheered when those colored American boys arrived." A strange silence closed on her face. She looked directly at the children, before correcting herself.

"I meant *Men,*" she said quickly. "I think Charlie was OK about fighting the Nazis. They were so vicious, what they did to the Jews and all. He didn't mind. But after the atomic bombs were dropped and he heard what happened to the people, and the city...what with poisoning the air and everything, he was never the same. After that he couldn't wait to get out of the service. That's all he wrote about until he was discharged. Somehow, I believe, the war is really what started him down...you know to being like he is now.

"How come Daddy didn't help him Mother?'

"He did, baby. Grady did everything he could do, even got him a job at the packinghouse for a while. But Charlie just wouldn't come to work on time, or he would show up smelling like stale wine, sweaty and unwashed. They finally let him go. You know he slept on that couch for a while right after he came home. I don't know what we could have done differently." She sounded sad and exasperated. "We even put a bed in the basement so he could have more privacy, and he tried it for a while...but it just didn't work out. He couldn't be caged in, said the basement was too dark for him. He needed windows and fresh air...I guess it felt suffocating, just like those Butterflies you kids keep in those jars." Mae looked at Nell, drawing her closer. Her eyes were soft, and at that moment Nell thought, at that moment, Mae was the prettiest woman in the world.

"Charlie's just got to be free Nell...that's all."

She brushed Nell's hair before continuing, "...like he was when he was in France fighting the Germans. Your Daddy give him money whenever we can afford it...that's the best we can do right now."

She sighed, got up and went back into the kitchen to check on the cornbread and stir the pot of greens cooking on the stove. Neither Nell nor Jacob knew what she meant about the atomic bombs, but they sensed it was something bad. Later that night, after she and Jacob talked about their conversation with Mae, she asked Grady about atomic bombs. It was after dinner, and he was dozing on the rickety old couch. He told her what he had heard on the radio about the bombing, and the Japanese surrender ending the war, and that seemed to satisfy her.

IT WAS NOT TOO LONG AFTER THAT, Charlie came to the tenement house begging for money so he could get a pack of cigarettes and something to eat. Grady was at work, and when Mae answered the door, she stifled a gasp when she saw him. Nell peeked around her mother at the strange looking man. A collection of stale wine, dried urine, feces, perspiration and dirty clothes colored the air around him. His tangled beard was mixed with gray and black hair, and his eyes, wearing a shocked look were blood red. His dirty hair was long and matted on his head.

"I'm hungry Mae. Can you help me?" He rocked back and forth unsteady on his feet.

"Oh Charlie," Mae said with a painful sound in her voice. It sounded as if something was squeezing her soul, and Nell could see the pain on her face as she protectively pushed her away from the door.

"No Charlie...no!" A sour taste rose in her mouth and, turning away momentarily, she struggled not to throw up. Nell wanted to comfort her, but rather stood there near the door angry with Charlie for the pain he was causing her mother. Mae finally gathered herself, and gave Charlie the few coins she kept in a handkerchief pinned inside her dress.

"Wait here," she said.

Nell stepped aside to allow her to turn, and followed her to the icebox. Nell stood silently off to the side of the icebox's open door warily watching Charlie from a distance. Mae looked through the old icebox and gave him a paper bag filled with the leftover food she found there.

After he staggered off in the direction of the Junction Nell tried to console her Mother, but the vision of Charlie stayed with Mae all day. "

She could barely wait for Grady to get in the house before she attacked him, the words spilling from her as in a torrent.

"We got to help him Grady...I don't care we cain't turn our backs no longer! I cain't rest knowing he's living like that!" Grady overwhelmed by her onslaught took her in his arms, he pulled her into the bedroom trying to calm her, but she pulled away.

"We got to help him Grady," she said as he closed the bedroom door. Nell could barely hear Mae's words, but a sense of shame pervaded her. She was now old enough to be concerned that people in the neighborhood knew Charlie was her Uncle, and she was ashamed he was living so poorly.

GRADY WAS ANGRY when they found Charlie sleeping at the Junction. Mae was more concerned for his health. Like an angry Bear, Grady rustled him to his feet while yelling in his face.

"Goddam it Charlie...Daddy and Mama got to be turnin' over in their graves. You cain't live like this no more. *I CAIN'T* take it no more," Grady said twisting Charlie's arm behind him. Mae helped her husband push him, stumbling, down the street toward home.

Nell remembered the resolve in her mother's face

when they left the tenement to find Charlie. Mae was uncomfortable with the confrontation, but was resolved to be there to help her husband any way she could. When Charlie tried to struggle away from the grip of Grady, Mae assaulted him from the other side. The sour, greasy smell saturating Charlie's clothes rubbed off on her, as he had to put her shoulder into his side to leverage her weight against him. Nell, frightened by their struggles with Charlie followed them from a distance once they reached the backyard. Her eyes were wide from the anxiety she was feeling.

After they had wrestled him in the basement door Nell stood at the top of the stairs calling quietly for her mother in vain.

Mae was too concerned the neighbors may have seen them treating Charlie so roughly, and she chastised Grady as they struggled to get him down the stairs to the single bed that was still in the basement. Earlier in the day she had prepared it with freshly washed and ironed sheets, sprinkling it with baby powder to help fight the damp odor of the basement. She gasped as Grady stripped the bed of the clean linen. He put one of Nell's old rubber sheets on the bed under Charlie, and covered him with some of his old work clothes, while Mae took off Charlie's old army boots. Breathing hard she held him down while Grady used two belts to strap him to the bed.

"Grady...don't we need to bathe him first? I'll get some soap and hot water," she said innocently.

"Not yet Mae, we got to get him sobered up first. We got time to bathe him. I'm not sure he even knows what's happening to him right now. Ask Nell to get that old army blanket out of his footlocker upstairs. It's pretty damp down here."

For the next week, each day before going to work, Grady would go down and check on Charlie. Each time

Charlie would curse and swear at him begging to be let loose from the belts. He would quiet down only after Grady gave him a decreasing dose of cheap whiskey before he left for work. Every night the house was racked with his screams when the monsters came and took turns attacking his mind. Nell would cover her head with the pillow to shut out the sounds.

During the time Charlie was in the basement, Grady only mentioned his condition to Nell and Mae briefly. He knew they were frightened by what was happening to Charlie, and especially by the noises he made at night. He explained the alcohol had taken over Charlie's life, and they had to get it out of him by giving him smaller and smaller amounts over time, and then keeping him away from it altogether. Each time he came up from the basement, he admonished Nell to stay way from alcohol and smoking weed.

One day he permitted her to accompany him to the basement, and she saw the pain in his eyes as he looked at his brother. Grady rarely spoke his pain, but simply rubbed Nell's shoulder in silence as they took turns feeding Charlie the soup and bread Mae had made for him. It was then Nell realized how much her father loved his brother, and how difficult it was for him to help Charlie through his ordeal. Each morning, she helped by bringing the pail filled with warm water so her father could wash Uncle Charlie's frail body. She watched, and helped as much as her father would permit, while he cleaned the vomit from the floor, and Charlie's waste from the rubber sheet.

Eventually the shaking, and the chills stopped, and Charlie's demeanor started to change.

After a few more days her father removed the belts.

With help, Charlie could walk up the stairs to use the bathroom on his own. His body didn't shake as much. Grady said he had gone through the worst of his journey back.

The following week while Dean was playing in the backyard, Grady asked him to assist with giving Charlie a bath, haircut, and shave. His body was still frail, and he needed support to stand in the tub for any length of time.

As Charlie got into the old tin tub, Dean wondered about the puckered skin that sunk into a hole on the side of his belly. It was dark, scarred, and looked like his navel. There was also a series of scars across Charlie's back. They stood out, slick skin, like laced strings cutting across his body. Grady and Charlie acted as though they were not there. Later that afternoon while he and Nell played marbles in the backyard he told her about Charlie's other navel and the stripes. She pretended to know all about them, but could hardly wait to ask Mae later.

That night Grady burned all of Charlie's old clothes including the army boots in the backyard as Nell, Mae, and Charlie stood on the back porch watching.

Over the next several days Mae and Nell took turns walking Charlie around the basement so he could regain his strength. Eventually he could eat by himself, and Mae started feeding him the same food she fed the family. Every now and then the monsters came back and teased his senses, but his mind was clearer and he recognized them for the passing hallucinations they were. He got stronger over the winter months, his mind became as clear as his eyes, and he apologized for the problems he had been to the family. Soon he started to put on weight, and could walk on his own. Mae made him promise to start going to church again.

He continued to stay with them, but chose to remain in the basement. Grady put in a kerosene heater to fight the dampness, and soon Charlie returned to work helping Mr. Barnes deliver ice, and cutting the grass, and cleaning the yard at Mrs. Meade's house.

"Were you there when they pierced him in the side"

CHAPTER SEVEN

*T*HE WINTER MONTHS always seemed to lag for Nell after the excitement of Christmas had passed. She was growing into a young woman; it seemed like almost overnight. She became more and more conscious of her body. She always wanted the door to her room closed, and when Mae wanted to get the dirty laundry from her room it always seemed to turn into a big problem for her. After a brief conference with her parents one evening they agreed she was old enough to do her own laundry, and could keep the door to her room closed at night. Nell was happy to have a place where she could be alone; she always closed the door with impunity whenever she got into a disagreement with Mae, but she was more cautious with her father and never challenged him.

Soon the other girls in the neighborhood, about the age of Rose Ann started to come into Nell's life, but she still enjoyed her times with Jacob. She especially enjoyed it when Dean, a classmate, began stopping by to play with them. Dean was a year older, and although he didn't know it, she, and the other girls had already chosen him as the best-looking boy in the school. Later, in the school year he won her heart completely when he stood up to the neighborhood bully.

IT WAS DURING RECESS, and Nell was playing a game of Tag with Rose Ann and two of the other girls in the class when she heard a loud voice. It was Dean.

"Hey! Cut it out. Give me my hat," Dean cried.

He was struggling against a much shorter boy. The boy, Maurice, had to jump in the air to be able to snatch the hat from Dean's head. In doing so he had intentionally pushed Dean onto the wet gravel of the playground, knocking his eyeglasses off. Dean looked around grappling for his glasses before he got up holding his side. He grimaced briefly. After dusting his clothes, he tentatively chased Maurice around the playground asking for his cap. Maurice simply laughed and dodged each attempt by the frustrated Dean to catch him. Finally tiring of the game, Maurice stopped and threw the cap into a puddle of rainwater on the playground.

Although he was shorter than most of the boys in his class, Maurice was two years older. He had flunked the third and fifth grade twice before passing on. A dark mud color, brutishly thick and muscular for his age, he enjoyed pushing the other children around. From the first day, when his family moved into the neighborhood he terrorized other children by taking their milk money, while they waited in the morning for the doors to the school to open. Sometimes he would catch kids as they walked to school insisting they give him money, or any other small valuable they had. At that time his shorthaired terrier, "Bully" followed him, and if anyone resisted he sic'd the dog on him or her.

Everybody watched out for him as they walked to school. Several of the younger boys had even talked amongst themselves about carrying broken bricks in their book bags to beat the "livin' shit out of him," if he ever touched anyone of them again.

As Nell watched Dean sheepishly retrieve his wet cap from the puddle. Maurice looked at the small group of children where she was standing. He started in their direction, and caught her eye. Smiling and winking at her, he turned off and approached a group of the older boys. They laughed loudly, breaking ranks so he could join them. Nell was scared of both, him and his dog. As she watched him laughing with the other boys, her mind drifted to a time last year when she told Jacob about her fears.

It was a Sunday evening, and summer vacation had seemingly abruptly come to an end. School was to start the following day. Jacob was sitting at the old upright piano in the church basement. They were waiting for Mae and Mrs. Turner to leave the evening service that was going on in the sanctuary upstairs. Nell sat close-by in a folding chair, and Jacob had been picking out a variety of tunes on the piano. He had a proud grin on his face as he played a few bars of Clair De Lune over and over.

"Listen Nell, I learned this from the school concert last year, when my class went to the symphony...you like it?" Nell ignored his question, and he was sensitive to her attitude.

"You in a bad mood," he asked concerned.

"I really hate school," she said, as if to herself.

"Hate school?" Jacob responded. His fingers frozen in the air. He looked up to question her. "Hate school, you must be kidding! I love my school," he said.

"Yeah sure," she sneered without thinking. "You go to a special school where they send a bus to pick you up everyday. That ain't all bad." He turned to face her as she continued. "I wouldn't mind being picked up. That way I wouldn't have to worry about Maurice and his devil dog Bully."

Judging by his reaction, she knew it was the wrong thing to say. Jacob wanted to, and had tried to go to a regular school with her and the other kids in the neighborhood, but, because of his handicap, couldn't successfully navigate the stairs in the school. As a result, he boarded a small yellow bus each morning during the school year with all the other physically challenged children. Some were slow learners, and he was concerned about being cast in that light. He and Nell usually caught a glimpse of each other as the bus passed her and Rose Ann walking down Fort Street to school. With an excited smile, he would wave to them from the rear of the bus. The difference in their school experiences was the first indication they would eventually have to go their separate ways on a more permanent basis.

Nell's words hung in the air in the church's basement punctuating the strange silence that had settled in the room. Jacob used his hands to push himself around on the piano bench. His crippled leg now pointed straight at Nell.

"Its really Maurice, ain't it?"

"Yeah," she confirmed his suspicions. "He took my milk money a lot last semester. I tried to stand up to him but he pushed me down, and sic'd Bully on me. He's a bad dog...tore my pant leg and broke the skin on my ankle."

"Did you tell your mom?"

Nell shook her head before answering. "I told her I got the tear on a loose wire in the playground fence." Jacob was looking at the floor, and seemed not to be listening. He finally looked up at her.

"I got it," he said excitedly. "Why don't you tell Uncle Charlie about Maurice, about what he did to you, to the other kids too? I bet he can stop it.... if you ask him!"

"No Jacob. Uncle Charlie's too big, and he'd probably hurt Maurice if I tell about him sic'ing Bully on me. I just know he'd do something to that boy."

"Hey, he's like your big brother, ain't he? That's what big brothers are for. Hey I wish I had a big brother. I sure as heck wouldn't be scared anymore...that's for sure. I'll tell Uncle Charlie," he said turning back to the piano.

"NO! Jacob, don't," she protested, but Jacob had

closed the conversation. He went back to playing the few chords of Clair De Lune.

Jacob finally did tell Charlie about Nell's predicament. After listening carefully about Nell's concerns, he would hurt Maurice, Charlie assured him Maurice would never bother Nell again. The next day on their way to school she and Rose Ann saw Charlie walking with Maurice. He had his arm around Maurice's shoulder as though they were old friends. Bully trotted along beside them. He growled incessantly, but kept his distance from Charlie.

In Charlie's free hand he carried a short broomstick with a sharp point on one end. Sporadically he waved it at the dog. When he left Maurice at the corner of the playground, Maurice had found a new respect for Nell and decided to keep his distance.

Although he picked on most of the kids in the class, Dean was a favorite target of Maurice. Nell and Rose Ann speculated it was because Dean had a honey brown complexion, light brown eyes, and a head of thick curly hair. One of two children, he was from an extremely poor family that lived across from the blacksmith shop in a small decrepit house not too far from the school.

As often as he could, Dean would earn extra money at the shop grooming the horses brought there by the various merchants to be re-shoed. His family lived off a monthly government check because his father had been killed in the war. At the beginning of the school year his mother received a clothing voucher for the children, every other year; she received a voucher so Dean could get an eye examination and new glasses. Although he had strikingly clear eyes, without the thick glasses Dean could not see well enough to do his schoolwork. Funny how things worked out, but it was Dean's glasses that eventually spelled the end of Maurice's terror in the neighborhood.

Two weeks after the afternoon when he had snatched Dean's cap, the gym class had been given free time out-side. Mr. Davis, the gym teacher had stayed inside to complete some paperwork. The class was free to have unstructured play near-by the building and close to the gym windows so he could monitor their activity from his office.

Dean went with a group of boys and several girls. They took two baseball bats and softball to play a pickup game on the baseball diamond. Before they went out they were wary of Maurice, and was happy when he went out with several other boys to the far side of the school away from the windows. They drew a line in the gravel and began to pitch pennies while keeping a wary eye out for Mr. Davis.

Eventually Maurice had either won all the pennies or tired of the game, and found his way over to the base-ball diamond where he stood watching the game. The game was tied. Each team had two runs, and Dean's team had the tie-breaking run at third base. There were two outs and Dean was coming up to bat. He had plotted where and how to hit the puny fast balls that were being pitched. Maurice watched silently from the sidelines until Dean approached the plate and picked up the bat. Suddenly he strides up to Dean declaring he was sending himself in as a pinch-hitter, and attempted to take the bat. When Dean turned suddenly snatching the bat away from him, he became angry.

What happened next seemed like an automatic re-action for Maurice. He lowered his head and threw him-self into Dean's chest lifting him off the ground. The bat dropped out of his hand when they hit the ground, and Maurice started pummeling Dean with unbridled rage. A thin stream of blood trickled from his nose. Dean some-how managed to push the angry Maurice off him, as a crowd of children gathered around them. Nell and her friends abandoned their game of Tag, edging their way closer to the scuffling boys. Dean's glasses had fallen off; and Nell quickly picked them up for safekeeping. She knew they would be the first things he would look for once the fight was over.

A small trickle of blood ran from Dean's nose as he sat up, aware that he had lost his glasses. He looked frantically around on the ground, as Maurice stood proudly back in the circle of kids gathered around them.

Aware of the crowd, he pranced around like prize-fighter shadow-boxing. Snorting through his nose, he glared at Dean.

"You want some more boy?" He yelled. When Dean didn't answer, he yelled louder approaching Dean as he got up from the ground.

"You want some more boy? I'll kick your little yellow ass some more...you want some more?" Dean ignored him, looking blankly at the crowd.

"Anybody see my glasses?" He asked hysterically.

"Here Dean, I got your glasses." Nell responded stepping forward into the circle. She held out the glasses. He and Maurice got to her at about the same time. Maurice snatched the glasses from her outstretched hand, and when Dean reached for them, he pushed him away. Laughing he turned his back to them, holding the glasses away from Dean who desperately tried to get them back. Maurice laughed louder as he spun around avoiding Dean's pleading and outstretched hands. Finally, he stopped.

"You want your glasses back?" He asked looking at Dean intently. He raised them out in front at arm's length, and when Dean approached he quickly snapped the frame, dropped the pieces to the ground and stepped on them smashing the lenses into the gravel. Defeated, Dean's shoulders dropped, and in shock he sobbed uncontrollably into his hands. His tears mixed with the bloody snot. It was smeared on one side of his face mixing with the dirt and gravel pressed into his face. Maurice smugly turned to walk away as the circle of kids broke deferring to him in their fear. He hesitated momentarily at the edge of the circle, hitching his pants up from the waist, spit on the ground and walked smugly away.

"I told you not to fuck with me Dean," he said the words over his shoulder.

After Dean picked up the broken glasses, he quietly picked up the bat from the center of the group. In a rage, he ran at Maurice screaming and swinging the bat with all his strength. The first blow caught Maurice in the back of the neck, and the second in the back of the head as he crashed to the ground.

"You broke my glasses! You, dumb ass-hole...*YOU BROKE MY GLASSES!*" Dean yelled at him as Maurice fell to the ground. Now Dean was on Maurice's back, his arms around his neck in a chokehold.

"I'll kill you. You bastard!" He screamed uncontrollably lifting Maurice's gurgling head from the ground in the chokehold. Drool ran from the corner of his mouth and he scratched at Dean's arms, attempting to loosen his grip.

Laughter, clapping, hoots, catcalls and other forms of praise came from the crowd. Maurice had stopped struggling, and his arms were weakly hanging onto Dean's arms. He was on the verge of losing consciousness when Mr. Davis broke through the crowd pulling Dean off him.

Nell's heart surged in her chest at the sight of Dean mastering Maurice.

After the fight, it soon passed throughout the school Maurice had lost to Dean in front of the whole class. The reign of Maurice was over. None of the kids shirked from his threats anymore, and he soon became just another kid on the playground, struggling to fit in where they would have him. Several months after the fight Bully was killed chasing a car down the street.

Mr. Davis arranged for Dean to get new glasses, but he patched his old glasses with electrician tape and occasionally wore them with pride throughout the rest of the school year.

NELL TOLD JACOB the story at church the Sunday following the fight. She could barely contain her excitement after Sunday School was over.   She pretended to be Maurice. Falling to the floor, in pretense, she cried out to Dean to stop choking her. Jacob, and several other children from the Sunday School class encouraged her performance. They all had suffered at the hands of Maurice, and laughed heartily at the images she was painting of the fight.

After the conclusion of Sunday School, a group of them skipped regular church services, and walked to the Italian sweet shop for lemon ice cones. Later that night Jacob accepted his relationship with Nell was changing. He could tell by the look in her eyes when she talked about Dean and, lately he had become a more frequent visitor to the backyard of the tenement house. It seemed the more Dean was around her, the louder and bossier Nell became in their play.

He knew they would always be friends, but now it would be different. He felt it in his heart. It doesn't matter, he thought, we don't catch butterflies anymore anyway, but we still have the Junction as our special place to go to in the summertime. She had promised she would not go there with anyone else.

"...Oh, oh, sometimes it causes me to tremble"

CHAPTER EIGHT

*I*T WAS THE FIRST TIME in months and things in the neighborhood seemed to be getting back to normal. Raymond had been tried and found guilty of manslaughter. Grady followed the case in the newspaper and kept the family apprised of how the trial was going. Nell was especially interested, checking with Grady each evening about what would happen to Raymond if he had to go to jail. When the verdict came back, Grady shared the news with the family.

"They didn't believe Raymond. He was defending himself...what a shame he was such a nice quiet man too."

"But he did kill Mr. Collins," Nell said quietly, "me and Jacob, we saw him!" Not understanding her father's statement, the tears welled in her eyes as she suddenly recalled the scene in Jim's Diner. Still reading his paper, Grady didn't respond, and she quietly left the room. Mae followed her into her bedroom and closed the door. The following week, Grady read in the paper Raymond was sentenced up to ten years in prison.

Bella, angry and hurt over the death of her father was in the court everyday throughout the trial. She continued to live at Mrs. Meade's house, but had not entertained any customers since the death of her father. After the trial ended she tried seeing customers again, but her heart was not in her work. The customers complained, and Mrs. Meade agreed she could stay at the house, but would assist James with the cleaning and cooking until she was ready to see customers again.

For Jacob, other things were happening that indicated his relationship with Nell was changing. He rarely saw her anymore except at church on Sundays. She had finally given up catching grasshoppers and shooting marbles. She spent more time with Rose Ann giggling, whispering about Dean, and combing each other's hair. Other times they stayed in her room looking through magazines at the pictures of girl's clothes. Mae told Grady she was finally becoming a young lady.

Jacob tried to spend more time with Dean and the other boys in the neighborhood, but was still disadvantaged because of his handicap. Those few times he saw Charlie, he would pressure him, without success, to allow him to go with him to the Junction. But Charlie, pleading work with the iceman, seemingly always put him off. It was not too long before he started sneaking off to the Junction to catch butterflies by himself. Sometimes on especially hot days he would fish from the old dock.

◆ ◆ ◆

IT WAS AN UNSETTLED and unplanned day for Charlie that Saturday morning before Easter. The sky was dark in the west and the smell of rain was in the air. The summer was coming on but it was still cool in the evenings. It always seems to rain around Easter, he thought. Looking at the sky as he left the tenement house, he decided to clean the yard at Mrs. Meade's early. The chickens she kept in her backyard continually filled the place with their droppings, and he knew it would be harder to remove them after the rain. He really didn't like the rooster challenging him in the yard, but it was a quick job, Mrs. Meade always paid well, and he was hoping to see Bella again. He had not seen her since the death of Carver. When he first started working at the house Bella always looked out for him, and those times when she was not busy with a customer she would fry them both an egg sandwich. Although Mrs. Meade didn't say anything, Bella could tell by the looks she gave them she didn't like her sitting in the large kitchen with someone dressed as poorly as Charlie. She knew Mrs. Meade was concerned her customers might get the impression Charlie was also a customer of the house. The primary concern for Mrs. Meade was for the business. If it mistakenly got around Charlie was a customer, she was sure she would lose some of her more influential customers.

She had built a reputation for servicing the highest types of clientele, and having the cleanest girls in the city.

Since Carver's death, it had been awhile since they had seen each other. Both had quit going to the junction. Charlie, now with a clearer mind spent most of his time with Grady planning to relocate to Pittsburgh at the end of the month. Other than going to court for the trial everyday, Bella had spent more and more time alone in her room when she was not helping James clean the house. One day while cleaning the backyard, and although he couldn't see them, Charlie overheard Mrs. Meade scolding Bella for drinking too much. He suspected Bella blamed him for what happened to Carver, and was intentionally avoiding him. He felt bad for what was happening to her, and he wished he could tell her before he left for Pittsburgh, he thought. He approached the side of the house, just as she opened the side door.

"Charlie, you're here early," she whispered. Happy to see him, she opened the door wider for him to pass. The rest of the house was quiet and shuttered behind her.

"Yeah, I thought I'd get the yard raked before the rain blows in," he said looking up at the sky. "You OK Bella?"

He asked the question, stepping into the side foyer; he smelled the stale alcohol on her breath. He tried not to notice the flimsy gown she wore. It barely covered her naked body. He averted his eyes and headed for the basement to get some old grocery bags, and the old bushel basket he used for the trash and droppings from the backyard. When he came up from the basement she was standing by the table in the kitchen. She softly called him as he started through the kitchen toward the back door. He stopped, acknowledging her in the dim light. Tears had welled in her eyes. Embarrassed, she raised her hands momentarily shielding her face from him.

"Charlie...I don't blame you for what happened to Daddy. I know you must think I do, but I don't...really! You did the best you could for him. We all did. I just miss him so."

Charlie's heart jumped in his chest. Her words pierced him. He had blamed himself more than she knew, he thought. But I could barely take care of myself, he thought defensively. She removed her hands looking at him through red swollen eyes.

"I want you to know that Charlie...I mean I did at first...but no more." She laid her head on her outstretched arm, as she sat down at the table sobbing quietly.

"Daddy's dead...Mama don't want me no more," controlling herself again she continued, "Nobody really loves me no more, not since Daddy," she said. "Since Daddy died I'm so alone Charlie...Daddy, can you hear me? God...I'm so empty!"

She put her face in her hands again sobbing. She's drunk, Charlie thought.

"It'll be OK Bella." He tried to assure her, as she

walked aimlessly around the kitchen wiping her eyes. Charlie stood frozen watching her, not knowing what else to say. She sat on the table again, holding her hand out to him. A deafening silence filled the room for what seemed like an eternity.

"Love me Charlie?" Was that a question, he tried to control his thoughts. "You love me...don't you?" She looked at him across the room. His heart started to beat in his throat when she opened her arms beckoning him. Frightened he looked directly at her for the first time since he came in the house. Her eyes wore a dead look, and were sunken in her face. She looked tired. Dark streaks of mascara trailed down her face.

"I love you Charlie," she said quietly. "You love me... don't you Charlie? Love me Charlie," she begged him, teasingly. "Please love me." Her head was coyly tilted to one side. "God...just love me once, for me...please. I'll be good."

She opened the top of her gown exposing her large reddish-brown nipples. Her breasts swelled extending themselves as she took a deep breath. It was a steamy morning and she pulled the gown over her thighs partially exposing her darkened passageway.

Charlie looked around the room, focusing on the sound of a revolving fan creaking down as it was turned off somewhere in the house. He could smell her musk, and beads of humidity started to glisten on both their bodies. He could feel it cooling his arms. It slid down his face.

"Whew!" He flicked it away unconsciously.

She slid to the edge of the table and opened her legs inviting him. "Just love me Charlie...just love me for who I am, and not what I am. Just cause I'm a whore don't mean I don't have feelings." She reached out for him. "Please. Take me with you to Pittsburgh Charlie...away from this, I cain't trick no more. I just cain't do it."

He could see the dark curls at the apex of her thighs, before she came to him. Her arms encircled him to guide him back to the table. His heart beat louder in his mind, and he could only think of all the wet dreams, and the last time he had tried, and fumbled poorly with one of the girls at the laundry last winter. After that every time she saw him at work, she would giggle quietly to herself and give him a knowing smile. The thoughts flooded his mind, but the sight of Bella's body made his body respond. She guided his hands; his fingers caressing the curls trying to remember through the years of drinking the importance of caressing a woman. He stroked her until his fingers were tired. Her breath caught in her throat, as her body moved rhythmically against his hand. Now he was only slightly aware of the smell of alcohol on her breath, but focused on her staggered breathing as she licked and nibbled at his ear.

He responded, and his mouth found her swollen breasts.

She moaned into his ear violently, struggling to unzip his pants, finally freeing him.

Adjusting herself on the table she laid back, her legs raised and opened the gown above her hips. Automatically, as a moth drawn to a flame, he closed over her. She moaned into the air, crossing both her legs, closing him into her embrace. His thrusts beyond the opening were short, violent, and alternately uncontrollable as she, with increasing intensity, purred into his throat. Her explosion left her sucking and gasping for air. It dragged him into her rhythm, and he too surrendered to the force of her crescent. She could feel him building inside her, harder and swelling larger and she covered her mouth with her hand grinding her hips painfully against him furiously one last time before collapsing back on the table. Fascinated by her body's reaction, Charlie rode her into his own violent and painfully sweet release. It exploded in his head jerking his hips forcefully into hers in a wild rhythm. Silence, shocked stillness, and spasms racked his body.

They lay there together trying to steady their breathing. She tried to hold onto him, wanting to keep the throb inside her while it remained firm. She felt it slipping away.

Coming to their senses again they both laughed softly looking around the kitchen. Charlie finally managed to extricate himself, and tumbled into one of the chairs near the table. He sat there fumbling to straighten his clothes watching the door expecting one of the other girls to come in at any minute. Bella straightened her clothes and without saying a word slipped silently out the kitchen door, heading up the stairs.

Mrs. Meade chose that moment to be walking down the stairs. They creaked with her weight as she moved toward her day bed in the parlor. A scowl was on her face when she saw Charlie in the kitchen. She didn't speak, but moved back to the hallway where Bella had hesitated on the stairs. They stared silently at each other from different levels of the staircase before speaking.

Feeling the tension, Charlie quickly left through the side door.

"I know...you want me to leave," Bella said.

"You damn right. You ain't made me no money in weeks, and I catch you in here fuckin' that drunk. You know, *DAMMIT!* You cain't fuck the help and keep workin' here. You know it's against the rules, you ungrateful little bitch!" Mrs. Meade shifted her weight. Her breathing was shallow with her anger. She put her hands on her huge hips, continuing, "...*in my house you damn little bitch?*"

"You just get the money together you been savin' for me. I be goin' to Pittsburgh with Charlie next week," Bella glared back; quickly gathering her gown around her, she walked slowly up the stairs toward her room.

"The nerve...fuckin' ungrateful bitch!" Mrs. Meade, visibly upset and breathing hard walked into the kitchen looking for traces of their heat.

◆ ◆ ◆

THREE DAYS LATER Jacob was dead. Nell was distraught when she heard about Jacob's death. She had just returned from the movies with Rose Ann. Charlie and Grady sat quietly on the couch. Charlie had his head in his hands. Mae sat in the big chair behind the heater. No one was speaking and Nell could sense the tension in the room. She sat on the floor at her mother's side.

"What's wrong Mother?"

"Jacob's dead!" Her mother wailed loudly breaking into tears. Shocked, Nell drew back looking at her in disbelief. But Mae's red and teary eyes told her it was true.

"I knew something had happened as soon as I walked in the door," she said laying her head in her mother's lap. Mae cradled her head.

"Jacob drowned earlier today, Nell. Dean came over to tell us. When he asked for you, I told him you were at the movies with Rose Ann.

"What happened...did he say what happened mother?" The warm mood she came home with was gone. Mae sighed deeply before answering.

"Dean told us, said he fell into the river from the old dock while tying to retrieve his fishing pole. It probably got caught on something in the water...they say he lost his balance dangling from one of the old pilasters trying to reach it before it floated away out of reach."

Mae stroked Nell's hair, feeling a conflicting flood of emotions, relief that Nell had not been at the Junction with him, and anger at him for going to the dock alone.

"He knew his mother told him to stay away from that place," she said angrily into the silence. Nell reacted. A pang of guilt warmed her face. She knew she always had the cooler head around the dock. She wished she had been there to caution him. It seemed, because he was a cripple, Jacob always wanted to walk the edge of risky behaviors.

"He was always trying to prove himself Mother. From the time we were first friends, I always cautioned him to do only those things he could do safely...you know without hurting himself." She shuffled her weight on the floor, fighting the impending tears.

"Why did he keep going there anyway?" She asked softly looking up at her mother.

Mae only sighed wiping the tears away forming in the corners of Nell's eyes. In the silence that followed Nell imagined her grabbing Jacob's hands as he slipped into the cold water. I could have saved him, if only I had been there, she thought. Every bone in her body told her it was so.

"According to the men in the Junction Charlie tried to reach him unsuccessfully with a broken tree branch. One or two of them even jumped in the river, but the undercurrent was too strong. It had pulled him down deeper under the rotting dock. He never came up again. When the river division of the police found his body, his pant leg was caught on a rusty spike in one of the wooden pilings just five feet under the surface of the water."

AT THE FUNERAL Nell was surprised to see Bella sitting with Charlie. She passed them following Mae down the aisle closer to the front of the church. Charlie was dressed in the clothes he planned to wear to Pittsburgh. Bella wore a white dress; a black scarf covered her head. She looked distraught, but nodded warmly at Nell when she passed. Their eyes locked briefly, and Nell wanted to go and sit with them. But Mae motioned her sternly to the front of the church. Before the service began she stood idly by their pew, not sure what to do or say, while Mae spoke quietly with Mr. and Mrs. Turner. During the service, each time Jacob's mother cried out in her pain, Nell struggled to contain her own emotions. Half ashamed of her emotional outbursts, she continually looked away from her mother to blow her nose and wipe at tears she thought would never stop. She was especially moved when Jacob's mother stood weakly at the side of the casket sobbing and shaking. It seemed, except for the vision of Bella's white dress, the entire service was filled with dark shadows of weeping women, tall men dressed in dark clothes, and loud music. Mae also wiped constantly at her own tears while constantly saying, "He's gone Nell...he's gone to a better place."

After the conclusion of the service, Nell walked boldly past the outstretched arms of the funeral director, who tried to stop her. She stopped before the sleeping Jacob touching his frail and darkened hand before they closed the casket. She felt empty, and a deep sense of unspoken guilt and anger filled her heart. Mae watched her closely, concerned for the long-term impact of Jacob's death on her young daughter.

When she and Mae, and the rest of the mourners followed Jacob's casket up the aisle toward the hearse parked outside, she looked for Bella and Charlie, but the pew where they had been sitting was empty. Her sense of guilt gnawed silently at her mind for attention. Yes, she acknowledged they had all let Jacob down, especially she and Charlie. More of his attention was given to Bella, and she had moved on to spend more time with Rose Ann. It was as if Jacob was the only one still caught up in the past, and that is probably why he was all alone when he died, she thought. She sighed loudly before the tears came again.

"You OK Nell?" Mae touched her shoulder.

❖ ❖ ❖

SHE FELT THE CAR SLOWING DOWN. It was Dean touching her shoulder.

"You OK Nell?" he asked again. Turning in her seat, she faced her husband, her eyes still closed.

"I'm OK," she said as the car took the exit from the Turnpike.

"The Bay Bridge is just ahead." Dean's voice chased the images from her head, and it was he, who had touched her shoulder to wake her. Looking past him out the window, it took her a moment to reconcile where she was. The landscape still seemed to be rushing past her. The light reflecting off the snow was strong and bright, forcing her to blink her eyes to adjust her sight. More snow had covered their surroundings and sporadic flakes covered the windshield. Painfully, she remembered the trip to Pittsburgh. The urn with Uncle Charlie's ashes sat on the floor between her feet. Thoughts of Bella flashed through her mind. She wondered what had happened to her, and between the two of them. They had gone to Pittsburgh with such promise she thought, as Dean turned the car into a small parking area near a bridge overlooking a receding lake. It was getting on toward dusk and the lights over the bridge were just starting to come on. She sat up more erect.

In the distance, she could see lights emanating from

cottages circling the shore of a large bay, and the rise of a tree lined horizon faded away into the darkness. The lights from the small cottages seemingly flickered in the failing light, but she knew it was the smoke from their fireplaces blowing in the snow creating the illusion. It was a long bridge, and its lights arched in a curve following the rise and fall of the bridge's surface as it jutted out over the dark waters of Lake Erie.

"There's a footbridge to one of the small islands near the foot of the bay," he said moving the car through the parking area leading to a space overlooking the foot-bridge.

"We can park there, take the footbridge out so far, and scatter some of the Charlie's ashes in the bay. The current will spread them along the Great Lakes, hopefully into the river past the old Hobo Junction area." He stopped the car, taking the urn from the floor.

"Charlie would probably like that," he said opening the door.

"It is a beautiful spot Dean," Nell said getting out of the car.

"My job used to bring me right by here each time I had to go to Cleveland," he said. "I always promised my-self I would stop here one day." The light was failing but they could still make out the sweep of the bay as it re-ceded inward from the lake.

"Majestic," Nell said. He is right about this spot, she thought as she followed him over the rise of the small footbridge. Dean carried the urn. They met an-other couple crossing the footbridge in the opposite dir-ection. The man spoke indicating the wind was picking up and the waves would soon make it too dangerous to be on the footbridge. Dean thanked him, indicating they would not be long. He passed the urn to Nell.

She leaned against the railing and raised her arms holding the urn to the dark sky. Without ceremony, she quietly poured half of the ashes   into the wind so they blew away from them. It was only briefly, but they watched the wind sweep the ashes out in a swirl over the bay before they disappeared into the darkness.

"We can give some of the rest to Mae for her flower garden," she said; "but I'll take the rest to Eden next week." She handed the urn back to Dean as they made their way back to the car.

"You want me to drive," she asked before they reached the car.

"No. I'm OK. Besides I think you need the sleep. You were breathing pretty deep for awhile back on the Turnpike."

"I am tired," she said.

The next time she opened her eyes, it was snowing harder, and through the steamed windows of the car she recognized the old gaslights lining the streets of the Commons, the historic district where she and Dean lived. After driving several more blocks, he turned again into the driveway of the old colonial they called home. Dean parked the car and reached over to see if she was still awake.

"Honey, wake up we're home." He reached over shaking her briefly and slid out the driver's side. Nell painfully unfolded out of the car. She stifled a yawn, stretching lazily.

"I'll unload the car tomorrow," he said following her up the stairs to the front porch.

Riding in the car while dragging herself through all those old memories of earlier days had been tiring. She didn't respond, but opened the front door and picked up the mail. She could tell by the look on Dean's face he was tired too. It had been a full two days and he had done all the driving.

"I want to thank you Babe for doing all the driving," she said hugging him and kissing his cheek. He took the mail and started to sort it, handing her an envelope from Hill at the news service.

"Probably my itinerary and tickets for New Orleans," she said heading up the stairs to the bedroom. She sighed with relief when she noticed she had a few days to rest before she had to travel.

The next morning, she checked her voice mail; there were two messages from Hill. He had arranged to put off the deadline for the story on drug trafficking until the middle of next month and informed her his office had arranged her itinerary, including three days at a small hotel in the French Quarter. He also called again later that same day emphasizing how important it was for her to meet the deadline with a professionally finished piece complete with great photographs. The Daily was doing a series on trans-generational drug use, and planned to run stories from various journalists from across the country. They had requested Nell do the lead-off story.

Later in the day, she called Hill's message service to assure him she could meet the schedule, and would send him the drafts and contact sheets as soon as they were finished, while Dean went on-line to search for Coon's Cove in Alabama. He was unsuccessful, but he did find a small town in Alabama called Eden just north of the Florida Panhandle. ******

The day before her flight to New Orleans Nell visited with Mae. She opened Uncle Charlie's footlocker to return the documents she had taken to Pittsburgh. Without Mae's knowledge, she took the photographs and letters form Charlie's Bible. She and Dean had discussed taking the photographs of Charlie with the young girl called Louise. She felt uncomfortable about her plans to disobey, and deceive her mother, but the note where Charlie insisted...' *The Cove was where he was happiest'* drove her curiosity. Dean, just as curious, encouraged her by searching the web for the small town of Eden on the Internet. He printed her a map, and reserved a car for her in New Orleans. Later that evening Dean placed Charlie's ashes into a large plastic freezer bag. He placed the photographs, and letters from the footlocker into a manila envelope, and placed these on the kitchen counter where Nell sat drinking a cup of tea.

"I took these out for you," he said pushing the freezer bag toward her. In his other hand, he held the manila envelope opening it so Nell could see it contained the letters and photographs from Louise.

"You can decide if you want to take these along," he said offering up the envelope. "They may come in handy." She sipped silently at the cup of tea, nodding her head.

"Regardless of what you do about the letters and photographs," he continued. "I agree with you. We owe it to Uncle Charlie to take his ashes. It 's such a simple request.If you can't find the Cove, I would just scatter them in one of the cotton fields down there in Eden." He sat on the stool next to her.

"I would go with you if I could, but my calendar is booked through the end of the year. You just be careful," he said bending over and kissing her lightly on her cheek.

"I will; hopefully Eden won't be much more than a day's drive from New Orleans. It's what Uncle Charlie wanted." She picked up the bag of ashes and the envelope, and looked lovingly at her husband before moving them to the chair on the other side of her. Dean poured himself a cup of tea.

CHAPTER NINE

NEW ORLEANS, AND EDEN, ALABAMA SOME TIME BEFORE
THANKSGIVING, 2002

*T*HE CROWD OF PEOPLE IN THE FRENCH QUARTER was raucous and happy. Laughter, music, and loud voices lifted above the throng of people milling in the streets. Occasionally car horns could be heard in the distance. There was, and has always been an attitude in the city that appeals to the curious and those with baser instincts.

They come to the city in a steady stream all year long culminating each year in record crowds during the time of Mardi Gras. Some think it is the food. Perhaps the music, or the noise but the sense of unbridled freedom in the French Quarter makes it a special place. Its a place where people crowd the streets, drinks in hand stepping happily into each other seemingly unconcerned about anything. It seems life is without problems. The environment is a great party and everybody is invited. With seeming determination, they collectively move toward some nonspecific place, as a churning happy wave. That night uniformed police directed traffic through and around the Quarter. Only emergency vehicles were permitted in the old cobblestone streets. Their red and orange flashing lights gave the area eerie, and changing appearances in the drizzling rain.

Nell sat in her dark hotel room high above the street, listening to the TV newscaster warn of a tropical storm bearing down on Louisiana and along the Gulf Coast. The newscaster was gauging the possibly of it become a hurricane before landfall. Anticipated landfall was within the next 48 hours, and heavy rain and wind damage was expected in New Orleans. Looking out the window Nell speculated about her planned drive to Eden in the morning. She had already completed the photo-shoot for Hill, but it was a pedestrian piece. Her earlier subjects were all in treatment programs, and not one acknowledged still using drugs. She still needed to include the raw side of drug addiction to have a sensational piece. She suspected prostitutes worked the streets of the Quarter during the evening hours. She thought briefly about doing some photographs from the hotel window of a girl at work. She also thought about trolling the streets looking for one, and hoped a pimp or a dirty cop would not protect her. It was important she still be strung out, and working the streets, so Nell could buy her cooperation for money.

If I pay her enough money Nell rationalized, the right girl could also provide an entre to get inside a drug house. She would need a heavy user; Nell thought ... one she could entice to take the chance to maybe get her inside a shooting gallery. This could provide balance for her other story line about the value of drug treatment.

The drizzling rain made the dirty streets look slick from her distance and small puddles of water gathered in some places pooling by the uneven curb. The TV newscaster was still talking about the weather, and Nell thought fleetingly about the impact of the possible hurricane, and wondered what lay ahead for her if she was stranded because of the hurricane. Well the trip to Eden could always be put off. At least I can stay here in the hotel and finish the assignment for Hill, she thought as she scanned the crowd below. As the hour moved on past eleven o'clock, she noticed a thin woman stumble out of one of the noisy bars down the street. She stopped to light a cigarette and stepped into one of the doorways. Nell watched with increasing interest as she picked at various men when they passed her. There was no presence of a pimp, and when a uniformed policeman came in her direction the woman quickly crossed the street and stepped into another doorway. She never approached a couple or another woman. She was on her fifth cigarette when Nell took her mini digital camera from the camera bag. Although it was smaller than a pack of cigarettes, it was a powerful little tool with a fast fixed-focus lens. She put it in her jacket pocket. She stuffed her hair under her cap and made her way out into the streets heading in the woman's direction.

As expected the woman appraised Nell as she walked toward her location. Nell suspected immediately she was strung out. She was painted to look about sixteen years old, but Nell knows she was older. Nell stiffened her walk to appear more masculine, and looked her way with interest as she approached her. She was extremely thin, and her hair was bleached a bright yellow, almost white color. Her features and color led Nell to believe she was of Mexican, or Indian extraction. As Nell walked past her, she touched Nell's arm.

"Hey, wann'a party? Thirty dollars!"

Nell hesitated and stopped. The woman's dull eyes searched Nell's face. She thinks I'm gay floated through Nell's mind as the noise and the crowd continued past them. Nell took a closer look at her evaluating her as a photographic subject. Her tight mini skirt barely covered her crotch, and her thin thighs were just a little larger than her legs. Her face was filled with freckles that the makeup covered in some places. But they stood out unabashedly along her thin nose line. She had long expressive hands. She used them when she spoke and she reeked of perfume. Nell had smelled the odor before somewhere a long time ago. 'Jean Nate' flashed in her mind. Bella and one of the teenage girls she had grown up with ...perhaps Rose Ann had worn the same perfume, she recalled.

"Twenty dollars," Nell pretended to be interested. "How much for the night?" The woman's brown eyes flashed excitedly in the darkness.

"Fifty?"

It sounded more like a question than a statement like she was bargaining to sell a souvenir in the port cities of the Mexican countryside. Nell mused expecting her to follow with the customary 'best price' closing.

"OK, but I'm hungry right now." Nell nodding agreement took her arm and led her to a small restaurant on Canal Street. The woman had highly agitated movements, a nervous smile, and she smoked incessantly. Nell stared with interest at the tracks on the back of her hands and on the inside of her arms as she scanned the menu.

"What's your name?"

"Sybil," she smiled. "They call me Sybil. I want a big breakfast. Hey you, is it too late to get breakfast," she yelled at the waitress.

Nell casually picked up the woman's hands turning them over so the light reflected off the pale tracks tracing her veins, before she snatched them away. Angrily, she put them in her lap under the table.

"Hey! What's up?" She eyed Nell suspiciously. "Who're you?" She scanned the room nervously with wide eyes.

"I'm nobody," Nell whispered. "Don't worry. I'm not the cops." A strained silence settled around them.

"How long have you been using?"

The woman stared at Nell like a frightened child caught stealing by its parents. She fidgeted in her seat. A dull yellow cast colored the whites of her eyes, and Nell thought, she looked tired.

"Awhile," she replied cautiously. "I don't do it every day, "she lied, looking away.

"How did you start? You're so young." She reminds me of Bella, Nell thought, remembering Charlie's ashes and the need for her to get to Eden. The woman smiled relaxing again.

"Young? Not really...I been on my own seems like forever." She hesitated before continuing. "Rico my high school boy-friend started me out. Probably so I would boost clothes and jewelry for him from the stores in the malls. That didn't last too long though. Cause after awhile they get to know you and they know ...what, looking like this," she looked down at herself. "Everybody knows I don't belong in them nice stores like Sax and Nordstrom's. In fact, the first time I caught a case, I was caught stealing women's purses from one of them nice places down at the River walk. Then he made me turn tricks just to pay for our blow, you know. I told him he should sell weed or something...but the bastard was too fuckin' lazy."

She lit another cigarette, and her emotions suddenly started to overwhelm her. Her shoulders sunk and they shook momentarily before she collected herself.

"If only I could go back...and do it all over again," she sighed. Silence settled between them as the waitress poured the coffee and took their order. She drank silently and deliberately. She was so mechanical, Nell wondered if she even tasted the coffee.

"Never been bothered turnin' tricks though," she said burping into her napkin. "The tourists don't complain. They just want to get off. Most are drunk anyway."

"What would you do differently? I mean if you could go back, and what happened to Rico?" Nell was intrigued.

"Gone. Quit usin' after he got out 'a prison."

"You on your own?"

"Yeah...hey you want to talk, or do it? It don't matter to me. It still be fifty dollars. Either way you gonn'a give me my money!" She opened her purse to show Nell the sharpen ice pick she carried inside.

I'll drain your windpipe Nigger. Don't you fuck wit' me." Her eyes flashed with mock anger.

"OK. OK, let's eat first."

"Just don't try to fuck wit' me. I...and I get paid before we leave this restaurant!"

"OK. OK, I understand!"

The woman watched Nell suspiciously as they each had two bottles of Red Stripe beer, a large bowl of gumbo, and fried grouper sandwiches with French fries. The food had a calming effect on both of them, and with encouragement from Nell, she spoke openly about her estrangement from her parents and other aspects of her life. She ate the food as if it was the first meal she had tasted in days, ordering key lime pie for dessert.

"Ain't had a meal that good since I went to my sister's house for Mother's Day."

"When was that?" Nell encouraged her to talk.

The woman's eyes soften and a thin smile spread across her face.

"Three years ago. I was just out of detox...the dinner was for Mother's Day but also my daughter. She and my Mom they were born on the same day. Just forty years apart," she laughed.

"You have a daughter? Have you seen either of them since that party?"

"No... Too ashamed. Fucked around and got strung out again right after that. I thought I could handle chipping on the weekends. It got out'a hand... still don't think I'm too bad though."

She offered to go to Nell's hotel with her, but Nell gave her five twenties, and had her sign a release form for the photographs. She took some available light photographs of her in the Quarter. Before too long, the shivering Sybil had struggled to control in the restaurant took over. Her nose started to run, and periodically she coughed in an uncontrolled manner.

"Cain't do no more...gettin' too bogue," she explained shaking as she lit her last cigarette. "I gott'a get a hit fore I really get sick. I got to go!" she looked helplessly at Nell.

"I'll give you another hundred dollars and a ride if you take me with you!" Nell insisted.

"Why?" She was focused. Concentrating on the possibility of another hundred dollars in such a short time. She faced Nell, wiping at her nose.

"Why? You want to take pictures? You cain't take no pictures where I'm going. They liable to kill both us! No, I cain't do it." She walked off back toward Canal Street looking for a taxi. Nell followed her.

"I won't take pictures, besides I'm out of film," she lied. "My car's right down the street. I have the money right here," she said patting her pocket.

"Show me," the woman weakened. "No, you got to pay me now," she insisted.

"I'll give you half now, the rest when we leave the house."

She hesitated, but followed Nell, tripping unsteadily over the cobblestone streets to the car back at the hotel. She blew her nose into the napkin she had taken from the restaurant.

"Listen don't say nothin' after we get there. Let me do the talkin'. And you'll have to buy some weed. Maybe smoke a blunt, or somethin'. Taft ain't gonn'a just let you sit in there. He'll get suspicious!"

"Why?"

"Why? Fuck you! I cain't stand no trouble. Give me my money." She started coughing again, and Nell could smell the sweat staining her underarms. Doubled over she stared at Nell extending her hand.

"Not until we finish."

"Then you got to promise me...you do what I say, or you get the fuck away from me right now...if you cain't do that!" Her voice elevated and her eyes flashed in the darkness.

"OK." Nell gave her the other fifty dollars. This was the first chance she had to do an honest portrayal of drug life as it happens. Nell knew it would be the center-piece of her work for Hill, and would possibly get her an award for outstanding photo-journalism. I need Sybil, she thought. She sensed Taft's was a place where she would find a conspicuous cross section of Americana, affluent suburbanites, urban poor and rural users, all trapped in an emotional time lock controlled by Taft, the man with the drugs.

She was concerned, but willing to make a purchase, and possibly smoke a blunt while she was in the house. That would be her last option, and only if Sybil let her know Taft was suspicious.

Over the three hours they spent in the house literally every cell in Nell's body was focused primarily on se-cretly documenting life inside a shooting gallery in the Crescent City. This house was set up in an old, seemingly abandoned piece of property not too far from the Louis Armstrong Park. The place had two levels. A mother and her three teenage children lived in the upper half. Two of the boys ran drugs for Taft. The place was ideally situated as it was in a poor neighborhood, and many of the people frequenting the place spent countless hours in the park peddling stolen merchandise, or trying to panhandle. Addicts gathered at the house at all hours to snort, shoot and smoke.   When Nell and Sybil walked in the door the smoke from the weed and crack pipes gave the place a blue haze. Nell coughed violently reacting to the strong acrid smell. She immediately felt some disorientation, and took shallow breaths trying not to fill her lungs with the putrid air. She sat on the first chair pretending to be sick. The place was dark and overwhelming, but she was determined to complete the assignment. She was thankful for the darkness, as it helped to conceal the fact that the small purse she carried openly in her hand was really her small digital camera.

She worked quietly. Still pretending sickness, stumbling from room to room. During most of the time Taft was mainly preoccupied with a group of young men wanting to trade several handguns for drugs. As she moved between the rooms, she stayed for a while in a back bedroom. Several young women sat on an old couch watching television. The smoke from weed and cigarettes had left a pale patina on the television and all the colors on the screen had a greenish cast. Taft's customers all sat, nodding in and out while attempting to have a conversation about the television show. In other rooms, people were snorting cocaine, while heroin was being used in the kitchen. One customer had passed out at the table and was sleeping quietly with his head on his neatly folded arms.

The scene reminded Nell of a bad movie, and to fit in she purchased and pretended to smoke several blunts while observing the activity in each of the rooms. She found Sybil, sharing the last blunt with her

She pretended to inhale the heavy smoke, quickly

passing it to Sybil who inhaled deeply. Taft, the owner of the house approached Nell suspiciously. She pretended sickness raising the purse to her head, and sitting quickly on the closet couch. He continued past her, but continued to watch Nell from a distance, but she successfullyexposed several frames of Sybil trying to raise a vein, snorting two lines of cocaine, and finally injecting a mixture of heroin and cocaine into the fleshly part of her butt-cheek just above her crotch. All the exposures were shot against the grainy backdrop of several other customers circulating a crack pipe. After awhile Taft started watching Nell very closely, and she knew it was time for her to leave. Without ceremony, she led the nodding Sybil out of the house. He watched suspiciously from the doorway as they struggled through the heavy rain to the car.

Nell walked Sybil to the front porch of her flat, and when she tried to get her keys from her purse several twenty-dollar bills dropped out. Excitedly, she crumbled; sitting on the wet steps in the rain and picked them up. Her thin legs were sprawled open in front of her, and with blank eyes she swore at Nell. The mixture of drugs and alcohol slurred her voice.

"You bitch...should'a left me at Taft's place! Mother fucker!" She yelled holding up the twenties shaking them at Nell.

"I still got money, you bitch...could still be partying! Shit," she cursed loudly as the wind whipped the rain stronger across the area. Nell fought the strong winds, but made her way back to the car. She looked back before she got in. Sybil tried to get up, but immediately sat back down again shaking the money in her hand, as in disbelief. Nell briefly thought about the life the young girl had chosen, and the similarity of her life to Bella's. She mulled their similarities as women, and the differences for choosing their respective lives. The differences were as vast as the differences had been in the community after the war. Bella was beautiful and sensitive, and worked to care for a father, and other men damaged by the war. Sybil, probably just as beautiful before the drugs, had been victimized by her search for acceptance and love, only to be used up and destroyed by the drugs and anyone calloused enough to take advantage of her.

"What a fuckin' waste," she muttered to herself, as her mind shifted, examining her time with the young woman.

"Did I take advantage of her? Yes." But, at least I paid her to help me, she said aloud. I didn't use her, she insisted in her mind, but her eyes started to swell with tears. "Fuck, "she exclaimed again and struggled to turn her thoughts to the drive to Eden. I'll leave tomorrow, she thought. The weather will be better. I need to be out of here. Wiping the tears from her eyes, she eased the car past Louis Armstrong Park, turning in the direction of her hotel in the French Quarter. The rain was blowing in sheets across the Park, and the streets were deserted.

◆ ◆ ◆

DRIVING EAST, HEADING toward the Florida Panhandle the next morning, she noticed how sluggish and inattentive her mind felt. Sleep the previous evening had not come easily, and she had sat up most of the night in the room listening to the storm outside. The thoughts dominating her mind drifted from memories of the old tenement house to the concern her Mother had shown about her going to Eden. She remembered that her Mother never talked about her childhood, only mentioning growing up in Mobile, once or twice. She wondered what she would find in Eden. Would she find Coon's Cove? Would it be like the old farmstead her Grady had described to her occasionally when she was a child, before sleep finally overtook her? Crossing into Florida she noticed the retention ponds along the highway were filled with water. Some trees were splintered and down, and several scattered buildings she passed had power lines sparking across their yards. This scene followed her until the middle of the afternoon when she turned north crossing the Alabama line near the eastern part of the state. Large stretches of forest along the interstate and occasional patches of plowed red clay with stunted cotton crops reminded her she was coming upon an area that depended mainly on business brought by highway travelers. Most of the billboards advertised local flea markets, and antique shops. She passed a truck stop flying a huge confederate flag. Its large sign advertised showers, southern food, and topless waitresses. Further down the interstate she passed long stretches of pasture, random storage sheds, and a store selling sexual toys, gasoline stations, more restaurants, and a string of small motels. They all seemed to be clustered at the edge of the small towns she passed.

She was pleased when she saw the exit for Eden. The area showed growth beyond most of the other towns. The billboards advertised real estate developments, dentists, doctors, attorneys, and an outlet store. Eden located near the southern border of Alabama near the Panhandle, had three exits from the interstate. She took the first exit to the outskirts of the town and proceeded down Main street, stopped for gas, and asked the attendant about a decent hotel where she could spend the night.

Later after checking into the Best Western Inn, she called Dean. He was happy New Orleans had gone well. She assured him she would be in Eden no longer than necessary to find Louise or one of the Robinson's. Later she called Hill. He was out so she left a message with his service. She had done all the photography using film. She had it developed before she left New Orleans, and planned to send him the photographic contact sheets by over-night mail. She promised to send him the accompanying story for the Daily by E-mail early the next morning.

She took a camera and drove through the center of the town. Approximately five miles long, the central area was mainly old storefronts, a new courthouse and jail, a new city hall, and the town was just beginning to draw the interest of real estate developers. Construction of new residential developments was advertised along the county roads leading into the square. She sensed the town's life had its own special rhythm.

The people walked and drove slow. They stopped at streetlights to exchange pleasantries, and seemed uncaring about time. It was the south of the past, and the future at the same time. It was different than the large southern cities like Birmingham or Atlanta. She had read about small towns like this, one foot stuck firmly in its confederacy past while at the same time striving to acquire the conveniences of the modern world. She passed a junior college, and a new mall. Both were busy with people and activity. Located in the center of town, they were near the courthouse, police station, and county jail. A new athletic field was also in the process of being added to the high school. Except for the professional folks who lived in large homes on the hill out near the county hospital, the outskirts to the town were composed of farms with large cotton fields seemingly stretching miles in both directions along a network of county and private roads. She decided to tour the hill section. The lawns were well manicured, and beautiful old spacious oak trees guarded the large homes.

Other than a few women and young girls standing at the bus stops on the main roads, there were few signs of black people in the area. When she turned into a cul-de-sac, she was approached by a private security guard and directed back to the main road. When a sign came into view indicating she was leaving Montgomery County she turned around returning to the hotel.

She had an early dinner by the outside pool and completed the first draft of the story for Hill on her laptop. After closing the computer, she lingered at the table drinking ice tea while watching a group of itinerant workers in the fields across the road from the hotel. They were a mixture of poor whites and brown families. Mostly, Mexicans, she suspected. Some of the younger children were crawling, as they chopped and weeded the fields until late in the evening. She later learned, most of the workers were illegal, and were brought in from as far away as South America every year. Each family was given a section of the field to care for and was paid based upon the yield of the crops from that section. Most lived in tents and their old trucks on designated land for the time they worked in Eden. She stayed out watching the workers until darkness, and the mosquitoes drove her inside to bed.

The next morning, she stopped at the local Bob Evans restaurant for breakfast. She was surprised to see more black people in the restaurant, but soon realized they were primarily tourists from the interstate on their way to someplace else.

After breakfast, she brightened when the busboy, a young black man, approximately seventeen, approached to clean her table. His large hands deftly removed the dirty dishes from the table placing them in the tray he carried. He had a wide grin when she spoke to him, a gold tooth flashing in the middle of his smile.

"You live in Eden," she asked. When he nodded, she

smiled and asked, "Where do all the black folks live around here?"

"Oh, you gott'a go south out the center of town, cross the railroad tracks near the old mill and the warehouses, and head out past the little colored area toward the Preservation bout eight miles or so. Most all us live over around the Cove," he responded.

"The Cove?"

"Un huh, Coon's Cove...near where the town started, down by the swamp. It's right near the National Pre-serve... place been there long before I was born. We all just call it the Preservation." He struck a chord, and Nell leaned forward intently in her seat.

"You wouldn't know a family...called Robinson's, Sangster's or maybe the Prad's? They all lived here a long time ago." She held his eyes.

"No Mam, sure don't. My parents, we just moved here about three years. Sorry." He said quietly.

"Can you tell me how to get there, out to the Preservation from here?"

"Sure, it's easy." He drew a map for Nell on a napkin after moving the tray of dirty dishes to the side of the table. She pushed two crisp single dollar bills into his hand.

"Thank you very much," she said as she left the table.

He appraised her with an admiring glance as he wiped the table with a damp rag before moving to the next empty table with his tray of dirty dishes. She could still smell the bleach from the towel he had used to wipe the table as she stood in line to pay for her breakfast.

❖ ❖ ❖

DRIVING DOWN THE TWO-LANE ROAD, Nell fol-lowed the crudely drawn map. It took her past the wealthy section of Eden. Large brightly colored homes sparkled amongst an array of Live Oaks and manicured lawns. Soon she crossed the town square and passed the small courthouse and adjoining jail. Several miles after she passed the jail the road turned south and down a severe hill before flattening out again. In this section she passed overgrown fields, random old shacks, seemingly endless old decaying bridges, and rusting railroad tracks. She finally passed a run-down isolated grocery store. It stangely sat out in the middle of a plowed field. Intrigued, she turned into the next crossroad. At the next stop sign she found herself on an unpaved road connecting to a series of other unpaved roads leading through a small cluster of houses. There were no sidewalks, and the small houses lined the roads were interspersed with overgrown vacant lots. She drove slowly through the area sensing its blackness. Near the center of the area there was a small white church with large stained glass windows on the side. Next to the church sat a small cinder block restaurant painted a teal blue color. When she passed it, the sound of Gladys Knight and the Pips' "Midnight Train to Georgia" escaped from the open door. Hickory wood smoking chicken and pork ribs filled the air. On the other side of the church was a small cemetery, and the headstones broke the grass and flowers into predictable patterns. Several of the casket vaults were visibly old and decaying. It seemed they were simply lying on top of the ground, and she wondered if the bodies were buried just beneath the surface. Suddenly she heard the loud whine of a saw cutting through wood. Driving further the sound of the saw grew louder, but soon it stopped and was replaced by the sound of small children playing in a vacant lot near the street. They were screaming at the top of their lungs chasing each other, while playing with a homemade teeter-totter. The sound of the saw drowned them out again, and she turned around heading slowly back in the direction of the restaurant, hoping to find an adult, perhaps one who might know Louise, or Miss Prad.

She stopped and listened for the direction of the sound of the saw. It was coming from a house sitting behind the restaurant, but further down a small crossroad. When she got to the intersection she turned and drove slowly through the maze of small shotgun houses lining the block. As she got closer to the sound she recognized it to be a circular saw ripping 2 by 4's. There was also the sound of hammers driving nails into wood. Loud voices could be heard intermingled with the whining of the saw, and the activity was coming from the rear of the house. Nell drove slowly past the house and parked the car across the street from the restaurant.

When she got out of the car, drawn by her curiosity, she looked up and down the street. Although a few of the houses were in disrepair, most had patches of grass and small gardens of flowers in their front yards. She noted a few of the places were very well maintained. The fence line was most noticeable. It stretched the entire block. Every house, although with different architectural details, had a fence and a gate. All the fences had ivy vines and a variety of flowers climbing them. Nell walked toward the noise, opening the wire gate she approached the rear of the house. She could hear the men discussing details of the next steps in whatever they were constructing. The saw started to whine again as they came into view.

Three older black men were at the rear of the house, each one dressed in tattered coveralls. Various tools, such as squares, levels, chisels, and crowbars lay about on an old concrete foundation. A box of nails, a hand saw and several hammers lay on the ground. One of the men, tall with large hands, and a grey beard was bent over a set of sawhorses cutting a 2 by 4. Several more freshly cut 2 by 4's lay on the foundation in a splatter of saw-dust. The other two men were smaller and younger. One looked thin and wiry, and the other was shorter with an exploding belly. They were adding an extension to the small house, and unaware of Nell's presence. They were focused on the whining of the saw. The noise filled the air as it cut through the 2 by 4. The tall man stopped the saw, straightened up, and blinking his eyes, looked her way to avoid the blowing sawdust.

"Boy! You shore a quiet one, ain't you," he said looking at Nell in surprise.

"Good morning," she smiled at his comment. He nod-ded, giving her an inquisitive stare, while putting the saw down on the foundation. The other two men had not noticed her. They were absorbed in aligning a 2 x 4 and nailing it as a support for an opening in the frame of the new wall starting to rise.

"I heard the noise from your saw," she said stepping closer to the foundation. "I'm from out of town, and looking for someone who might know the Robinson, or maybe the Prad family. They used to live around here someplace." The tall man arched his back stretching, while exhaling a tired sigh into the air.

"Robinsons? Maybe a long time ago, you probably mean Big Poppa and Shugababy. Used to live over yonder by the Preservation. They all dead Miss. Been dead...goin' on a long time now!" He appraised her more carefully.

"Miz Eva be the only one still livin' I know of. Why you want to know bout them folks?" He challenged her as he picked up a wooden yardstick and put another 2 x 4 on the sawhorse. After taking a measurement, he straight-ened up and pointed at one of the other men, who were now eyeing her suspiciously.

"LD there probably remembers them folks you askin' about." He nodded in the direction of the other two men. Nell turned, appraising the man called LD. His back was to her,They wereHe was the thin wiry one.

"He's Miz Eva's nephew, one of them cousins back in the family some way or other." Nell cautiously, appraised the man called LD when she turned toward him. His thin face looked strong;he had strong features. They stood out sharp against his skin. His broad nose sat on his face like a budding tulip, and his full lips wore a purple cast.

"You ain't from round-bouts here. What you want about the Robinsons? They dead, best be left where they be!" Nell heard the agitation, and the challenge in his voice, but she quietly met his eyes. Except for the purple of his lips, his skin was the color of reddish-brown mud. His hair that could be seen coming from under his straw hat was gray. It stood out trailing down the back of his neck in little ringlets. The humidity had put a wet sheen on his face, and his perspiration stained the collar of his undershirt.

When the saw started again, he nimbly stepped from the foundation to face her. He was breathing heavy, and wiped at his face with a large handkerchief. She guided him away from the noise of the saw.

"I suspected most of them might be dead by now," she said. "I'm just trying to find someone who might have known my Uncle Charlie Campbell. My Mama said he used to come and spend time here in Eden helping them out on the plantation."

The two men on the foundation had turned away to align and nail another 2 x 4 in place, when LD eyes suddenly lit up as if he had been struck by lightning.

"Then you must be Grady's girl? Well I be!" A glint of recognition flashed in his eyes. "Let me look at you," he said taking the large print handkerchief from his pocket again. He shook it vigorously to remove some of the sawdust before using it to clean the glasses hanging from a string around his neck. Smiling, he tilted his head back appraising Nell through the thick glasses.

"Damn if you ain't Mae's baby girl...looks like you could be Shugababy's child too, got her pretty black color, her sad eyes and full mouth." He laughed exposing his teeth again. "What you doin' way down here child?" He outstretched his hand.　　　" Yes, I'm Mae's daughter, Nell," she said. He sat on the edge of the foundation, and took a deep breath before speaking again.

"You shore takin' me back a long way, didn't ever think I'd see a Campbell back down here again...ever!" He stood, extending his arm, circling her shoulder. It was covered with sawdust, but she gladly accepted his embrace. A broad smile broke across her face. Finally, she thought warmly, perhaps he can help me find Louise.

"LD Johnson," he said, "it is really good to see you. Your Mama and me, we be first cousins. Miz Prad, she be our oldest livin' auntie. Big Poppa he be our Grand-Poppa, not Grady's family at all. He and his young brother Charlie, they stayed with us...just before he married Mae. Loved Charlie like he wuz my brother though." His words caught her crosswise.

She heard them, but had difficulty absorbing their meaning, and stood quietly struggling to process what he had said. It was clear she knew nothing about how her parents grew up. He must be wrong she thought. She was sure Mae had told her that her Father grew up in Mobile. LD looked at his watch.

"Come on, we just bout breakin' up here for lunch, let's walk down to Ruby's."

INSIDE THE LITTLE TEAL BLUE restaurant, they sat at a table near the window. It was larger than she had thought and had a quaintness provided by old photographs on the walls, and overused and mismatched furniture. The sounds of James Brown filled the space blaring from a jukebox along the wall. It reminded her of the places her daddy had described to her when she was a child and the two of them sat on the back porch of the tenement house long ago. Above the crusted fried food smell, she could also make out the distinct odor of stale beer. The place was only about twenty feet wide, but extended deep into the rear away from where they sat. At the very back of the room sat a stage with a ring of Christmas tree lights strung around it at the top. There was a microphone in the center of the stage and several large speakers on each side ringed it. An old upright piano was off to the side against the wall, and a well-worn set of drums sat near it. A small dance floor of red linoleum had been laid over the concrete foundation, and red and blue bulbs hung from three ceiling fans extending down the middle of the room. In the front of the restaurant a small kitchen ran along the side just inside the front door.

LD asked Ruby, the proprietor to turn down the juke-box and ordered two pulled pork sandwiches for lunch.

"Ruby's got the best food in Eden," he said as they waited. "Specially these sandwiches. You wait. You'll see."

"Good. I'm hungry," Nell, said as she watched the rotund woman prepare the sandwiches. They sat silently salivating over the huge sandwiches. Finally, LD spoke, while sucking at a string of the pork caught between his teeth.

"Goodness, ain't seen or heard hair from your family for such a long time...not since we heard bout Grady passing. How's Mae and Charlie doing?"

"She is doing just fine. But Uncle Charlie has passed on," she said quietly. LD was accepting of the news, as if he had expected to hear what she had said.

"God bless Charlie, we all called him Nappy. He wuz a good man. He be the main reason I learned to read and do figures to this day. I wuz younger than him by bout three years. But he came by lot'sa evening after we finished workin' in them fields out there. It would be dark as the devil outside, but sure enough Charlie would always show up knocking on my Ma's door. If Charlie didn't come by, Ma wouldn't let me go by myself. Anyway, we'd take the lantern, leavin' Mama in the dark, and walk together to the little school room up in the ole slave quarters, and when lessons wuz over he would walk me back." Nell was intrigued and sat forward in her chair listening intently.

"You be talking about the little Sangster's school; you know Louise?" She held her breath anticipating his response.

"Yep...shore it wuz! You know Louise too? You must'a been out to the Preservation?" He looked surprised. Nell shook her head from side to side.   "NO, haven't found the place yet." LD continued sucking at more meat caught in his teeth.

"Louise's mama and Miz Pete, they started the little place for the colored chil'rens. My Ma couldn't always pay the weekly dime they charged, but them women runnin' it never turned nobody away. They made it work somehow."

"Louise white?" Nell asked. Her mind had moved beyond the talk about the school.

"Yeah, she white all right," he responded; "her folks, they just like all us. Poor as dirt. She couldn't read or write neither. Her Mama and Miz Pete had 'most twenty or more us kids in that little ole place. Part of it still standin' over there in the Cove."

Nell dropped her eyes, and her mind raced back to the letters Louise had written to Charlie. LD's words were like pins sticking into her brain. She tried to gauge his age, and thought of Mae, and her reticence the day they found Charlie's photographs. She had questioned Mae's attitude at the time, but had not concentrated on it. The thought at the time had disturbed her, wondering about her Mother's motive, and she pushed it from her mind. Now she wondered, is LD the key to Mae's past reluctance? She pressed him for more information.

"LD, are you talking about cabins where actual slaves lived out there in the Cove?" She was fascinated by the possibilty of walking into a historical artifact.

"My Daddy and Mama didn't live out there, did they?" She asked him, finally understanding now she really knew nothing about her own roots. She wondered briefly why she never asked before, or wanted to know before now about the family history. His response shook the thoughts from her mind.

"Yass mam! Those be the ones...the ole slave quarters." He ignored her question about Mae and Grady. "At that time when we wuz kids, must'a been thirty or forty of them old places. All that land out there wuz the old Sangster plantation; belonged to Louise's great great-grandfather. When I wuz born though, most the land had been taken by the state 'cause of taxes. The portion left wuz trusted into an e'state, for the descendants of the slaves that worked them fields from the first time them white folks brought them to Alabama. That e'state wuz trusted to ole Marsh, Louise's daddy."

A strained silence grew up between them. Each felt awkward as they sat there in their private thoughts. They glanced past each other into the distance as his words sank into their consciousness.

"You're kidding," she finally said. She quickly grasped the storyline underlying LD's words. I need to go out and see this Preservation she thought.

"I got'a get back," he finally said looking at his watch, and standing up. "If you gonna' be here more than a day or two, you ought to try to get out to see Miz Eva. She can tell you more than anybody else down here 'bout life back in those times."

"You mean Miss Prad. She live out in the Preservation?" He nodded as Nell followed him out the door into the bright sunlight. "I'd like too, and I'd like to come back and see you too. I want to learn as much as I can about how my parents grew up," she said anxiously.

"You come anytime," he smiled; "my house the red one down the street."

"How can I get to the Prad place from here?" LD continued walking, picking up his pace when he heard the saw whining again. He slowed up when she stopped at her car. She could tell he was anxious to get back to work.

"Can you tell me where Miss Eva lives," she pressed him again before getting into the car.

"She live close by, not too far, the little grey cabin in the Preservation," he turned looking back in the direction of the paved road she had taken into this area.

"Just go back to the main road, make a right turn and follow the fence line...you'll see a fork leading to a dirt road. Just follow that to the turn-around. She lives up there in the little house at the turn-around." He watched as Nell turned the car around.

"Just follow the fence line," he yelled at her. "Tell Mae, I'm OK down here!" She waved her thanks back at him, but had no idea what fence line he was talking about, but she proceeded as he had instructed. When she turned onto the main road, signs indicating the Alabama National Preserve started to rise along both sides of the road. Eventually, she saw the tall wire fence lining the Preserve. It protected and separated the pines, poplars, and lush ground vegetation from the traffic along the road. She could only sense the depth and beauty of the Preserve as she drove along the fence line. Her mind drifted to thoughts of the photographs of Charlie in front of the old schoolhouse. She wondered what she would find when she met Miss Eva, and would she find Louise, or any of the Robinson family still living in the area. The road suddenly forked into two rutted tracks, one going left the other veering to the right.

Did he say turn right or turn left? The question nagged at her mind as she instinctively turned the car around heading back in the direction of the town square, and her hotel. We'll try this tomorrow, she thought. I can get an earlier start.

After an early dinner at the hotel, Nell sat outside by the pool. A family with three small children played in the shallow end, so she found a lounge chair at the deep end, and faced away from the noisy children so she could enjoy the setting sun. She had considered calling Mae, and Dean, but felt uncomfortable talking about LD. It was as if she had stumbled upon some forbidden family secret. Was this why Mae had discouraged her from coming to Eden; couldn't be, she thought, LD's not enough. Perhaps it's because it's the history of the south, she concluded.

Eventually a few other travelers noisily took to some of the other scattered lounge chairs to enjoy the lazy evening. Their robust conversation scattered her thoughts, and she turned her attention to a few of the migrant workers still working in the fields. Must be the last harvest she thought. How long in the season does cotton grow, she wondered; but her mind soon returned to her meeting with LD. He was an interesting character she thought. She struggled, but she couldn't recall hearing his name in any of Mae's or Grady's past conversations. It was like he mysteriously appeared out of nowhere. Suddenly it dawned on her, she had never met any of her Grandparents, and she remembered hearing her Mother discuss the death of her mother only once. It was with the preacher at the small church when Nell was a child. Nell could only remember photographs of Grady's

Mother and his Grandmother hanging in the hallway of the old tenement house. There was no picture of Grady's Father. She had seen one picture of Mae's Mother, and one of her Father in his WWI uniform. Her mother had large breasts, full lips with fair skin, and light eyes, but contrasted with her father who was strikingly handsome with coal black skin. Mae kept these and other photographs in a scrapbook buried deep in her closet.

She felt strangely betrayed by her parents, but more by Mae. Now she suspected the family history had been consciously hidden from her. She thought back over her life, searching, trying to remember if she had ever seen a picture of, or heard any comments about the town of Eden, Coon's Cove, LD, or Miss Prad before Uncle Charlie died. But she could only remember, as a child the few letters that came sporadically from Eden, and Mobile, and in response the money, and packages of second hand clothes Mae, and Grady would send south each year

Later she turned off her cell phone, and had another restless night, wondering if she should call Dean to talk about her feelings. She resisted, as images of her past family life trailed through her mind over and over again. Exhausted, she finally fell asleep just before dawn.

"...Oh, oh sometimes it causes me to tremble"

CHAPTER TEN

NELL WAS IN NO HURRY to leave the hotel the next morning as a cold rain had blown in from the Gulf during the night. It was expected to last most of the day. After a leisurely breakfast, she sat in the lobby and called Dean. He was happy to hear from her, but pretended anger at her for not calling sooner. He peppered her with questions.

"Hey, where you been? Why did you turn your cell phone off? Must'a called you six times!" He accosted her, "you didn't even call Mae! What happened? That's not like you. You meet one of those hot southern boys last night," he asked, changing his tone. "Mae called me six times already wondering if I heard from you." She didn't answer his questions.

"Dean, now I think I know why Mae was not too excited about me coming to Eden."

"Probably for the same reasons I was concerned;" he reponded. "Most of the south is still dangerous for people with our mindset."

"No, no. It's more interesting than that. I met a long, lost cousin," she said excitedly telling him about her meeting with LD. He listened intensely.

"So, so what? Mae told you might find some long, lost family folk down there."

"Yeah, but I thought they would be my Dad's people. This is one of Mama's cousins...and he said Mama and Daddy lived down here once, in the Cove. I always believed Mama lived all her life in Mobile, and Daddy and

Charlie only went to Eden for just a short time, you know while helping out their Grandparents, Shugababy and Big Poppa."

"So!" Dean didn't understand Nell's concern, "so what's the big deal. You just need to do what Charlie asked and come on home." She heard the impatience in his voice, but ignored it.

"Mother lied Dean, Shugababy and Big Poppa was Mama's Grandparents, not Daddy's and I think she lived most her life in Eden growing up in the Cove." Dean had moved on from the conversation.

"You need to call her, and Hill. He called yesterday looking for your proofs!" She dismissed Hill's concerns.

"Yeah, he's always antsy. I mailed the contact sheets before leaving New Orleans. He should have them soon. I'll call him later today, but I need to know more about this area before I talk to Mae. It could be nothing, but as I think back on it she always shut down any questions about the family when I was young. She just intentionally lied to me all those years. I know I need to confront her about it, but I just don't want to put her in a position where she will lie to me again."

"I'm sure Mae must have a good reason." Dean attempted to be objective; "when are you coming home?"

"Soon as I find Louise and Miss Prad; but today it's raining too hard to try to find the Cove. I think I'll go to the library this afternoon and get the storyline together for Hill. I took about twenty exposures inside the drug house, but only about seven of them are usable. Hill will need some work on them; I should probably E-mail my comments on these to him sometime today. I'll see if I can find any thing at the library about the history of Eden too, before I look for Miss Prad. I'll call you later tonight."

"You be careful," he cautioned.

The library situated down the street from the courthouse and other municipal building smelled of moldy of old leather and dusty books. Several older women from a nearby senior citizen residence manned the counters. Nell was directed to a section housing the Eden historical collections. The young librarian overseeing this section smiled when Nell approached. To Nell the room seemed overcrowded with older white people sitting at the few tables sorting through old books, and at machines viewing files stored on microfiche. After discussing her needs with the librarian, she found a section of books that told the history of Eden, and areas south of the confluence of the Coosa and Tallapoosa rivers. The librarian also advised Nell a machine would be available later in the afternoon if she wanted to view black history data in the census tracts, and the old newspapers stored on microfiche. Nell declined to reserve a machine, but spent several hours researching the names of the Campbell, and Robinson families in the area.

She finally found a tattered book on the history of the Campbell family, and was surprised as she glanced through the small volume. She found old photographs of white people dressed up in period clothing. There were also photographs of blacks working in a cotton field while a white man stood close by, astride a large horse. She was even more surprised to find white members of the family with names like Charles, Grady, and Nellie Mae. Her search of the Robinson family proved to be just as fruitful. The name "Mabel, and Samuel four-year old twins, son and daughter of John Henry Cromwell" was the inscription under the photograph of two small fair skin children sitting in a black woman's lap. Except for their color they both surprisingly looked like Mae. The resemblance made Nell catch her breath. Her mind questioned kinship; she had heard of an Uncle Sammy in the past somewhere. Had he stopped at the tenement house when she was a child? She pushed the thoughts from her mind, but on a subconscious level she was intrigued by an unthinkable prospect.

She finally closed the book, and opened her brief case to review a copy of the contact sheets she had sent Hill. The photographs were grainy. They would require some work in in the lab, but she was still pleased with them. She opened her laptop, and typed the first words of the storyline.

THE FOLLOWING DAY, it was late in the afternoon when Nell took her lightweight jacket and left the hotel. A November breeze cooled the air, but the bright sun hurt her eyes and she quickly retrieved her sunglasses from her purse. A subtle headache, from lack of sleep, slowed her movements, but she rolled the windows down, and turned the car in the direction of the Cove. The humidity from the rain was extremely high she thought as steam drawn by the sun arose from the street. She flicked the moisture from the bridge of her nose. In case she couldn't find Miss Eva she had put the plastic bag containing Charlie's ashes in the case with her camera gear and her laptop, and planned to spend the day taking photographs and writing about the area. Inspired by her discovery at the library yesterday, she sensed she would find a wild beauty in the Preserve. When she turned onto the road leading into the small black community, she saw small groups of people from a distance. She could smell the smoke from the little teal blue restaurant and remembered LD's words about the fence line. The distinctive warmth of the people in the community impressed Nell more than anything else. They are like, in a special world of their own, she thought, and it seemed the people on the hill don't even know these people exist down here. Maybe they have gotten so used to the poverty, they have forgotten about them. Thoughts of their exotic richness, their old age, and wrinkled black skin against the green fields and blue sky ruminated through her head, and was capturing her imagination. This place, what with its overgrown fields, and remnants of old abandoned shacks and slave quarters were made for a photographer's holiday she concluded. She felt her emotions surge, as the fence line came into view. She wondered what Miss Prad's house would look like, and what it would be like living in one of the small places.

When she took the fork in the road to the right she saw the old woman. "A surreal painting," flashed through Nell's mind. The area appeared desolate and undeveloped; it seemed the woman was the only other person alive on this side of Montgomery County. She looked like a tired and lonely stick-like figure sitting on a large rock by the side of the road. Leaning back into the wire fence, her eyes were closed and perspiration glistened on her skin. A plastic grocery bag, the weight of its contents anchored it to the front of her neck, hung to her side. Two other bags of groceries sat on the ground beside her.

Nell stopped the car, inquiring if she was all right, and might need help.

"Sure, I'm all right...just restin' a spell...that's all!" The old lady opened her eyes wide examining the intrusion carefully. Bracing herself against the fence, she struggled to her feet, while holding the bag with one hand. She smoothed the wrinkles from her dress.

"I'm sorry mam for disturbing you...but I didn't

know if you were all right and all sitting by the side of the road like that," Nell said. "Can you tell me, is Coon's Cove up this way?"

"I can show you," her voice was strong. I got to go that way. It's right by my place. I generally walk it wit no trouble, but today I'm whupped by this humidity," she said moving stiffly. "It ain't too far. I'll show you," She took the bag from around her forehead, and leaned over painfully to pick up the other two bags of groceries.

"Leave that ma'am. I'll get them," Nell said walking around the front of the car. The old lady insisted on carrying the smaller package. Nell opened the car door before retrieving the packages. The old woman helped her settle the groceries into the back seat. Standing back, Nell appraised her carefully.

It was hard to tell her age, Nell mused. She wore a clean white apron over a neat faded print housedress. It had a faint odor of talcum powder, and the collar and cuffs were starched. A pair of worn blue tennis shoes covered her feet, and her thick snagged stockings were rolled down to just below her knees. She had carefully placed a knot at the top of each one to keep them from rolling down her thin legs. A small Bible peeked from the pocket of the apron, and her store-bought teeth clattered when she spoke. A small stream of saliva crept down the side of her mouth. She casually pulled a small white handkerchief from the sleeve of her housedress and wiped her mouth. Swallowing hard she removed her teeth wrapping them carefully in the handkerchief before putting them inside her pocket next to the Bible.

"Can't stand these things no way," she said loudly, referring to the teeth as she spoke. She looked Nell up and down while speaking. Finally, with a deep exhale she settled into the front seat, seemingly happy for the ride.

"Only put them in when I go to town, and church most days anyway." Squinting her eyes, she stared at Nell over her thick glasses again.   "You be a stranger in these parts...must be lost, you too far away from the highway," she declared.

"Mighty glad you came by though...reckon you be wondering what an old lady be doing out here with all these groceries, all by herself."

"You're really loaded down all right," Nell responded.

"Well the jitney, it just brings me so far, jest til the gravel road runs out. I usually walk home from there. I generally don't have this much to carry though. Some these things belong to my neighbor close by. Don't know why she can't do her own shopping anyway!" She looked ahead squinting her eyes against the setting sun.

Nell looked at her out of the corner of her eye, noticing how straight and tall she sat in the front seat. Her skin was the color of coal and smooth as a fresh black olive, and her veins stood out full and rich in her long hands. Her thinning gray hair was pulled neatly into a bun at the back of her neck. In those places where the hair was thin, the pink color of her scalp was a shocking contrast to the blackness of her face.

Nell drove slowly, and carefully down the rutted road. It lead into an area that looked like a mixture of rich, dark fields, and swampy wetlands. The road was worn and uneven, and some of the holes were so large Nell had to maneuver close to the drainage ditches on the side of the road to pass.

"It can be pretty tough getting around in here," she said.

"Yeah...gets really rough sometimes after a big rain," the old lady laughed. "This here all happened when the Union Army destroyed that big dam, high up on the Coosa back during the war...flooded all this good rich dirt, but no body can grow anything much here anymore... Swamp's too unpredictable when it rains."

"Swamp must be close by. I think I smell it," Nell said steering the car back into the rutted road again. The old lady simply grunted an acknowledgment. They passed a few small shacks dotting the landscape in the distance. Nell was interested.

"Anybody live in them old shacks?" Nell asked, nodding out the window.

"Some folks do...them old shacks left over from sharecroppin' when all this land was part of the plantation. Rich old white folks owned all this here land...all the way back north of the Preservation a long time ago. A few old slave shacks, some still kind'a standing further in, is nearby my place. Most pretty much rotted through by now, though."

Nell felt a surge of excitement. The warmth of the failing light gave a distinctive glow to the area. Her camera was on the back seat, and she wanted to stop and take some photographs, but decided she would return the next day. She sensed there was much more beauty to see of the area. The shacks were weather-beaten, decaying, and scattered into the high brush near the swamp. In the rear-view-mirror Nell could barely see the top of the closed cotton mill and the warehouses back near the town's center. Coon's Cove sloped downward away from the railroad tracks that brought dry goods, new appliances, furniture and the mail into Eden. The same tracks had also taken most of the cotton bales north to Tennessee to be processed and spun years before. From there the bales were primarily shipped north to the textile mills in the Carolinas, and on to Europe. Because of this proximity to the downtown section and the industrial heart of the town, Coon's Cove, despite its abandoned poverty, had city water, some sewers, and power lines.

They passed a footpath that led away from the main dirt road into the Preserve and to most of the shacks. A few of the abandoned places had deteriorated, and weeds and wild vegetation had grown up the walls, spilling from the broken windows and doors. Some of the other cabins had small neat clearings around them, and the owners struggled to grow flowers and an assortment of vegetables in the small spaces.

The people in the area, mostly old, called out and waved at them as they drove past. There was a southern singsong cadence in their voices, and Nell sensed, despite their poverty, they were kind and welcoming. As she gazed into the distance, the landscape on each side of the road reminded her of one of the French Impressionist paintings she had admired over the years. It was an unplanned stretch of pasture dotted with the colors of wild flowers, pine trees, and wild brush. As they got closer to the strand of pine trees where the dirt road ended, remnants of a decaying stone fence ran along the road, and she could see trails of old limestone, partially grown over with low weeds leading off into the pasture. Most of the stone path disappeared into the undergrowth, but one section was still intact in the brush. It followed down a rise in the fields to a stream, where the stream emptied into a creek. The songs of the animal life around the creek could be heard over the hum of the car motor.

"My place be just up ahead in that turn-around where the road ends... up there." The old lady leaned forward in her seat pointing at a small cabin that seemed to be sitting in the middle of the road up ahead. She had been so quiet, and Nell had been so preoccupied with dodging the ruts in the road, and admiring the natural beauty of the area she had almost forgotten where they were going. She refocused on the old lady admiring her carriage as she leaned forward. It was one of a woman who had maintained her health well for her years.

"The road, is it wide enough so I can turn the car around up there," Nell asked.

"You can park up there," the old lady said. "There's room right near the front yard." She pointed out the designated area as Nell slowed the car while approaching the area. After she managed to maneuver the car into the small space off the end of the road she noticed the cabin was sitting off from a small cul-de-sac. There were two-foot trails leading from that point. They forked off in different directions, into the woods and down toward the swamp. Nell looked around as she turned off the ignition. Three other little cabins were scattered off in the woods not far from them. As she got out of the car, the sound of water running over rocks in the distance grabbed her attention. Her eyes, drawn to the sound immediately found the creek, glistening off in the distance. How soothing and peaceful, she thought, watching the old lady slowly emerge from the other side of the car.

"Louise lives over there," she said pointing in the direction of one of the small places in the distance to the right of hers. As they unloaded the groceries, Nell found herself staring at the small place wondering about Louise. She wanted to ask the old lady about Louise, if she was white, what did she look like? Did she know Uncle Charlie? Images of the old photographs and the letters from the footlocker stirred in her mind, but she held her questions. The old lady continued talking as she made her way around the car and toward the cabin.

"She's the one I got them other groceries for, sometimes she's just too lazy to get up." she declared angrily over her shoulder opening the gate to the small front yard. "Mr. Barnes lived over there in that other place," she said pointing in the direction of the closest cabin down the trail in the brush leading from her back porch. "He lived there until last summer, but he died. I think his place is up for sale now...not sure anybody'd want it though. It's about as bad as old Coot's place," she said nodding her head at the last cabin furthest out near the creek. "Strange though, Coot still comes down here every January...stays all winter getting away from the snow and cold up there in New York, so he says. I think it's for the fishing. He just loves to fish these swampy streams down here in the Cove. That's his place over yonder by those big pine trees next to Swallows Creek."

Nell looked in the direction the old lady had indicated. She could barely make out the shabby brown cottage. It sat in a small clearing in the middle of the pine trees where they parted in a large semicircle encasing the beginning of the creek. What a peaceful place Nell thought. It's no wonder he comes here for a refuge if he lives in New York.

"Come in daughter;" the old lady was holding the front door open for Nell as she carried the last of the grocery bags into the small place. The old lady took it from her and proceeded to the kitchen area. Nell wondered about her age. She was so active, and reminded Nell of Dean's aunt Mattie who still lived by herself at ninety-five years old. The old lady must at least be as old as Aunt Mattie she thought when she heard a scratching sound coming from the other side of the door.

"That's Mr. Fred," she said emptying the last of the bags. "I want to thank you daughter for the ride...sure helped me a lot. You want'a glass of cold water, maybe sit a spell out'a the humidity?

"Don't mention it," Nell said. "A glass of cold water would be fine and," she hesitated, "maybe you can tell me a little bit about this area." The scratching at the door became more insistent.

"OK, OK Mr. Fred!"

A large gray cat greeted them as soon as the door was opened. The cat purred solicitously and slightly arched its back, circling them as the old lady ushered Nell into the small kitchen area. The place smelled of fried bacon and fresh herbs. Nell could make out the odor of sage. It made her sneeze. Old linoleum on the floor, though worn in spots near the sink and the stove, gave the kitchen floor a nice clean look. The bedroom and the living areas were combined. The floor in that section of the cabin was bare, but two carefully placed throw rugs broke up the plainness of the floor. One was placed at the side of a small white spool bed, and the other was facing the fireplace in front of an old worn couch and a rocking chair. A stack of cut firewood sat neatly in a rack nearby. Nell was surprised to see the fireplace and the cut wood. She had grown up believing the south was always warm, only recently accepting ice storms in the winter could cripple the area as much as the north.

"You can sit there if you like," the old lady said motioning to a small table in the kitchen area. A vase of fresh cut flowers sat in its center. Nell was pleased their perfume helped modify the scent from the sage and the fried bacon when she sat down. The old lady went to her bed, and removed the small Bible from her pocket. She placed it carefully on the pillow before going to the back door, opening it and latching the screen in place. Nell looked out onto the small back porch. It leaned away from the back of the cabin. Not very steady, she thought, as she moved to open the screen door for a closer look.

"Don't you go out there!" The old woman's words were sharp. "That old porch is just falling-down," she continued. "I don't use it no more, kind'a afraid it will just fall down completely and hurt somebody. Louise said she's gonna' help me fix it one day. That'll be the day," she laughed. "Maybe if she can stay out'a that still-liquor long enough. I'll probably have to get somebody to come up here and fix it one day."

She turned away dropping a treat for the cat hissing to get its attention as she walked past Nell toward the front door. It was still open.

"Come on! Scoot! Move Mr. Fred." She scolded the cat, dropping another treat closer to the door. The cat that was politely rubbing its nose against Nell's shoes immediately followed her and the trail of treats.

"Oh, that's a good sign. She be marking you. She likes you!" The cat obediently took the last treat, and as encouraged bounded quickly down the front steps, across the yard disappearing into the undergrowth beyond the clearing.

"She?"

"She's a she all right. I only named her Mr. Fred cause I couldn't stand having two women in the house at the same time, specially now since Lovie 's passed on. Oh! That man was the beating of my heart," she said closing the front door. "We were married more than sixty years. Don't know how I made it this long without him. Been dead now going on thirty years. At first I thought I would go crazy, but thank God for Louise, she moved in and stayed with me for a while. She helped a lot." She hesitated before exclaiming, "why don't you sit over by the door." She moved one of the wooden chairs from the table closer to the back door, patting the back of the chair indicating Nell should move.

"There's a better breeze blowing up from the back of the house in the evening," she said. Nell sensed the old lady was pleased to have company.

"Me and Lovie, we been married just about sixty-five years when he passed on, you know." She filled two jars with cold water from the refrigerator. Drinking deeply from one of them, she sat the other on the small table.

"For you," she said, turned and started putting the canned goods into the little metal cabinet next to the old gas stove. Nell quietly sipped slowly from the cool water. It was refreshing, and she also began taking cans of sardines, peas, and pork and beans out of the last bag. The old lady stopped her.

"You can leave those things, they be for Louise. She be coming tomorrow to pick them up."Nell took the jar of water and went back to the screen door looking out on the ramshackle porch. It led to a small garden at the rear of the old place. Sipping from the cold water she listened as the old lady continued to talk nonstop. Nell surmised from the way she was talking, quickly and with an elevated tone, she was a lonely person, and was happy to have someone with which to share her stories. It was all about her past life, and how she spent each night listening to sounds in the old place she swore were being made by Lovie, her late husband.

"He's just watching out for me, you know. You believe in spirits daughter?"

"Oh, sometimes. I'm sure things happen to us we can't explain," Nell responded remembering Mae's comments about Grady coming to her at times. "Yes, I'm sure they're looking down...sometimes guiding and protecting us," her thoughts turned to Uncle Charlie. "I'm sure they know what we are doing all the time," she continued. "... And sometimes, I believe, they help us make good decisions. I know the spirit of my Dad hovered over me for many years after his death...always encouraging me until I got through graduate school. Then just as quickly he left, and I haven't felt his presence since." The old lady nodded in agreement as she filled an old blackened teapot with fresh water sitting it on the stove over a low flame.

"I can hear Lovie most times when the weather is getting scary, specially when there's hurricane warnings. One night he came and stood at the foot of my bed. I swear he shook the whole bed to wake me, told me to get up and go to the root cellar. When I got up I could hear Mr. Fred crying loudly next to my pillow. The wind and rain lashed at the house, rattled the branches on the trees...and the windows in the house whistled all shrill-like. Me, and Mr. Fred, we got to the root cellar just in time, before lightening struck that old dead tree in the front yard, and one of them big branches fell on the roof." Nell looked at the old lady with concern.

"You were OK, right."

"We made it just in time. I was lucky cause some of the rafters from the roof just crashed all over my bed. I specs I would have been killed if it weren't for Lovie waking me like that." She looked at Nell over her glasses, sitting at the small table.

"You know 'bout Jim Crow, daughter? Lovie fought it till his dying breath!" Nell shook her head as she responded.

"I heard my parents talk about it when I was a kid. But I don't really appreciate what it means...something about how the laws in the south applied to black people. Right? Jim Crow laws kept black people from voting, running for public offices, and such. I know there was something about literacy tests, and poll taxes," she looked at the old lady seeking confirmation. "I probably know more about the Ku Klux Klan." The old lady sighed deeply.

"More than just laws daughter. Was the things them laws kept alive...kept slavery-like situations goin' on for colored folks down here and everywhere else in this country for years. And the Klan, down here they'd lynch a colored person...man or a woman just as soon as looking at him if we didn't act right."

"Act right...what was acting right?" Nell asked.

"Colored people couldn't buck this here system down here, couldn't even be a part of it...just always had to stay a boy, or an uncle...an auntie, you know...always a Nigga holdin' on to nothin' but dear life!" Tension crept into the space surrounding them. Nell could sense the history this little cabin contained. The stories this old lady could tell would make a book, she thought as she

172

watched the old lady through partially shaded lids. The old lady grunted loudly biting her bottom lip. Her voice was rooted in old anger when she continued.

"Jim Crow and the Klan, they dominated everybody's life at that time. Just crushed you down, suffocating the life outta' you...specially the colored's...cheated you out of your share of the crops at the end of the year, and --to white folks walking you right off the sidewalk in town. Better not look a white person in the eye; you'd be an uppity Nigga. That's what they called my Lovie, an uppity Nigger!"

"Couldn't look them in the eye," it sounded incredulous to Nell. "I had heard about some of the other stuff, but what were you supposed to do when you talked to them."

"You didn't talk to them, they talked to you...at least before Dr. King came...Why! I'm surprised you don't know that. What they teach'n these days." She moved to the rocking chair, shaking her head. The chair creaked as she rocked it back and forth.

"It was all over back in those times...in everything, separate drinking fountains, toilets, schools -- and colored girls, once they got to be eleven or twelve, they just weren't safe nowhere. Sometimes not even in their own homes. No honey it was not just the vote. Huh! I'm sure that's the way they want it remembered. Luckily there was some who just didn't put up with that kind of treatment. Don't think I'll ever forget Miz. Sangster, Louise's mother...and Miz. Pete, Lovie's mother. They both looked out for me when Mama died. My brother and his wife they saw bout the place for a while. But the Klan chased him off. The only thing left to help me wuz them two old headstrong ladies."

Nell felt her heart suddenly beating in her throat as she heard the names. She leaned forward listening intently.

"Miz. Pete...Lovie's Mama was the prettiest colored woman I'd ever seen," the old lady continued. "It was cause of her, we started talkin' on, bout the school for the children down here in the Cove. She couldn't get anywhere until she went to see Miz. Sangster, a white woman, whose husband wuz a direct descendent of the people who owned most this land before the civil war. She, and her husband wuz known to be a good friend to the coloreds. It's a wonder them old white folks didn't kill her for what she did for us colored young'uns."

Images of Uncle Charlie's photographs began to surface in Nell's mind. She stared deeply at the features of the black face rocking back and forth in the chair. Looking away she wondered if this old lady could have been one of the children in the photograph standing in front of the schoolhouse. Her mind drifted. She couldn't wait to call Dean and Mae. They wouldn't believe she had been so lucky as to find this place so quickly. Uncle Charlie would be happy here, she thought, a slight smile creasing her lips. The sound of the teapot was shrill against their silence.

"Oh, the water's hot!" The chair creaked louder when the old lady got up. She was deliberate in her movements now, and slowly crossed into the small kitchen area where she placed slices of fresh lemon into two teacups filling them with the hot water. Returning, she held the hot teacup out to Nell at arms length in front of her. Nell sipped the hot liquid carefully enjoying the citrus flavor of the fruit.

"So now...who was Mrs. Sangster," she asked inquisitively, wanting to confirm her suspicions.

"Louise's mama! She wuz Louise's mama. She be a small woman just like Louise, but she had long dark hair. Bout five feet tall, I'd say...very small, all over, but tough. She was big on helping the coloreds in the Cove. She, herself, was raised not too far from the Cove. Was poor as dirt 'til she married Louise's daddy. He came from a bloodline in these parts goin' back before the war over slavery, but She wuz called white trash by most them folks living up in Eden, specially them living up on the hill." The old lady blew at her tea, sipping it loudly.

"They sharecropped a small plot just north of the swamp down there with the coloreds. They grew a variety of vegetables they sold at a vegetable stand on the state road leading to town. They'd been friends with the Pete and Prad family forever. When the crops were poor, her daddy hunted with my Daddy, Big Poppa, to keep food on the table. All them, they worked together in them fields out yonder, planting, hoeing, and chopping cotton. At the harvest, her husband wouldn't let those crooked white people at the mill cheat them out of their fair due for the work, He watched out for Big Poppa, and any of the other coloreds at the mill when he was there." The old lady cleared her throat loudly, spitting the phlegm into a piece of wrinkled toilet paper she took from her apron pocket.

"S'cuse me daughter. All that hot lemon water helps with my sinuses," she said before continuing.

"Though...they had threatened to kill him many time, old Marsh Sangster...he died with the fever back there at Louise's little place leading to the swamp." She poured more water from the old teapot, filling Nell's cup after hers.

"There's more lemon slices if'n you want one," she said sitting in the old rocker. It creaked again with her movements, and she became silent remembering those days alone and in her own head. Nell increasingly conscious of the silence interrupted the old lady's thoughts by clearing her throat. The old lady stirred and began speaking again as though she had never stopped talking.

"Mrs. Sangster...oh she was the most strong-willed person I'd ever seen, you know like I said she was Louise's mother. Between her and Miz. Pete, they did a lot of good things for people living in the Cove. The best thing they did was to start the school for the colored children living down here. The only other colored school was way on the other side of Eden.... way out in the other County. The only way to get there was to walk through the white section and the town square. You had to walk in the road...couldn't walk on the sidewalk, not even in town. They also called the sheriff for nothing. The men... They picked at us when we passed them as they walked on the sidewalk, specially the colored girls. Once you got to school, then the coloreds over near the church they picked on you. They thought they were better off, 'cause we wuz so poor down here in the Cove."

Nell sat quiet as the old lady talked; she tried imagining her Uncle Charlie as a young man living in this area. He would love that creek out there and the overgrowth of the Preserve, she thought, remembering the time he spent in the simple wilderness of Hobo Junction. Her mind rejected her train of thought. That's too simple, she immediately remembered. It was not the wildness of the Junction that drew Charlie there each day, it was the alcohol and his devotion to Carver and the other men forced to live there. It was the same energy she had sensed among the men in the lobby at the veteran's hospital in Pittsburgh, she concluded. The old lady stirred again from her own thoughts.

"One day Miz. Sangster," she said laughing aloud, "she just went up to that storage bin in the white school in Eden, and took one of them McGuffey readers. Mostly they were just sitting there in a box anyhow, and shonuff she helped start the colored school in the corner of one them old abandoned slave shacks. There was twelve of us young-un's started out back then. We all had to sit on the floor, and some bales of hay most that first year. Louise...she went to our school...the only person in the school that weren't colored." The old lady clapped her hands loudly while looking up at the ceiling. She clapped them again.

"Praise the Lord for Miz. Sangster! She wouldn't let Louise go to that white school. Them uppity cracker kids, they made fun of her clothes and things, even when they saw her in town. She went barefoot and half-naked like the rest of us, cause other than two or three other white families, she wuz the only white child our age kept living down here in the Cove." She laughed to herself again, her small eyes twinkling as she continued.

"At first Miz. Sangster, and Miz. Pete had to teach them first classes themselves, and they did too --in spite of them threats. Miz. Sangster, she was quite something else. A firebrand my Mama said."
Nell, who sat quietly near the back door listening intently, and enjoying the slight breeze. It was now softly moving the white curtains in the kitchen area.

"Why, my goodness daughter...I'm just babbling on like I lost my mind."

"No mam...no such thing, please... tell me more about the school. It must have been hard starting a new school, especially a colored school at that time." Nell searched the old woman's face. It was relaxed and she started to rock slowly in the chair.

"It helped if you were tough!" She clapped her hands again, turning slightly in the rocker. "Miz. Sangster...she was tough, something else God bless her soul. The Klan would have tarred and feathered anybody else. Her, the most they did was burn a cross in her yard, stand outside at night threatening her, and calling her a Nigga lover. But that's all they did. All of them scared to death of her husband. Strong as a bull and mean as a scared snake when he had a drink or two of corn liquor, he wasn't afraid of the devil himself, 'cept maybe Miz. Sangster," she laughed slapping her knee. "He sho-nuff kept most the Klan ruckus under control down here in the Cove for a long while."

Nell went back to the refrigerator and refilled their jars with cool water, and the old lady drank deeply loudly smacking her lips.

"Thank you, daughter." She smacked her lips again savoring the last drops of the water on her tongue before speaking again.

"It really all started with Lovie's Mama, Miz. Pete. She'd been talking about starting a school for the children in the Cove for a long time...surely most' of that first year. When Miz. Sangster got involved it became the hottest topic for discussion by the women after Church each Sunday. Some of them refused to let their children, go to school in an old slave shack, but Miz. Pete, I'll never forget it...she told them all, its better to go to school in a field rather than not having no learning at all. A few had even wanted to use the church for the classes until Elder Haley said the Lord wouldn't be pleased with them using the house of God for anything other than praisin' him. Unknown to the women he also told the men he was afraid of what the whites would do if the school interfered with the children working in the fields at the other plantations.

The old lady coughed several times, clearing her throat she loudly expelled a wad of phlegm into the toilet tissue.

"S'cuse me daughter," she coughed again. "Lord I ain't talked this much in years," she said, her eyes glittering as she looked at Nell. "It's good to have company." She struggled out of the rocking chair toward the living area. Nell, started to arise, but the old lady encouraged her to remain seated.

"Stay! Stay, I just got to get something for this cough."

When she returned to the rocking chair, she brought

with her a small orange colored bottle. It was filled with sliced lemons, lemon juice, honey and whiskey. She took a long swig of the liquid.

"If this tonic puts me to sleep daughter...you just stay long as you like, and just close the screen door behind you when you leave. Oh! If Mr. Fred is outside the door when you leave just let him in too." She sipped the liquid again before capping the bottle and placing it on the floor next to the chair.

"We all did the best we could, you know the colored, could in those days. It was hard for all us back in those times. Course...we were lucky. We had Louise. She could get things done, being white and all, when we couldn't. She was tough too. I'll always love her for that part. She helped many a little colored child learn their letters. Don't get me wrong, I don't like everything she do...but God knows, she's just like my sister." The old lady sighed deeply. The chair creaked beneath her shifting weight, and a creeping silence settled into the room.

Uncomfortable, Nell shifted studying the fading light on the old lady's face. It was a warm mellow light, and she imagined how a shot of her face would look as a photograph.

"You've really had a full life down here. I can tell," Nell said. "Regardless of what happened in the past the Lord has blessed you with a long life. A lot of people don't get to enjoy their memories, like you." Reluctantly the old lady agreed nodding her head up and down.

"That's right daughter, she agreed." Silent again, she closed her eyes, and started rocking the chair again. Her face gave little indication, but her mind was searching through the pain in her past life.

Nell sat quietly by the open back door, thinking she should leave if she was to get back to town before dark. She cleared her throat attempting to get the old woman's attention, but only the noise of the rocking chair continued the conversation with the silent room.

Nell wondered if the old lady was asleep, but respected her silence by sitting back watching the darkness creep into the small cabin. Her mind drifted to Mae's concern for what she would find in the Cove. Is this what Mae was concerned about, a little old lady that could be her great-great grandmother? I'll have to tell Mae, she thought, nothing to be ashamed off here. In fact, I think there is a real story here on life in the Cove.

The darkness came without warning, as the sun had dropped quietly beneath the top of the pine trees. The sky lost all but the faintest hint of light emanating from the horizon far below the tree line. Suddenly the creaking of the chair stopped. The old lady looked around as if awaking from a drugged sleep. She smiled at Nell.

"Lord be!" she exclaimed. "Dinner will be ready in a minute daughter," she said without pretense. "You can use the wash bowl next to the bed to freshen up." Nell respectfully followed her directions as the old lady moved toward the sink to wash her hands.

"The water should be good and hot. That was the last thing Lovie did, putting in that hot water tank, fore he got real down and sick.... heated by 'lectricity and all. Still use the tin tub to take a bath though. Fact a' matter that's the only time I go out on that back porch, to get the tub." She laughed. "Just don't have enough room for everything I need, but I'm doing fine anyway."

She turned on the small lamp in the kitchen area and showed Nell how to fill the washbowl with hot water from the kitchen sink.

"Gets mighty dark out here after the sun goes down. I kind'a reckon you best stay the night," she said removing several bowls of left-over food from the refrigerator. Nell protested, but the old lady raised her hand, shaking her head.

"It'll be all right. Don't have much space here, but you can spend the night at Coot's old place. It ain't

180

much, but you make a wrong turn out here in the Cove, you could end up stuck out there in the Preservation. I'd be worried sick bout that." Nell could see the concern in her face. She's probably right Nell thought and decided the wiser move would probably be to stay.

"You sure it's all right. I don't want to put you out," she said reaching for the outstretched hand towel.

"Not at all... The best thing to do. Mr. Coot always leaves a key when he goes back north," the old lady responded. "You're welcome to use the place. He's neighborly like that...won't mind a bit. Besides what he don't know, won't hurt him," she laughed again. "He won't be coming down here for another month or so...just hope it's not too stuffy from being shut up." Nell was sure she was intruding, but immediately removed the feelings from her mind. She was pleased the old lady had offered the place.

"Thank you, Mam, you're probably right. It is too dark out there for me to try to find my way back to town," Nell said reconciling herself to her building excitement about possibly spending more time with the old lady.

Perhaps she knew Uncle Charlie. She could be talking about the same Louise that knew Uncle Charlie. They were all around the same age, she thought. Maybe I can learn more about life in the Cove, where Uncle Charlie lived, and did here...could help me determine the proper place to scatter his ashes. Maybe she knew Big Poppa, and Shugababy too. Nell's mind was speeding. She struggled to conceal her excitement and anticipation by thinking about the natural beauty of the Cove and the Preserve she had observed while driving up the road to the old lady's place.

She still had two rolls of film left and her digital camera for backup. Staying over would give her a chance to shoot some film at first light in the area. She surmised the high humidity would bring light that would be soft and warm in the morning, providing exotic hues and colors to the vegetation and the old cabins. The old lady interrupted her thoughts.

"Food's warm," she exclaimed. "I hope it ain't too simple for you...and I hope I didn't talk your ear off. Lord knows sometimes I just blab on too much when I get company. You too young to be interested in stuff an old lady talks about."

It was a dinner of black-eyed peas cooked and seasoned with smoked neck bones. Raw onions, cooked okra, a mess of fried cabbage and pan-fried corn bread. She sat the filled plates out for them garnishing the meal with fresh cut tomatoes. They ate at the small table in the kitchen, and she brought out one of the lamps from the living space so she would have additional light to eat by, and more than the overhead lamp provided. Occasionally the moonlight peeked from behind the clouds and it added a sense of warmth to the scene.

They were quiet throughout the dinner. The old lady ate with her fingers as much as with her fork. Nell relished the food, and took a double serving of the fried cabbage.

After the dinner, ignoring the old lady's protests, Nell washed and dried the dishes. She was just finishing the last of the pots when the old lady approached her with a rusty looking key and a large flashlight. She smiled, handed them to Nell, shaking her head in disbelief.

"You know you's in my house most the afternoon and I don't even know your name. Don't matter though...been a long time since I enjoyed somebody so much. I'm Eva Prad. Miss Eva is what everybody hereabouts call me... What's your name daughter?" A warm smile creased her face.

Nell's heart jumped in her chest as soon as she heard the name, Eva Prad. Here she was standing in front of her, the lady Mae had talked about. She could be part of the family somehow. Her mind struggled with asking the old lady a series of questions, as she walked in front of Nell to the front door. Nell looked at her watch. It's too late now, but tomorrow. It'll be better tomorrow. Her mind settled itself.

"What do folks call you daughter?" Miss Eva repeated the question. Soliciting an answer, she turned to face Nell at the door.

"I'm Nell Campbell. Just call me Nell." She mumbled awkwardly searching the face of the old lady for any discernible hint she might have Campbell blood coursing through her veins. Her mind flashed to the conversation she had with Mae about Mrs. Prad just before she and Dean went to Pittsburgh. *'Eva Prad's her name...I think she's either a cousin or something...'* Mae's words rattled in her mind. Miss Eva broke her thoughts by extending her long thin hand. They shook hands and following Nell out to the front porch, Miss Eva told her the easiest way to get to the Coot place.

"Just take the footpath going left out the front yard daughter. You can leave your car parked out front. It'll be al'right...right there, "she said. Don't nobody ever-comes up this way with devilment, cepting maybe the sheriff's deputy on patrol now and then. Just wanting to boss over somebody when he comes," she laughed. "Nobody down here pays him no mind."

The old lady stepped back inside the cabin closing the screen door behind her. As she moved, the light from the house cast her shadow across the small porch like an abstract dancing figurine.

Nell heard the words, but her mind didn't track them. Her heart was beating too violently in her ears. She stood outside the door for momentarily, letting her eyes adjust to the darkness before turning around to face the old lady.

"Mam, would you be the same Eva Prad that knew a Charlie Campbell a long time ago?" The words stumbled out of her mouth.

"My Mother told me about an Eva Prad from these parts that could be related to the Campbell family," Nell hastened to add. "That's the main reason I came to Eden...to find out about my Uncle Charlie." The old lady's eyes flashed as she stepped back, moving to shut the inside door. She pushed it up as if she was encouraging Nell to leave, but didn't fully close it.

"Charlie Campbell," she said, in thought, leaning forward, her weight against the slightly cracked door. She was silent, her eyes still studying Nell suspiciously. A slither of light from the opened door cut a path across the porch and into the front yard. Nell started toward the car afraid she would lose her bearings when Miss. Eva finally closed the door.

In the darkness, crickets were singing their songs, and other creatures made noises in the distance. She followed the thin path of light to the car. After Nell reached the gate, and was beyond the yard, Miss Eva called after her.

"I can't say I remember no Charlie Campbell." Nell noticed a distinctive chill in a voice that, earlier, had been warm and friendly.

"They be having a revival at the church most the rest of the week," she continued. "If I ain't here when you get ready to go in the morning, just slip the key under the front door. I'll get it when I get back."

"Yes Mam. Good night Mam." Nell was disappointed in the old lady's response, and hoped it hadn't shown in her voice. Miss Eva watched her apprehensively until she opened the car door before she softly closed and locked her front door. The light from the car, the only light piercing the darkness surrounded Nell as she reached into the car. She took out her jacket, the bag with Charlie's ashes, and her camera gear. Leaving the car in the turn-around, she turned on the flashlight. It cast a strong beam and she walked slowly up the path toward the Coot's place. Enjoying the sounds of the night, she wondered what she would find when she got to the old cabin.

"...Tremble, tremble, tremble"

CHAPTER ELEVEN

*T*HE COOT'S CABIN was built on a slight rise in the swampy terrain. It had been built years ago as an overseer's cabin when the area had been a large plantation. It stood close to the creek on a small-elevated plot of land covered with gravel and small stones. The elevation and the stones provided the plot with drainage, a sense of stability, and served to keep the marshy wetlands back that surrounded the cabin on three sides. The elevation also provided a view of the creek standing behind it, and looking out from the small-screened front porch, the sweep of the view extended back to the interstate.

Beyond the small-screened front porch, the door opened into a simple one-room structure with a small adjoining water closet containing a toilet. There was an old faded mirror on the back of the door to the water closet. A separate alcove from the larger living space served as a kitchen. As soon as Nell opened the door, the damp moldy smell of the place greeted her. She coughed. The place smelled moldy from the humidity, as well as dusty from being closed-up for a long period of time. She traced the flashlight along the simple space. There was a sink, storage cabinet, a small stove, and a small hot water heater in the small alcove. A single bed and a small wooden table and two chairs dominated the center of the room. A single bulb lit the entire room. It extended from the ceiling in the middle of the room over the table, and was rigged with a long string so the light cold be turned on and off from the bed. Nell turned it on and the dim light filled the room. The only window in the large room was across the room from the door. Another smaller window was behind the toilet in the alcove. The other fixtures in the cabin were a wash basin, and a small wood-burning stove fitted into a crude fireplace.

Nell was drawn to several faded photographs of small black children sitting on the chest. A crucifix hang on the wall behind the bed, and a small picture of Jesus, torn from a magazine, was thumb tacked to the wall in the small alcove. Several magazines on fishing gear lay on the table. They were covered with a thin layer of dust. As she looked in the cabinet, she could hear the bullfrogs down by the creek. They sounded as if they were in the room with her.

There was a can of old coffee, several cans of pork and beans, canned milk, canned sardines, a jar of dry cream, and tiny mouse droppings on the shelves. She looked further in the bottom of the cabinet and found the small coffee pot, sugar and flour stored in old glass Mason canning jars. She turned the water on in the sink. The old pipes gurgled, and shook as a brown fluid spewed forth into the sink. She reduced the flow, and let it run until soon it was running slow and clear. She filled the coffee pot with fresh water, sat it aside, and tested the bed. She pulled back the spread, and sheets checking them with the flashlight for insects. They covered an old soft mattress lying on top of a firm box spring. She was surprised at their quality. They were both clean and sealed in plastic against the dampness in the place. A smile crossed her lips as she climbed in the bed without undressing. She pulled the spread over her. It had been a long day and she suddenly realized how tired she was.

Before she drifted off to sleep that night she cracked

the window hoping to reduce the dampness and musty smell of the place. The stars were alive in the sky.

It reminded her of the time when she and Charlie sat on the back porch at the tenement house late one night. It had been too hot to sleep that night. It was a cloudless night and the stars filled the sky, just like tonight, she thought. It was just the two of them and Charlie told her about Bella going to Pittsburgh with him.

"We gonn'a get married Nell. I ain't sure she loves me...but I need somebody. We both needs somebody."

"Uncle Charlie...it's going to be all right. I just feel it. Mae says so too," she said shuffling her weight to look at him closer.

She remembered he looked so reflective before he responded, as if he was still struggling within himself.

"I just got to stay on the straight and narrow, Nell. I'll be all right if I can just do that! I know it ain't gonna' be easy...but Bella... she's gonna help me," he said soberly.

"Bella! How could she help Charlie? The question rattled in her mind. She thought of Sybil. Wasn't she just like Sybil, the streetwalker in New Orleans? They themselves need too much..."

The thought trailed off, but the words rang in Nell's head as she remembered Bella waiting for Uncle Charlie and Grady as they walked down the alley that day long ago. Nell tried to recall Bella's attitude when she joined them on their way to the bus station. Did she stumble when she took Charlie's arm...had she been drinking, or was she just excited and happy? The thoughts stayed with her until sleep finally overtook her.

Just before sunrise the soft chatter of the birds' calls stirred Nell awake. As she sat up she struggled to remember where she was, finally remembering her day in Eden and the last evening with Miss. Eva. She sat up on the side of the bed wondering how she would brush her teeth, and, at the least wash her face. Turning on the overhead light, she looked though the drawers of the old chest. Surprisingly there were several clean well-used washcloths and towels in one of the drawers. Somewhere off in the distance the sounds of the birds became louder as more of them began to add their distinctive calls, piercing the silence. Soon other sounds of different wildlife in the swamp folded in practically drowning out the birds. As the sunlight suddenly flooded the area she lost the ability to distinguish the different sounds and soon she lost her sense of the background sounds completely. The sun streamed into the windows of the small cabin. She made a pot of coffee. While it brewed, she washed at the sink. Later she heated one of the cans of beans and sat by the open door of the cabin taking in the view of Swallows Creek as she drank the strong coffee and ate the beans. After the second cup of coffee, she loaded one of the cameras, and called Dean. He fumbled with the phone before he finally answered.

"Yes...hello."

"Dean, it's me. I know it's early. I'm sorry. I must have awakened you?"

"Yeah...It's OK," he growled. "You OK? I thought you were going to call me last night. Mae is asking about you." He sounded more awake, and she could hear him as he groaned himself to an upright position.

"Hey Babe," her voice smiled. "Guess where I am?"

"Honey," he responded. "I love you, and miss you but why are you calling me so early? Are you at the airport?" He cleared his throat before continuing. "Nell its just after five o'clock? You're not still in Eden, are you?" She ignored his question.

"I'm in a little cabin in a place right next to Eden called 'Coon's Cove'. It's a wonderful place Babe! You would love it! You remember the time we were driving through Maine on our way to Quebec City and the car broke down?" She could hear the alarm clock go off and sensed him reaching across the bed to turn it off.

"Yeah, sure. How could I forget that weekend? We broke down in the middle of nowhere, near Skowhegan, Maine...yeah a trucker gave us a ride back to that little place near the lake," he yawned in her ear. "S'cuse me I really slept hard last night. Yeah, I remember that little tarpaper shack, and that whole weekend. Thank God, we had that bottle of Smirnoff, and you was so horney. I never would have gotten through the weekend without it...all that desolation."

"Same kind of place Dean," Nell was excited. "I'm in the same kind of place, more civil, and more room than the other place...but basically it seems I am living that whole weekend all over again, but without you."

"Did you find anybody that's a part of the family? Louise? Did you find Louise?"

"No, no Louise, but I did find one of Mae's Cousins, a man called LD" She hesitated, "and Miss. Prad. An interesting old lady, she's a friend of Louise, I think."

"Do they remember Uncle Charlie?"

"LD certainly does, but Miss Prad, she says she don't know no Charlie Campbell!" Nell laughed. "But I don't believe her."

"Nell, thats exciting," his voice sounded excited. "How old is she?"

"Don't know; could be late eighties, nineties, maybe. Too hard to tell. She looks older than Mae though."

"She could be senile, or maybe just had a hard life," Dean suggested. "Maybe just can't remember things that happened a long time ago."

"Not this lady," Nell laughed again. "She can remember. Hey, did you get anything from Hill on my contact sheets yet. I E-Mailed him the story two days ago."

"No, nothing!" She heard him stretch again as he slipped from the side of the bed. "OK...Nell, I got to get going…driving Mae for her errands today. I miss you Babe."

"I miss you too, but I won't be home right away. I think I'll take a couple of days here and finish the corrections Hill will have on the story line. Besides I want to spend some more time with Miss Prad."

"I really wish you wouldn't. You be careful Babe. It's still the south."

"Yeah, I hear you. I really got to tell you about New Orleans too, when I get home. Listen, if you hear from Hill tell him he can call me on my cell, but he should have received everything he needs by E-Mail already. When you see Mae today, bring her up to date on Miss Prad, but don't tell her about LD I will try to call her later this afternoon."

"OK, you be careful down there," he admonished her again. "I love you."

Nell put the phone back in her jacket pocket, looking out at the creek in the distance. Thoughts about uncle Charlie slowly crowded her mind again. Her eyes fixed on the glistening surface of the creek, and it seemed she could see images of Uncle Charlie sitting on the bank with the men from Hobo Junction.

It was as if she and Jacob were children again. She watched them, as if she was a separate person apart from herself. They chased and caught a lone butterfly; just as they had the day they met Bella. Jacob sat near the shoreline away from the men watching her, as she held the Mason jar up to the sun. The butterfly inside moved its wings gently and patiently while resting on the weeds they had stuffed into the jar.

Suddenly, without warning, Jacob struggled up from the ground and took the jar from her. He removed the top and turned the jar upside shaking the butterfly free. It struggled to catch a current of wind and soon flitted away. He turned and threw the empty Mason jar into the quiet current of the river.

"We're too old to catch butterflies Nell. That's the last one. We just makin' killing them for no good reason," he said looking at the men in the Junction. They were sitting quietly in a circle as they always did while waiting for Bella to bring the sandwiches from Jim's Diner. Except she was not there, and she wouldn't be coming. As designs change in a kaleidoscope, it seemed the men changed instantly from the placid circle waiting for Bella into an angry mass of flailing energy. They began fighting over the last drink in a small bottle of cheap wine. Then they started arguing amongst themselves about who had been the bravest in the war. Uncle Charlie was the loudest. He had raised his shirt, and was pointing vehemently at the wound in his belly and the scars across his back.

The image scattered when a crane landed in the shallows of the creek, and Nell quickly transformed back to reality. But she wondered how many of the men at the Junction had been wounded like Uncle Charlie. It was a common sight seeing displaced veterans wandering the streets in those days. There were many state hospitals for the emotionally ill at the time, but few people wanted their loved ones locked up in those places. She thought briefly of Carver, and the last pictures she had taken of the homeless Vietnam veterans sleeping on the Mall across the street from the White House.

Suddenly feeling despair at the memory, she stepped from the porch, looking down the trail in the direction of Miss. Eva's cabin. Charlie's ashes briefly crossed her mind. Where would it be appropriate to scatter them; her mind drifted. Maybe in the pasture out there or maybe if she could get close enough to the creek. That would be the best place she thought. Her mind was unsettled. She needed to talk to Miss. Eva or maybe LD some more she accepted, settling her thoughts.

As she turned to close the door to the cabin, she caught a glimpse of a doe stepping quickly through the hazy light heading down to the creek. Nell took the 35mm camera out of the camera bag, put two rolls of film in the containers on the strap. The air was brisk and damp. She put on her light jacket and started out down the trail toward the creek. She followed the doe into the undergrowth until the footing started to get too soft and mushy, and she had to return to the path. She watched as the doe disappeared in a distant strand of pine trees out at the edge of the creek.

Nell was concerned for snakes as she walked, but was intrigued by the swamp. She was also concerned about the possibility of getting lost. All of the area was similar, except for a huge Live Oak tree that appeared unexpectedly every now and then. So she stayed on the path worn into the undergrowth.

Soon it became obvious the path formed a circle eight pattern. It went by several old deserted and decaying wooden shacks. Most had rotted roofs, porches, and their doors had been removed. They were built in a large cleared semicircle as if they all shared a large front yard. They were all one-room cabins except for one that was sitting off, away from the rest. Its door was jammed tight, so Nell looked in the window. It had two rooms.

The fireplace in the larger room was decaying, but unlike the ones in the other cabins it was still intact. Remnants of partially burned wood and glowing ashes in the bed of the fireplace led Nell to conclude the place was still being used. It was more preserved than the other cabins, and had an air of caring about it. An old splintered wooden door balanced on a bed of bricks was in front of the fireplace. It was covered with a worn mattress, and crumpled bedding. A pail of water sat on one side of the bed, and an old rusty slop jar sat on the other side. The second room in the rear had a large window, and was empty except for several old benches scattered about the floor.

She knocked on the door of the cabin, calling out into the silence.

"Hello! Any body here?" Nell called out again, walking into the center of the large yard. She scanned the area for anyone who might have been around, but to no avail. She took several photographs of the area, concentrating more exposures on how the larger cabin was settled into the brush. Finally, she followed the path further, and when she saw her car parked in the turn around, she realized the path would take her back to the road down by Miss. Eva's place.

Walking down the path she saw the doe again. She was off in the distance grazing on the wet grass in a small clearing near the shoreline of the creek. Nell braced herself against the nearest tree and took several exposures of her as the cautious animal looked across the clearing in Nell's direction. When the doe moved off and was partially hidden by the brush, Nell proceeded slowly down the path towards Eva's cabin and the car.

She knocked on Miss. Eva's door several times before concluding that Eva was not home. She didn't push the key under the door as she had been instructed, but decided to see if the old lady would permit her to use the Coots place a few more days. She waited in the car awhile hoping Eva might show up, before she decided to drive back to thelittle teal blue restaurant for breakfast on her way back to the hotel.

"...Were you there when they crucified my Lord?"

CHAPTER TWELVE

*T*HE NOISE FROM THE the little teal blue restaurant greeted Nell before she even reached the door. Most of the tables near the window were taken. Ruby greeted her as she put another rasher of bacon on the hot griddle. "LD be back by the stage if you be lookin' for him."

"I'll take the special," Nell nodded. She filled a plate with bacon, grits and scrambled eggs from the buffet, before proceeding toward the rear of the restaurant. LD stood up to greet her as she approached. She encouraged him to keep his seat, but he stood long enough to pull out the other chair at the table.

"Good morning." A broad smile creased his face.
"Good morning, LD;" she settled into the seat across from him, "I need to know more about my Uncle Charlie, LD. I only have a few more days left to be here," she said. "And I really want to know about my mom and dad's life down here too." The smile drained from his face as he stared intensely through her.

"Mother never talked about living here, in fact she covered it up...like she was ashamed," she said.
The old man's face darkened as he cleared his throat.

"If Mae didn't tell you, she shore won't like me tellin' you. She must'a just wants to forget it all." He looked through her again.

"I's'wuz just a young'un, only remembers pieces,

but Shugababy, she tell us the story long fore she died. Your Daddy he came here first, more than a few years too. Your Uncle Charlie, he came after they opened the school. At first it wuz good for him, and everybody but later, Mae and Grady, they had to leave. The Klan, they would have killed Grady sure as I'm sittin' here."

"Klan! What? What you mean...the Ku Klux Klan?" Nell put her fork down, leaning forward again.

"It wuz just before he left, when they whupped Charlie too. He wuz just a kid, but they whupped him just like he wuz some kind 'a animal or somethin'." LD bit his lip, and sighing deeply stared across the room out the window.

"They whipped Uncle Charlie? The Klan whipped Charlie?" Shocked she sat back in her seat, her hands in her lap. She sat silently sorting through what she had heard, before following LD's gaze out the window. Finally struggling to control her breathing, she touched his arm.

"Tell me more. What happened?" He looked down collecting his thoughts and feelings. The memory of that day was fresh again in his mind. He pulled his hand back reacting to her touch. She could tell he was still affected by what had happened to Charlie. As he spoke his eyes stared through her.

"Was all about that trashy white woman where Charlie and Grady worked sometime doin' handy work, you know cuttin' grass and such. One night she told her husband, Charlie stole some her jewelry. Came out later... was all a lie, but it wuz too late then. Everybody in Eden, 'cepting her husband knew she wuz sneakin' around with one of them boss men over at the mill. She gave him that jewelry so he could go to Mobile to gamble on them river boats."

LD's voice broke as he cleared his throat nosily and blinked his eyes rapidly to clear them before continuing.

"...It all came out later. While playing poker on them riverboats he lost her ring and a bracelet to one of them boys that lived over on the hill in Eden. He recognized the ring 'cause it had a cross on it made out'a them little diamonds. Shugababy say the man who won it brought it back and give it to her husband a few days later."

"That's crazy! You mean they knew Uncle Charlie didn't steal anything, and they whipped him anyway? Nell looked out the window again in disbelief biting her lower lip. She spoke again, this time with her hands.

"SO? Why did they whip him then? He didn't do anything."

"Neva mind. In them days whuppin' and lynchin' wuz common, child. Crackers did whatever they wanted, specially to the coloreds. Why, right down over yonder," Looking out the window he nodded his head in the direction of the center of the town.

"Right over there in Eden, they used to have signs all over some the streets telling coloreds not to be caught in town after dark." Silence settled between them.

"That was a long time ago," LD, said conscious of the silence, "but they whupped him anyway." Nell felt her stomach tighten, and she resisted the mounting anger she was feeling. LD continued.

"Charlie resisted when the sheriff came to get him. It wuz a natural reaction. He hadn't done nothin' plus he wuz just a kid...maybe twelve, thirteen years old. They knew he hadn't done nothin' but they tied him to the hitching post in the center of the square. All us heard they gave him maybe eight or so lashes of rawhide... made him count out loud after each one. Some them licks cut his back open." Nell grimaced at the words. LD shuffled in his seat.

"Shugababy say most the white people in Eden, even the little kids, they come to the whuppin' lots of laughin' and drinkin' like they wuz at a picnic...a celebration or somethin'. All the coloreds be too scared to go to town that day and for a long time after that."

As LD spoke Nell remembered Dean describing the scars he had seen on Uncle Charlie's back long ago in the basement of the tenement house. The gall started to rise in her cheeks. That discussion with Dean had intrigued her all these years. She had buried it deep, yet still close enough to the surface to be resurrected at a time such as this. Dean had talked about the pained look on her father's face as they helped Charlie with his bath that day. Grady never said a word, but she always suspected he knew what had happened to Uncle Charlie.

"I remember we wuz all scared," LD broke into her thoughts recapturing her attention.

"Was there a trial, she asked weakly."

"No mam...They say when they pull Charlie from the jail he had a wild look in his eyes. Stumbling, and screaming, he resisted all the way. They had to drag him to the hitching post. They lashed him so bad the blood ruined his shirt runnin' down his back."

"But...he was innocent, she protested, "and they whipped him anyway? That's fucking crazy!" LD didn't answer, and let the silence settle between them again. She swallowed hard, looking away, as the realization of what he was saying hit her. She sunk into the back of the chair in pained silence.

"Big Poppa, and your Daddy" he said after a while, "they wuz plowin' the last section of the field out near the pasture when Louise and Shugababy come runnin' to tell them 'bout what the sheriff wuz gettin' ready to do to Charlie. Ole Marse Sangster's brung them on the tractor trailer right to the square. Big Poppa jumped off the back of that tractor fore it even stopped. He snatched the whip from the sheriff's hand and without flinching pushed him backward. The sheriff drew his revolver, but Big Poppa stood up to him throwing the whip to the ground. Big Poppa went straight off at the sheriff protestin' what they wuz doin' to Charlie. He even offered to give up his share of the crop to pay for the jewelry, but the crowd wanted to see blood, and the sheriff knew better than to disappoint them. It wuz like a carnival in the square...filled with a sea of laughing white people and they children. Many of them sat on the shoulders of they fathers' so they could get a better look at the whuppin'." LD shuffled in his seat before continuing.

'What you doin'!'Big Poppa yelled at the sheriff. 'I'll pay for the damn ring'. 'If'n that ain't good e'nuff for you.... you just got to spill blood...then whup me. Charlie ain't done nothing!' Big Poppa had barely finished speaking, when three of the sheriff's deputies overpowered him. Dragging him forward they tied him to the hitching post next to Charlie, and the crowd went wild when they turned the lash on Big Poppa. The sheriff cracked that whip cross Big Poppa's back hard as he could...did it four times one right behind the other...split the skin right open fore he gave the whip to one of his deputies.

"Here Deke..." He said between gulps of air, while stumbling to the side of the hitching post where he tried to catch his breath.

"You hurt this here Nigga real-bad, you hear?" The crowd cheered loudly when the deputy cracked the whip across Big Poppa's back. But before he could level the lash again, Ole Marse Sangster pulled his shotgun of the tractor and fired it into the air. The crowd scattered away from him and he leveled the gun in the direction of the sheriff and them deputies.

'That's enough Deke...you ain't gonna whup Big Poppa no more. He ain't done nothin', and y'all know Charlie ain't stole nothin'. He used the gun like a knife cuttin' hot butter to move through that crowd callin out to your Daddy who wuz also on the tractor. The two of them cut Big Poppa and Charlie down, put them on the bed of the tractor trailer, and drove through the crowd back over those railroad tracks out there, back to the Cove."

LD turned slightly in his chair and looked over his shoulder. The crowd had thinned out in the little restaurant, and he became aware of how his voice now seemed too loud for the place. Lowering his voice, he continued.

"They took Charlie back to the little shack in the Cove so Shugababy could nurse them cuts on his back, but they hid Big Poppa back over there in the swamp for a while 'til they could sneak him out'ta town. Good thing they hid him out too, cause the Klan came to get him two days later sure as we sittin' here.

"Your Daddy and Mr. Sangster...they took turns, and stayed with Big Poppa every night for the eight, nine days. They made a blind of broken branches and leaves in the crook of one of the larger trees, changing his dressin' and watching out for the Klan. That whip cut Big Poppa, and Charlie so deep they bound their wounds using fat back, turpentine and tree moss to draw out the infection and help the wounds to heal faster."

"How did Shugababy deal with everything that was going on?" Nell could only imagine the stress she would have been feeling under those circumstances. LD grunted.

"She be strong as a rock...even though she was big with a comin' child...every day she struggled through the marsh just when the sun was low in the sky, and brought a canteen of fresh water, some corn bread, and a small pail of syrup. Big Poppa didn't want her too, but she ignored his protests. 'Go on back Shuga' you riskin' the baby. Grady or Sangster be comin' soon!' She just ignored his concerns, and would wait with him until she heard the familiar whistle from one of the men. They always arrived just before sunset so she would have enough light to make her way out'ta the marsh before the warm moist blanket of darkness covered the swamp.

"They say every night Marse Sangster went to stay with Big Poppa, while Louise and her hound dog, Cajun stayed at Shugababy's cabin until he comes home the next morning. She always brought her rabbit gun with her vowing to shoot anybody messing with them."

Nell had sat quietly listening to the old man, but her mind was spinning. She alternately stared through him, and at the floor of the restaurant.   Her mind locked on the face of the little girl in the photographs with Uncle Charlie, and the simple words in the letters she had written. They were warm celebrations of a friendship and a life she now knew, she wanted to know more about.

"Though Louise wuz young," LD had started to speak again bringing her suddenly back to the present,"her father...he knew he could count on her and Eva to follow his directions. They had to look out for things and help Shugababy while the men were gone. That little Louise wuz somethin' else too, just like her Mama. She always had a stern determined way about her, even as a child when she said she would do somethin' she really meant it.

"The plan...I wuz told, wuz to get Big Poppa back on his feet, and get him out'ta the Cove before the Klan or the sheriff found him. Everybody knew they would lynch Big Poppa if they found him. They finally did come, three nights later lookin' for him"

LD silently stared into the distance again, remembering what Shugababy told him later about that night the Klan rode into Coons Cove looking for Big Poppa.

IT WAS A CLEAR WARM NIGHT. There was not a cloud in the sky, and a refreshing breeze rustled the pine trees surrounding Swallow's Creek. All the people living on the plantation had been on edge since the Big Poppa stood up to the sheriff, and nobody had been out enjoying the pleasant weather that evening. Seemingly everybody had gone to bed early, closing-up their small cabins. It was past midnight when they came, and a quarter moon was the only light in the area.

Louise, Charlie, and Eva were asleep on the floor of the small cabin. Cajun stretched out next to them while Shugababy slept fitfully on the other pallet. Charlie, and the dog heard the noise first. When Cajun started barking he struggled to sit up on the pallet, trying not to disturb the bandages on his back. He quieted the dog and listened more intently. The sound of horses was coming from the direction of the pasture. Shugababy heard them too; she knew they were comingstraight to the cabin. She bounded from the pallet to awake Louise and Eva, hurrying the children out the cabin. They all ran back toward the lowlands leading to the swamp. While Eva led the way, Shugababy helped Charlie get to the drainage ditch cut at the foot of the swampy area.

"Where's Louise and Cajun," she asked Eva, breathing hard from the exertion.

"She didn't come Mama. I saw her take the dog round to the back of the cabin."

"Oh Jesus...maybe she'll hide in the pine trees down by the field toilet," Shugababy consoled herself. "You' all stay down outa' sight and be quiet," she waved for Charlie and Eva to get down in the drainage ditch, and struggled to lower her self carefully to the damp ground, groaning as the child growing inside her kicked in protest.

Louise had taken her rifle and went around the back of the cabin to the side away from the pale moonlight. She stood waiting and watching in the shadows as four men on horseback approached. Their white robes rustled in the wind and stood out against the dark night. She knew Eva, and the others would be safe in the drainage ditch. They were the same ditches the men on the plantation had dug, and lined with crushed stones so heavy rain during the hurricane season would run off away from the pasture and the area where the cabins were located. Her daddy had always told her when she heard anybody coming at night, and if she was at home alone, she should take her rifle and hide in the brush, or the drainage ditches away from the cabin. When she turned ten, he taught her how to load and fire the gun and had taken her squirrel hunting whenever he found the time. She became an excellent shot and many times was responsible for putting meat on the dinner table.

"I just get so upset thinkin' about it," LD finally said loudly.

"What do you mean?" Nell asked.

"Painful memories...just thinkin about painful memories." He stretched out his hands curling and uncurling the knotted fingers. Arthritis had affected his hands crippling the little finger on both hands.

"It wuz that bastard Clay Cromwell, one of your Mamas... Mae's cousins on the other side. Neither one of them ever owns up to it; but his daddy owned the gin mill. He wuz a mean man, just like his daddy and granddaddy before him. Family's one of the first in Eden long ago, even when Alabama wuz a wilderness. His cracker Grand-daddy, Henry Isaacs Cromwell had one of the largest plantation in Eden, over a hundred slaves. He wuz the first head of the Klan too, hated everything colored 'cepting them black women on his plantation...Clay wuz just lke him, 'cepting they say he wuz only crazy after that pretty black girl working at his house. All the old folk's wuz glad when he disappeared too...gone just like that!" He snapped his fingers loudly.

"Where did he go, and what do you mean Mae's cousin?" Nell leaned forward again. Thoughts of the photographs stored in Mae's closet popped in her head again as she asked the questions. She recalled one portrait of a fair skin man Mae had said was her uncle. It was signed Samuel Cromwell. His features were distinctively different from Mae's. She remembered he had a patrician nose, straight hair and thin lips. Intuitively she knew the answers, and she quietly accepted the image of young black women used by white men at will during slavery. Now she understood Mae's reluctance for her to come to Eden. Her anger flashed in her eyes questioning LD. He ignored her question about Mae's cousin.

"What you think I mean! He's gone, just disappeared sudden like, years ago. His horse showed up without him one night at the gin mill. Sheriff looked for him weeks on end. We all believe a gator got him one night while he was coon hunting."

"I mean tell me about him being Mae's cousin," Nell was dismissive about Clay's disappearance. "You know what I mean!" LD shuffled in his seat again swallowing hard, staring Nell down.

"Happened all the time down here in them days. There wasn't nothin' nobody could do about it either."

"Bullshit! I'd die first!" Her eyes stared through him.

"Like I said" he continued, "...just four of them came lookin' for Big Poppa that night...rode right through the pasture bold as the devil, and set the Sangster barn on fire, 'fore they rode on to Big Poppa's place. They wuz angry with Ole Marse for takin' up for Big Poppa, and I suspect they knew he had hidden Big Poppa out some where out on the plantation. Louise told us later, she could see their white hoods and sheets flowing in the nighttime breeze as they rode their horses at a slow gallop toward the cabin. The sky in the background gave off a red glow, which grew larger and larger in the distance, and she hoped they had not set their cabin on fire. She said, she anxiously watched as Shugababy had to partially drag Charlie to the drainage ditch because of the beating he had received."

Nell conflicted about hearing anymore of the story turned away from LD and moved to stand,but LD reached out his hand restraining her.

"You need to know this girl!" He took her hand pulling her back into her seat. "I know it's ugly...but its part your history too...as much as Charlie's."

"I just didn't know all this happened to Uncle Charlie...and in my own family," she said returning her attention back to LD.

"Like I said, Charlie wouldn't have made it if it wasn't for Shugababy. They had barely made it to the ditch just before the Klan stopped outside Big Poppa's place. Louise stood at the rear of the cabin in the shadows. She said, she leveled her rifle at the throat of the closest horse, cause it wuz the biggest target. The man sitting astride its back would be her second target. The horse pawed the ground and snorted reacting to the growling of Cajun. The dog moved back and forth by Louise's side. The hair on Cajun's neck stood rigid as he strained against the leash she had tied to a young sapling at the side of the cabin. She said she recognized Clay Cromwell's big bay horse when he took his rifle, and pushed open the gate to the yard. He urged his horse into Shugababy's garden just inside the fence line. The rest of them stayed outside the fence

"What did Louise do?" Nell asked.

"She yelled out to them, what you all want Clay. I know it's you and the Reese boys." Clay Cromwell pulled the big horse up at her voice.

"That you Shugababy? We just want to talk to Big

Poppa... Big Poppa, you in there?" LD imitated the white speech patterns of the south.

"Big Poppa ain't here," Louise responded,"but he say you just go on now and there won't be no trouble."

"That ain't Shugababy. Sounds like that little Sangster trash," he said. "Big Poppa what you doing? You hiding behind a little white gal's skirt tail? " They all laughed.

"You come on out'ta there Nigga! You come on out now...or we burn this here shack down, and all them little Nigga coons wit' you. You got trouble boy, big trouble," Clay yelled in the direction of the cabin.

Louise stepped out slightly from behind the cabin. The moonlight reflected off the rifle she had leveled at the chest of the man sitting astride the nervous horse. He saw her movement and turned to face her.

"We don't want no trouble wit you little gal, but we do mean to have that Nigga, Big Poppa. We don't care non-bout that boy Charlie. But he shouldn't ought to have stole that jewelry from the Boricks house."

"You just get out'ta here! Ain't nobody stole no jewelry, Louise said loudly. "You all just get off this property now! My Daddy be coming into town tomorrow, and he'll straighten this whole thing out. G'wan now... Git I say." She held her ground, never lowering the rifle.

"We want Big Poppa you little Nigga lover! You better get on outta the way!" A voice from out near the fence called out. "He's got more than a little ole whuppin' comin' now! He cain't be messin' wit the law like that!"

"Exasperated, Louise fired off a round from the rifle into the air before yelling, "You just git Clay. I ain't kidding.... don't make me shoot you now!"

"Cajun broke the leash and ran barking toward the horse in the yard. It skittered sideways away from the dog's charge, rising on its rear legs. The rider struggling to keep the horse under control spurred it backward away from the growling dog and out the open gate where he paused.

'You fuckin' little bitch…You tell your Daddy to have Big Poppa at the sheriff's office tomorrow, or we be comin' back to take this here place apart. You got fair warning now.'

"The sound of the horses leaving, on the dirt road was a welcome sound to Louise. She felt proud for standing up to them, but she also knew the red glow flickering in the sky came from her Daddy's tool shed and the barn. She hoped the animals had gotten out through the broken door in the rear of the barn. Fears for the future of the sharecroppers flashed through her mind. Her daddy always said they would all be lost without the animals and the tools they had amassed over the years." LD pushed himself back from the small table stretching his legs out in front of him.

"Shit," he said, looking at his watch. "S'cuse my cussin' but I gotta' get goin'. We still be puttin' the walls in down the street today. But," he said, sucking air through his teeth. "This little piece of meat goin'ta annoy me 'til I take these damn teeth out tonight," he digressed momentarily. But Nell was still taken up with the story about Charlie.

"So. What happened with the fire?" she asked as he stood up to leave, still sucking at his teeth.

"Oh, all us on the plantation worked to put out that fire. We worked most the night, but we lost all the tools and things in the sheds and the barn. It wuz bad," he paused jabbing a toothpick into his mouth. "Weren't too long after that most them folks, 'cluding your Mama and Daddy drifted off up north following other family members to work in the car plants. Heard some ended up in the packin' houses too. A few went to the coal mines in West Virgini. Matter a fact that's where Big Poppa ended up. A few stayed, like my parents and Eva; most left though."

"It's a wonder anybody stayed after that...I would have been scared to death. But you stayed! How many others stayed?" Nell asked. LD stroked his chin as he looked around the room.

"Let's see...I stayed cause my Daddy and Mama stayed. My Daddy was a good carpenter and, you know he could get work here and there in town. Louise's Daddy, Marsh, he stayed even after his wife ran off wit one them Karcher boys. Let's see Eva and Shugababy...oh bout ten families stayed, I guess."

He tried the toothpick again, accidentally breaking it. He crumpled it in his fingers before placing it on the table. "I guess I'll just have to wait until tonight to take care of this," he said softly as to himself.

"Sounds like Mr. Sangster was a decent man. What happened to him, did the Klan ever drive him off?" Nell was curious.

"Oh, the Klan had threatened to kill him many times. At least, this was long before Clay disappeared. They never did though, he died about two or three months after the fire, one day in the shallow water up in the Cove in Swallows Creek." He motioned his head in the direction of the swamp.

"In the swamp, what happened?" Nell shuffled in her chair.

"A hungry gator grabbed the milk cow one morning when she wandered down and was drinking from the creek. Usually most of the stock stayed away from the creek and drank from the shallow streams running through the pasture. But it had been real dry that year... most of the streams running through the pasture had dried up. Even the grass in the pasture was all brown and dried up.

"Ole Marse, on his way to the fields heard the cow's

cries and ran with his shotgun to the creek. The gator had the cow by one of her front legs and was struggling to pull her into the water. They say the old shotgun either misfired or he had forgotten to load it.

"Anyway, he went into the water beating at the gator with the gun barrel, and the gator turned on him. That day everybody 'cept Shugababy had gone to work the fields cause she was expectin'.

"She heard his cry for help and got there just in time to shoot that gator with Big Poppa's old colt. Screaming she emptied the gun into the gator's skull, and though she was big as a house and barely able to keep her own balance, she managed to keep Ole Marse from sliding into the creek. But it was too late. He bled to death right there on the creek bank. Shugababy tried, but she had to run too far before she found help. Some of the other men, and me, and yore Uncle Charlie...we wuz choppin' dried cotton stalks not too far from the burned barn. You should talk to Miz. Eva about yore Uncle though before you go. She grew up right there, wit' Charlie. If she will talk about those days, I hear she's not too friendly these days. Sometimes that old lady can be downright mean," he chuckled.

"LD," Nell, holding his hand slowed his departure. "Y'all ever find out why that lady lied on Uncle Charlie?"

"To get even wit' Grady, 'cause he refused her advances. She finally told it," he said. "Just before she died. She wanted him...said he was too good looking to bed down wit a black woman. She was angry cause she said he scorned her...and you know a Nigga couldn't scorn any body white in those days."

"I'll be dammed! You got to be kidding! LD, so she accused Uncle Charlie for something my Daddy wouldn't do! I am surprised she found him attractive. Daddy was as black as I am. We were raised believing black was ugly." LD smiled, "I know! That's what they say alright," he said moving toward the door.

"I need to take some pictures of you later," she called after him. He waved his hand as the door closed behind him.

"Please," she called after him. After he left, thinking about what he had refused to tell her about Mae, and what he told her about Uncle Charlie. Nell now believed she could understand his drinking. It probably went a long way toward erasing some of those painful memories for him. They probably pained him for years, she thought. Remembering his ashes in the car, he really belongs here, she said under her breath, trying to settle her mind.

NELL REMAINED IN THE LITTLE RESTAURANT awhile thinking about Mae and Uncle Charlie. Could his drinking be a result of these experiences? The alcohol probably went a long way toward erasing some of those painful memories. They probably pained him for years she thought, remembering his ashes in the car. Does he really belongs here, she wondered to herself. Then she thought of Louise's letter. There must have been some good times too, she thought. Her thoughts about Mae's history were sympathetic. She knew her mother had this violent disain for fair skin blacks, always saying they were 'uppity'. All these years, Nell had concluded Mae rejected that part of her family because of her dark skin. She pushed the thoughts from her mind, ordering two bar-b-que dinners to go and drove slowly back to the turn-around leaving the car in front of Eva's yard.
When she knocked on the door, Eva opened it slowly, suspiciously.

"Thought you'd gone back north," she said coldly. She was dressed in a bright yellow print dress, and held a orange yellow hat in her hand. She eyed Nell cautiously.

"You didn't leave Coot's key like I told you. Did you," she asked.

"I left it at the cabin," Nell lied. An awkward silence grew up between them.

"Thats a pretty dress," Nell said as the old lady pinned the hat in place. She warmed breaking the awkwardness.

"Goin' to the revival tonight." Nell's heart dropped with dissappointment; Miss Eva was going to church tonight. LD had only peaked Nell's curiosity about Uncle Charlie's life in the Cove. She hoped the old lady would be able to tell her more, and now with her going to church tonight she would have to wait a bit longer.

"I brought you some dinner," Nell said brightly trying to ease the tension between them. A hesitant smile crossed the old woman's face as she accepted the outstretched food.

"Why, how nice ...thank you daughter!" Nell could feel the mood changing, as she continued, "...and I want to thank you for letting me use the Coot's place. I hope I can stay a few more days, if it's all right." Mr. Fred approached Nell from the rear of the cabin. The cat purred solicitously. "You're welcome to stay as long as you like daughter. The old place just be sittin' up there anyway. Somebody might as well make use of it. This Ruby's bar-b-que be the best around. I'll eat it tomorrow. They gonna' have food at the church." Miss Eva resisted Nell's offer to drive her to the church.

"I walk to church all the time," she said closing the door. They parted ways after she closed the gate, and Nell reluctantly made her way back up to the Coot's place wondering why Eva had said she did not remember Uncle Charlie, as her cell phone rang. It was Hill.

"Hey sugar." He was in a happy mood. "I got your stuff. It all looks great. I'm sending the package to the Times this afternoon, but I wanted to make sure you had a signed release for all the photo's."

"Come on Hill you know I got a release. It's a hard copy. I'm sorry I didn't include them. I can fax you copies if you like."

"OK, just needed to check, send them on when you get a chance, just in case the Times want them. Where are you anyway? You know you're off the clock." He said it with a chuckle, but she knew he was serious.

"Hey, I know I'm off the clock. I'm in Alabama... In a place called Eden. You know like the Garden of Eden...It's almost garden-like too, but like I have always said there is usually a dark side to beautiful things," she smiled into the phone. "I think there might be a story here Hill. I'm going to be sending you some images and a query on another story soon...just as soon as I get a better feel for the life of the place."

"OK that's fine. I hope you approach it from a light perspective for a change. Send it along. We'll look at it. Hey as soon as we get a sign-off from the Times, I will send your contract to accounting." After Hill hung up Nell immediately called Dean, and spent the next hour bringing him up to date on her conversation with Hill, LD, and what she had found out about Uncle Charlie. Afterwards she called Mae, and found her surprisingly pleasant, even after she told her about her discussion with LD, Mae could feel the excitement in Nell's voice. It reminded her of the excitement children display when they are surprised with a new toy.

BUT MAE'S MIND didn't stay in a happy place after she hung up; rather it drifted to one of those times when she and Charlie sat behind the heater in the old tenement house. It was the day before he was to report to

Fort Wayne for induction into the service. All that day Charlie had been in an anxious mood. He even ignored the pestering of Nell, and left the house early rather than play with her. He returned only after she had gone to her room to do homework and the house was relatively quiet.

Grady was still at work, and dinner was cooking on the stove in the kitchen. And Mae, as had been her custom when he was anxious, took his hand and encouraged him to talk about what was on his mind. When he finally opened-up, she became so immersed in the conversation, the water in the pinto beans almost dried out. It was that day when he told her about his feelings for Louise.

His feelings for her had haunted, and frightened him from the very beginning of their friendship; and Shugababy had constantly cautioned him about playing alone with Louise. She always made sure Eva played, and went to the small school with them. He accepted they were attracted to each other. It was in the quiet look of her eyes when they played together, or those times when he helped her and Eva pick blackberries in the Preserve. He never told anyone about those feelings until he anxiously told Mae that day at the tenement house.

As she had sat in the rocker listening to Nell describing the Cove, her mind recreated the scene in the Cove as Charlie had described it to her that night long ago. It was as if he was in the room with her again, sitting on the floor next to the old rocker. The fear in his voice was what held her attention at first.

"I know we shouldn't have done it," he said, "but it was like I wasn't in control of myself. I shook, couldn't stop the shaking Mae. Scared! Have you ever been scared, of something you wanted, Mae?" His eyes stared deep into hers. He needed to know if she really understood what he was feeling, and had gone through at the time. It was the first time he had used Mae's name in a long time. She simply looked at him relishing the sound of her name.

"I had to leave her when she really needed me Mae," he continued. "We were both so young and didn't know no difference...but she was so nice. We used to meet after sunset, sometimes after supper out in the pasture. All the mules, horses, and the cows would be in the barn, except for the old bull. He always slept down by the fence along the trail, and if we were quiet and stayed upwind we could have the place to ourselves. Sometimes we would sneak into the old schoolhouse."

"I only meant to kiss her at first...but we didn't stop there." He looked away, and took a deep breath before continuing. "We went further...but I don't even think I got it in her. I'd never done it before...neither one of us had. She wanted to do it as much as I did." Silence filled the room. Mae reached over and stroked his hair to let him know she understood.

"It was the first time we had ever gone that far." He sat back looking across the room. "That was one of the nights we went to the old schoolhouse. It was safer, we thought, cause' we could come and leave separately. She usually left first. But... That night I left before she did. That's when that Cracker Cromwell caught her crossing the pasture on her way back home."

"Did he see you boy?" The concern showed in Mae's voice, "Is that why you didn't go down there no more?" She leaned forward, looking Charlie defiantly in the eyes. He sensed her concern, and mistakenly mistook it for disappointment in him.

"Yeah...that's why. But don't tell nobody, not even Grady about what happened, please! I guess I'm just scared now...maybe cause I'm goin' to war, and may never see her again. I need God's forgiveness.They both sat quiet in the glow of the heater. Each preoccupied

ness. Finally, he went to the front door of the tenement
house. He stood there silently for a moment looking out
at the dirty snow on the front stoop, before opening the
door. Silently he walkedoff toward the river road. She
watched him leave, before going to tend the beans on the
stove and to mix the cornbread. Grady would be coming
home soon. She wondered briefly if she should tell Grady
about Charlie.

And, that day, as she listened quietly to Nell speak of
the Cove, the old rocker creaked on the hard wood floor,
as it had long ago. She already knew about Louise and
Charlie, and that Clay Cromwell had mysteriously disappeared. LD had written her about it just before Charlie
moved north to live with them in the tenement house.

CHAPTER THIRTEEN

*T*HE SPORADIC IMAGES of the three days Nell
had spent in the nasty throat of New Orleans
floated in her memory after she hung up the
phone. She continued up the path to the Coot's place. In
her mind she reviewed the photographs she had taken
of her subjects, like Sybil the young prostitute holding
her stomach on Ramparts street, when she complained
about withdrawal. Some of her images at Taft's place-
showed various stages of addiction and were ugly; but
she had wanted to show the rawness of a life controlled
by drugs. She welcomed the images in her head as she

216

sat on the front porch of the cabin watching the light filter through the pine trees. She simply needed to be away from the story LD had told her about Uncle Charlie if only for a little while. She sighed deeply. She knew it would be back. It was too consuming.

Uncle Charlie's ashes lay in the freezer bag on the table in the center of the room. She had put them there that first night and they had lain there undisturbed ever since. Moving to the table, she opened the bar-b-que dinner, and sat staring alternately at the ashes, and around the small room while she slowly finished the dinner. I'll know what to do with them when the right time comes she thought.

After dinner, she moved back to the front porch and looked down at the small cabin where Miss Eva lived. She had told Dean, that of all the different places she had been, the Cove was the most special and relaxing place she had been. She wanted to stay longer, but knew she needed to get back home; all the while she needed to know why Miss Eva had said she could not remember Uncle Charlie. Then I can go home, she determined.

That night she slept poorly. Images of the sheriff whipping Uncle Charlie crossed back and forth across her mind. Looking to settle her mind she imagined him, as he looked the day he came back home from the war. His uniform was clean and neatly pressed. All the color-ful ribbons were on his chest, but suddenly in her mind, someone, a white hand ripped off his hat and thrown it to the ground. When he turned around his uniform was torn across the back from the lash. She could hear the lash crack in her ears and she screamed with each blow, but Charlie smiled at the sheriff refusing to react to the sting of the whip. It was as if he didn't feel the rawhide cutting his skin.

Nell tossed and turned on the old bed throughout the night, and the morning light found her exhausted. She spent the day trying to start a first draft of a query on a story about life in the Cove. Her thoughts were not easy and, after going down to the restaurant for breakfast, and a carryout she spent the day sitting on the floor of the cabin's front porch. Her back braced against the wall, she spent most of the day enjoying the sights and the sounds of the swamp around her. Alternately she dozed in the warm humid weather.

Sometime before nightfall, an unfamiliar sound awakened her. Frightened she scrambled to her feet, peering anxiously into the creeping darkness. Probably the deer, she thought stepping over the laptop and entering the cabin. She sat on the old bed yawning. The laptop still lay open on the floor of the porch in front of her; its LCD had turned itself off, and its darkened empty page stared into the cabin. It was the last image Nell noted before falling backward, sprawling across the old bed. Soon she was deep in sleep.

TWO DAYS LATER, following her routine to get food, the quiet mysticism of the Cove still held her prisoner, while she managed to complete a draft query on Coon's Cove. She E-mailed it to Hill. Writing it had been difficult because she had the recurring thoughts of Uncle Charlie being whipped strapped to a hitching rail. Only this time she could visualize the faces in the crowd cheering with each flick of the lash. When she needed to remove these images from her mind she would walk to the front door of the cabin and become consumed with the subtle beauty of the Cove.

She had told Dean she would leave two days ago, yet she was still there feasting on the sweet air, and raw beauty of the place. Occasionally she also found herself thinking about what the Cove would have been like when Uncle Charlie lived there.

She would look at the landscape imagining it changed

to a rich field where the smiling children from the old photographs probably played and sang songs in the evening. As she sat on the screened porch looking out over the swamp, she could visualize those same children among the high stalks of cotton plants as they swayed in the breeze. At other times, she imagined groups of families, both black and white, working the fields, moving in rhythm through the rows singing work songs and sweating in the heat of the sun.

Finally, the following morning, Nell accepted she was addicted to the place, when she took a towel from the cabin, and scrambled down the exposed roots of one of the old oak trees to bathe in the clear water spring that bubbled up from the earth on a small rocky bluff slightly below, and about fifty feet from the cabin. The spring fed down an incline eventually splashing over the edge into Swallows Creek. The tree's deep roots partially exposed, hung down to the small bluff that slightly projected out over the dirty green waters of the creek. Leaving her clothes on the rocks, Nell took a quick and stimulating bath in the warm spring, before sitting on one of the large rocks to enjoy the sun on her body. From where she sat she could see where the creek ended and drifted off into a series of small streams finally losing themselves into the marsh in the distance. Further on, the creek continued as a larger stream meandering through the undergrowth. If she looked to the east, she could see the overgrown rolling field of the old Sangster's pasture.

Swallows Creek was a large body of water at the beginning of the swamp, seemingly enclosed on three sides by tall pine, and sporadic magnolia trees.

The swamp was bordered by an elevated dirt road that led to the beginning of the Alabama national Preserve. Beyond the road, the pasture stretched over a rise into the distance, disappearing into the horizon. Occasional Live Oak trees sprinkled with Spanish moss stood large like guardians of the area.

The place had captured the artist in Nell. It was the colors, she thought. It was always, even in the evening --filled with hazy colors caused by the vapors of humidity being sucked up by a seemingly constant blazing blue sky dominating the daytime weather. But in her heart, she knew it was more than the colors. It was also the sounds of the marsh. It was a place where cranes, raccoons, snapping turtles, bullfrogs, crickets, and red-necked black buzzards were daily companions. Their sounds always filled the air. The nest of an osprey could be seen at the top of one of the pine trees near the cabin, and a pair of peregrine falcons would sit daily on one of the dead trees searching for game.

As she ordered her carryout dinners from the small teal blue restaurant each day, the locals in the small area cautioned her about the predators that might be around the cabin. They told her about the alligators and the snakes in the swamp, and that black bear from the forest sometimes came down to the Creek for fresh water when the streams turned into dry beds during the dry season. Nobody mentioned the swamp deer, but Nell had already seen them on her first morning.

It was a place where she was told, the loud sounds of mating alligators filled the late spring nights. Every evening just before the light settled in the western sky, she would sit on the front porch and watch the egrets nestle in for the night across the creek. They settled into the same dead tree. From a distance, they looked like a large bouquet of white gardenias. And every morning when the darkness gave way to a muted sunrise, she enjoyed standing on the front porch again to watch for the occasional doe and fawn walk toward the creek. With their ears constantly flickering at the various sounds of the swamp, they carefully ate the young shoots of grass turning green in the pasture. Later she placed salt in a plate closer to the front porch hoping she would get a chance to see them up closer.

LATER THAT NIGHT, the beauty of the Cove was disturbed when a strange noise suddenly awakened Nell. At first it sounded like it came from the direction of the creek. Frightened she sat up in bed, but found it difficult getting her bearings, and knowing where she was. It was the same feeling she had experienced when, as a photojournalist she traveled to a lot of cities in a short time frame. It was common for her to awaken sometimes in different cities, and different hotel rooms in a matter of days. Even at home, if she was startled awake at night from a deep sleep, it could be a struggle to remember where she was and why. It was one of the reasons she finally started free-ancing, and quit taking so many assignments from The Courier Magazine.

When she finally realized where she was, she checked her watch against the slit of moonlight crossing the room through a small crack in the window shade. It was just after 1:00 AM in the morning. At first the noise sounded like a wounded animal. However, when she heard it again she became certain it was a woman's voice screaming squalls of angry words.

The sound continued sporadically, lifting over the quiet night, like a persistent intruder into the small cabin. Nell sleepily struggled from the bed and moved to the door so she could hear the sounds better. When she opened the door, the sound was clearer. Frightened, she peered into the darkness. It was hard to determine the direction of the sound, but she could make out the words, "stop...please stop, help me...Daddy! Daddy! Oh God, somebody please! Help me please!"

The words were distinctive, intrusive, and the voice was pleading. Nell's first thoughts went to Miss Prad, but she was sure it was not the melodic voice of the old woman. Rather the hardness of the sound reminded her of the whiskey-laced voices she had heard recently in the bars in New Orleans.

The voice called four or five times into the darkness before ending with a scream of rage. It seemed to move through the marsh and the woods in waves before silence finally settled in again. Nell stood frozen at the door. Minutes later she jumped at the sound of gunfire, twice in rapid succession. Nell quickly ducked to the floor expecting a shell to crash into the cabin somewhere.

"A shotgun?" Nell's heart pounded in her chest as she questioned herself. An eerie silence followed the gunshots. It closed over her, and she stayed on the floor still peering out the front door of the cabin until her heart slowed again. A ripple of sporadic laughter and crying continued intermittently as Nell struggled to her feet. Standing behind the partially closed door she finally exhaled loudly. The sounds in the distance continued as a low sobbing moan, but got softer and softer and seemed to be receding away from the Preserve.

Once Nell realized the sounds were not coming from the trail she accepted she was in no immediate danger, and she tried to get a better fix on the direction of the sounds. It seemed they came from the other side of the creek away from Miss Eva's place. The sobbing continued. Finally, she managed enough nerve to move to the front porch of the cabin to see if she could see anything.

Off in the distance down near the Barne's place she could vaguely make out a moving figure dressed in what looked to be a white shirt, or short gown. It was evident from the size it was either a small woman or a young girl. The moonlight reflected off her short pale legs and her hair. She was thrashing about as if she was struggling with an unknown force.

Nell heard her utter the words, "Stop, No! No," as she fell to the ground. She struggled up, running and screaming again as if away from some unseen apparition. She finally fell to the ground again settling into the thick ground cover. She lay there emotionally spent, while her pale legs, the only part of her now visible, rolled from side to side in an undying rhythm. Eventually they too dropped from sight, and everything became mysteriously quiet. Nell sat on the floor of the porch.

"Shit! What the fuck was that. Am I dreaming?" She mouthed the word silently, pinching herself. She was frightened by what she had seen, but at the same time she was intrigued. She kept staring in the direction, searching for the spot where she saw the figure fall into the brush wondering if it would get back up.

"What the fuck was that?" She said aloud shaking her head. She still stared at the spot where the figure had sunk into the ground cover. However, she never saw it again. Finally, she closed the cabin door and checked her watch. Although it seemed like the activity in the field had lasted a long time, it was only 1:14 AM. She sat on the side of the bed staring into the darkness for a long time before drifting off to sleep, only to wake up again expecting to hear another scream fill the air. She would alternately sit on the bed, and then on the floor while staring out the cabin's window into the darkness. It was just before sunrise when she found deep sleep, and the cabin began to lighten with the sounds of sunrise. It was mid-morning when she finally crawled out of the bed. The most pressing thing on her mind was to get Miss Eva to talk about Uncle Charlie. Nevertheless, it was difficult to push the vision of the figure from her mind, and wondered if Miss Eva had heard the noise.

"...Were you there when they pierced him in his side?"

CHAPTER FOURTEEN

*I*T WAS LATE THE NEXT MORNING when Nell finally met Louise. She was sitting on the steps to Eva's back porch smoking, when Nell knocked on the front door. Nell was frustrated, because for the last few days Miss Eva had been spending all of her time at the church's revival. When she returned to her small place it was late at night. Nell had respectfully kept her distance, but she still anxiously hoped for an appropriate moment when she would be able to spend more time with the old lady. Unsuccessful to this point, and shaken by the events of the night before, she was feeling uncertain about how long she could stay in the Cove. She still needed to find an appropriate place for Charlie's ashes, and there were many unanswered questions about Mae, LD had raised for her.

Resolved she knocked at the door again, louder this time, feeling tired from last night's frightening experience. When no one answered, Nell knocked again, finally accepting the old lady was not at home again. At a minimum, she should do something to express her thanks to Miss Eva for allowing her the use of the Coot's place. All these thoughts were bouncing around inside her head as she turned at the sound of the voice.

"Who the hell's knocking so damn early in the morning?" The drawl, accompanied by a smoker's cough, had an unmistakable hard edge to it. A woman muttered to herself as she walked from the back yard around the side of the cabin. She coughed spasmodically as she approached Nell, who was immediately attracted to the deep blueness of her eyes. Although they also had red veins standing out in them, they were the most striking feature of her face. They were big, widely set, tired and happy at the same time, and rimmed with long curly lashes. The rest of her weathered and bloated face was almost nondescript. The nose was straight with small nostrils. It capped a small underdeveloped and extremely thin set of lips that broke her full cheeks into dimples when she smiled.

Nell quickly concluded from her freckles, the woman had spent years in the sun. The wrinkles around her eyes were deep set, and her teeth when she smiled showed signs of excessive tobacco use over the years. Her age was apparent, but it was obvious to Nell, at one time in her life; she had been an attractive woman. An occasional reddish strand stood out, bedded inside of the short grayish blond hair cupping her face. She had a small frame and was dressed in a dirty pair of blue slacks. A print shirt, opened at the neck hung outside the slacks. She was barefoot, had a hammer in one hand and several long nails in the other. She appraised Nell intently stopping just short of the front yard.

"You Nell?" She was direct.

"Yes, I'm Nell." Nell responded surprised.

"Got to be Nell, I ain't never seen you before round here. Eva said you might be comin' around. I'm Louise, Eva's friend. Come on out back," she said leading Nell around to the back of the small place. As Nell followed the small woman, she wondered if the shock showed on her face. Her mind started to whirl through all the images of Louise she had entertained and discarded. The woman appeared to be all those things and more, except she was shorter and thinner than Nell had imagined. Her movement and stature made Nell think of the figure she had observed in the pasture last night. Nell entertained the thought guardedly, as the woman stopped at the steps to Eva's back porch, turning to face Nell.

"Good morning," Nell said, "I was just looking for Miss Eva." Louise extended a small hand after wiping it on her baggy pants. The smell of alcohol and cigarette smoke surrounded her like a cloak. Her hand felt cool, as Nell shook it gently. Louise turned looking at the back porch again.

"Eva ain't here right now. She went to collect the eggs lay'd by the hens this morning. S'cuse the way I look," she said brushing at her hair with both hands.

"I was just nailin' back one of them steps on the porch that come loose," she said walking toward the back. Nell followed her. At that moment, Mr. Fred purred at Nell's shoes. She had not noticed him until he started rubbing his head back and forth on her shoes and her legs. He followed Nell purring loudly as she walked forward to examine the porch, where Louise crouched down to finish pounding the nails into the loose step.

"That might hold it for awhile," she said stepping on it gingerly, testing the step before moving to the porch. She opened the screen door beckoning for Nell to follow her. Nell hesitated, remembering Eva's warning about the safety of the porch. She looked again carefully at the slanting back porch. Louise opened the door even wider.

"Come on. It won't fall. Come on in." The hardness in her drawl had disappeared.

"Evie told me you might be comin' sooner or later, and if you wanted…I should let you in. I be goin' just as soon as I nail that old shutter back in place for her. Hurricane season you know. Can't never tell when one will blow this far inland I just live right down the road; just make yourself at home. Evie should be comin' along any minute now. Course she don't walk as fast as she used to," she laughed stepping back on the porch.

"One day soon I got to fix them pilasters under these floorboards. They rotted clean through." She stomped carefully on the floor of the porch. The four by four pilasters supporting the floorboards of the porch had rotted through. They were now simply rotted old stubs partially sticking out of the ground. The lack of support for the floorboards had caused the porch to sag pulling its roofline away from the rear of the house.

"Fuckin' firetrap. Don't know why she insists on stayin' here," Louise muttered as to herself. She nailed several scrap pieces of lumber into the old rotted pilasters. Nell watched silently from the small kitchen area of the cabin. Her mind told her, *this is Uncle Charlie's Louise'*, and that she should talk to her. Conflicted, she looked down at the floor wondering if he should try to open a conversation about Uncle Charlie, but what if she treats me like Miss Eva did when I asked her about Uncle Charlie? Hesitation froze her thoughts.

"Shit...this ain't gonna work too good." Exasperated, Louise laughed standing up briefly looking at Nell. She realized the sag in the porch was too far-gone for the patch job to be effective. "Will have to do though 'til I get to town." Louise continued muttering to herself as she toiled over the pilasters.

Perhaps I should offer to help her with the repairs Nell thought, but held back, unsure what Louise would think about her intruding. She bit her lip as she watched. Finally, Nell walked to the edge of the porch, and blurted out.

"You know...I can help you if you tell me what to do. I think you might know my Uncle Charlie!" Louise finished putting the last nail into the board and moved to the side of the house picking up an old shutter from the ground.

"Come hold this," she said looking at Nell with cold eyes. "Who's your Uncle again now?"

"Uncle Charlie...his name was Charlie Campbell."

"Sorry, don't know a Charlie Campbell. Does he live in Eden? Nobody by that name live over here in the Cove" Nell tried not to show her frustration with the response. Doubts flashed across her mind. Maybe she's not the Louise in the pictures with Uncle Charlie. Nell stared at women intensely as she nailed the shutter back in place. She could be the same woman. There was a faint resemblance to the young girl in the photograph.

"You Louise Sangster, ain't you?" Nell confronted her more directly, startling the woman. Her eyes flashed angrily when she answered.

"Yeah, I be Louise Sangster. But I still don't know no damn Charlie Campbell, Maybe, he's one of the new folks over in Eden," she said tugging at the shutter testing its resistance. Satisfied she turned to face Nell hanging the hammer on her belt.

"Wait a minute," Nell said walking quickly back to the car. She remembered the envelope containing the letter and the old photograph of Louise with the small child. When she returned, Louise was sitting on the back steps smoking a cigarette. Nell handed her the picture first without the letter, and sat down next to her. Louise stared silently at the photograph, her hand shaking slightly as if the picture was too heavy for her to hold up. She visibly swallowed hard.

"Nappy!" It was a quiet utterance. Unbelievable, she thought. Her eyes blinked rapidly focusing on the small photograph. She was visibly shaken, and sat frozen in place. Only her chest moved rapidly up and down.

"Nappy?" This time she stumbled over the name, her breath catching in her lungs. The ash from her cigarette inched closer to her fingers and the heat forced her to finally drop it to the ground. Nell was conscious of the reaction, but focused primarily on her eyes as they now stared blatantly ahead into her memories Louise struggled to control her heartbeat.

"Where did you get this picture?" She looked tentatively at Nell suspiciously through wide eyes. "Who are you?" The question attacked Nell, and her first thought was to be defensive. But she only reached over silently and took the photograph from Louise's limp hand, before offering her the letter. Louise took it but sat there with it unopened in both hands. Nell was uneasy with the silence. It was like a cloak wrapped around them, closing them in on each other. When she dared to look at Louise again she had closed her eyes and silent tears inched slowly down her cheeks. Instinctively Nell touched her knee.

"Uncle Charlie is dead Louise."

Louise struggled awkwardly away from her touch, walking away deeper into the backyard. She placed her face in her hands, and sobbed quietly. Her back faced Nell, who watched her shoulders shake with grief. Nell sat there quietly watching her pace around in the back yard, the letter still clutched tightly in her hand. Reluctantly she went to Louise and embraced her, not knowing what else to do.

"I'm sorry," she said. Louise clung to her, and Nell could feel her spastic breathing against her chest. Louise pulled away. In better control of herself she sat on the steps of the porch staring absently at the ground. The letter dropped to the steps beside her.

"Did he die in the war?" She asked Nell leaning over to brace her head in her hands against her knees. She fished in her pocket for a tissue to dab at her tears.

"He did, he died in the war." Nell lied remembering the condition of Charlie when he came home from service. Her simple lie seemed to sum up the promise of his life after the war. It was the war that killed him, she concluded momentarily thinking of the death of the butterflies she, and Jacob caught as children. They lived for a while in the old Mason jars, she acknowledged, but they really died the moment they were touched and controlled. The same was true for Uncle Charlie. There were earlier times when he stayed by himself, and she could remember seeing him brood a lot when he was younger, but it was as if his spark for life died within him when he came back home from the war.

"He wuz my love. He and Evie wuz the best friends I had...ever!" Louise sobbed while wringing her hands, struggling with her emotions. Still breathing heavy she dried her eyes with the crumpled tissue before blowing her nose. She stood facing Nell for a moment. It seemed she wanted to speak, but no words came forth. Dropping her head, she turned and started walking down the side of the house toward the front yard. Nell followed her. She is Uncle Charlie's Louise! I can't let her leave now, Nell panicked.

"Don't go," she called after Louise, following behind her. "I want to talk to you; I need to talk to you about Uncle Charlie...please!" Louise stopped, and turned abruptly.

"What for? He's dead now. It won't bring him back." She was more composed. Nell noted her words now had a hard edge to them. The tissue had fallen apart, but she blew her nose into it again looking at the disarray of Eva's back porch.

"I just need to know things," Nell said. "He wanted me to come here with his ashes, and I have to finish this journey for him. You can help me. Please?" Louise walked past her, back toward the porch taking the hammer from her belt again.

"Can you help me get this here porch back up for Evie? You said you would." It was as if she suddenly remembered what she had been doing before the conversation about Charlie. Nell knew from her own experience with death, she had simply put the issue away for more personal grieving in a private way later while alone.

"She can't even use this porch safe-like no more!" Louise continued. "I could really use another set of hands with this here porch right now, and be finished with it for good. Always' patchin' and patchin', tired of all the damn patchin'." She sounded exasperated. She was through with talking about Uncle Charlie, but Nell could tell from the look on her face, there would be more discussion about Uncle Charlie if Nell stayed to help with the porch. She admitted her skills were limited, but Louise seemed sure, they would be able to repair the porch. She nodded her head in agreement, when Louise walked back past her toward the porch again, but Louise didn't notice.

"Hell! I cain't do this all by myself." She looked at the porch defiantly crossing her arms in front of her. "Evie's rheumatism too bad to help out any more. She looked at Nell. I'll bet we...you and me together, we could get this back up in no time if you help me." She leaned over and started pulling at the porch's pilaster closest to her. It didn't budge.

"These damn things are just too heavy for me." She grunted looking at Nell. Her blue eyes were piercing.

"I said I'll help you," Nell picked up the hammer lying on the ground at her feet. "We need a crowbar to get that piece out. You got any other tools?"

"Evie got Lovie's old tool box in the house some-where." The blue eyes softened as she took the hammer from Nell hooking it back on her belt. A flush came over Nell. She now knew she had committed to help Louise with the porch. Can't be that hard if I can find the stam-ina? The thought briefly nagged at her. She felt physic-ally tired from the lack of sleep the night before, but she was excited about the opportunity to spend some more time with Louise and Miss Eva. She estimated they could finish the porch, perhaps over the next day or two. She made a mental note to call Dean and Mae later to bring them up to date, while looking again at Louise. The small woman lost in her baggy pants looked too fragile to do heavy work, but Nell suspected Louise was as hard as nails. Even so, she can't do this work all by herself, Nell concluded.

"OK," Nell said. We'll have to get those side boards straight and reattached to the back of the house. Maybe we can talk about Uncle Charlie, I mean Nappy while we work." She glanced at Louise. A small smile partially crept across Louise' face, but was quickly replaced with a sense of sorrow again.

"Nappy's dead," she said, dropping her cigarette, and turning away breathing deeply.

"Well, let's get started," Nell finally said.

They looked over the slanting disrepair of the porch evaluating the amount of work it would require. It was a small porch, no more than eight feet long and running the width of the small house. Nell quickly calculated the supplies they would need to do a good repair job as they planned, and the two women quietly discussed the cost.

"We cain't afford that!" Louise said loudly to herself. A frown creased her brow.

"It'll be OK. I'll take care of it. It's the least I can do," Nell said.

The frown slowly slipped from Louise's face. She quickly broke into a happy laugh while dancing her way to the steps of the porch. Reaching under the bottom step of the porch she pulled out a bottle of clear liquid.

"Better than vodka," she said opening the bottle. "To Nappy, May the wind always be at your back!" She said solemnly, taking a short swig from the bottle. Handing it to Nell, encouraging her to drink. Nell grudgingly took the bottle swishing the contents around inside. The aroma of distilled corn floated up from the open bottle.

"Too soon in the day", she said turning away from the strong odor, as she handed the bottle back to Louise. After sipping bravely from the contents, Louise placed the bottle hastily back under the porch when they heard Eva approaching from the side of the house. She was singing softly and alternately talking aloud as to herself. Louise cautioned Nell about the alcohol, placing her small finger to her pursed lips; she shook her head not to mention it. They watched Eva as she walked with short deliberate steps, proud of the fact that --for her age she didn't use a cane for support. "A stick", she called it. She had walked back from the small hen house in Louise's backyard, and she carefully carried the eggs she had collected at the hen house wrapped carefully inside a clean white napkin. It was folded so the eggs inside would not move as she walked.

"Mornin' Nell...see you two met already," she chuckled at Louise. She paused alongside Nell, adjusting the napkin with her free hand.

"Sure hope everything been all right up at the Coot's place for you. What with the revival goin' on at the church, I plum nearly forgot all about you." She laughed briefly.

"Evie, she's gonna' help me fix the porch," Louise said loudly. It sounded like she was shouting. The old lady walked past them before stopping again at the back- porch steps.

"That's good. Been mighty humid these past few days. Be good to sit out in the evening breezes again. She was breathing heavy.

"Hope you all can stand some leftover biscuits, scrambled eggs wit' some peach preserves for breakfast...don't have no more bacon." She frowned at Louise, as she continued speaking.

"But …I think you probably need a strong cup of hot water wit' some lemon, or a big cup of black coffee 'fore you do anything else…one or the other!" She said, carefully mounting the steps heading toward the back door to the kitchen.

After breakfast, while Eva washed the dishes, Louise and Nell discussed their approach to repairing the old porch. Later she quietly listened to them measuring and talking, as she pulled weeds from her small garden at the rear of the yard. They planned to save as much of the old porch as possible. But agreed they would need a few things, such as ready-mix concrete and several two by fours.

"Is there a lumber yard nearby?" Nell started around the side of the house toward the car. Louise followed her.

"You cain't get that concrete mix by yourself, be too heavy. I better go along with you…so you won't get lost." Nell followed her directions, heading the car out the yard into the rutted road back toward the little teal blue restaurant. Louise guided her back across the railroad tracks, past the small colored section, and on into the business section of Eden. Just before they reached the railroad tracks Louise pointed out places to Nell important in her childhood.

"The remains of the old barn where Mama and Miz Pete started the first school for the coloreds in the Cove stands just over there." She pointed at a burned and decaying block structure looking like what had once been a large barn. Although now abandoned, it had originally been a tool shed, and had been enlarged over the years as most of the original building had been changed. Pieces of the sign 'Sangster's School House' still showed through on the smoke-stained structure. It stood out above the side door to the building. Two small homemade stained glass windows were on each side of the door. Immediately to the side of the structure was a small cemetery. It was a place filled with tall oak trees growing in what looked like a planned pattern across the space. There was no fence, and many of the old head-stones lay crooked and uneven in the soft ground. An occasional sprig of plastic flowers around some of the headstones brought the only bright colors to the area. Further down the road she asked Nell to stop the car, where she got out, encouraging Nell to join her. They stood close to the drainage ditch running along the road.

"My Daddy's family used to own all this land." Louise swung her outstretched arm out, sweeping the pasture in front of them. She turned as she spoke indicating, all the land they could see, at one time had been owned by a long line of Sangster's and Cromwell's. As Nell followed her sweeping arm, her eyes settled briefly on the pine trees in the distance surrounding the Coot's place. Pieces of the cabin's front porch, and chimney peeked through the surrounding brush in the distance. The chimney sat serenely silhouetted against the pines, and Nell's mind instinctively flashed on the noises and the images she had experienced the night before. The imagery flooded her mind, momentarily blocking out everything else. Louise walked away from her along the drainage ditch, continuing to speak about the area. Not listening anymore Nell concluded what she had experienced last night was not a dream. Her mind mulled over the idea until Louise broke her thoughts when she returned touching her arm.

"Did you hear what I said?" She looked at Nell questioningly.

"Yes. Yes, I heard," Nell lied. Looking out across the pasture back toward the Coot's place, her mind struggled to return to the attention of Louise. She went on pointing out the few remaining remnants of the old plantation, the remains of a partially decaying fieldstone fence, the remnants of the barn and school, and the burned-out skeleton of what had been the big house. The chimney from the old fireplace still stood like a blackened witness to the ravages of time and decay that had grown up around the old place. There were the remains of a large burned porch with what looked like four large charred columns, collapsing onto the overgrown underbrush.

"Is that the old Sangster big house?"

"Shore is...My Great, Great Grandpa left it just where it stands today. The Yankees burned it after the war." Louise brushed her hair from her face. "They said he couldn't afford to rebuild the place. The war hurt everybody; good white people too...just like some the coloreds.

"Sounds like he was a real strong man."

"He wuz a good man," Louise sighed. "He eventually died trying to make life better for all the Cove folks...lots of people in town didn't like what he was doin'...but they never broke his spirit. Yes, he was a strong man...moved into one of the slave cabins after they burned the big house and kept right on goin'. That's where me and my Daddy lived for awhile, his Daddy lived there too."

"LD told me the story about Uncle Charlie being whipped in the town square. You know about that?"

"I knew about that...Everybody knew about that!" Louise turned away looking at the water sparkling in the drainage ditch. "Yes, I knew about that." Nell sensed the tension in Louise's voice, and wished she had not broached the subject, realizing too late it was a painful memory for Louise.

The ensuing silence eventually created an awkward space around the women.

"What I didn't understand," Nell needed to break the silence. "What I don't understand is what happened to

Big Poppa? Do you know how he got out of town?"

"Not sure when he got out...But he did get out. Broke Eva and Shugababy's hearts though when they found out he had to leave. My Daddy found out the Klan wuz gonna' follow Shugababy one night to the blind in the swamp. Nappy's big brother Grady and my Daddy, they helped Big Poppa catch a freight train goin' out'a town that same night. Big Poppa ended up working in the coal mines of West Virginia. Started sending money back to Miz Pete so Shugababy and Eva could come join him as soon as the baby was born."

"How'd that work out? Did they ever get to go join him?"

"No, never did...least Shugababy never did," Louise said walking away. She looked somberly back up the road in the direction of the Cove. Hesitating she turned and took Nell by the arm walking back toward the heart of the Cove. When they stopped again, she tried to direct Nell's attention out to the remaining fieldstones of an old well out near the remnants of the old slave quarters in the pasture.

"Can you see those stones out there?" Louise pointed in the direction of a small patch of yellow wildflowers in the pasture. "The stones close to the ground now," she said. "They mostly wore down from time or fell down cause of the weather." Nell could only see the color of the wildflowers, and the scruffy undergrowth where Louise was pointing. Louise pointed out an old oak tree.

"Look," she said, "they right near that tree...just a little to the right of that big old oak tree."

"Sorry Louise, but I can't see anything other than the brush and that little patch of color from the wildflowers out there." She was disappointed because Nell could not distinguish anything from where they were standing.

"Doesn't matter. I know where it is. That's all that counts. This place has a lot of bad memories for me."

Heavy in thought she kicked at one of the small tufts of weeds growing in front of her. Silent, Nell looked away, out over the landscape enjoying a soft breeze stirring the heat. Her mind mulled what Louise meant by 'bad memories' as she turned toward Louise.

"Bad memories? I don't understand". Silence followed them as they turned back toward the car.

"You know Grady is my Daddy."

"I figured."

"You were probably too young to be much affected by what went on back then," Nell said.

"I wasn't too young...Just too innocent." Louise wiped a thin bead of perspiration from the bridge of her nose, stepping away from the tuft of grass she had been kicking before continuing. "The innocent just got to stick together...if they do, then they got power. Together they can make everythin' be all right. That's what I believes." The silence seemed to grow louder around them.

"What you believe Nell? Evie believes in the Church and the other life after we die. I think she knows better but, for her, believing in a heaven probably explains away all the evil she lived through down here. Me, I think we got to believe in ourselves to overcome evil. My Daddy taught me that!"

Nell didn't answer. She didn't know what she believed anymore. She thought about Mae, questioning her Mother's motive for hiding her life in the Cove. Both women were aware they had stumbled into the edge of a discussion close to the surface for both of them. Louise needed to back away from it more than Nell, but Nell's silence forced her to continue talking. She changed the subject.

"They burned Daddy's barn down cause, he helped Big Poppa. But your Daddy did too! He helped Big Poppa too".

"That's probably why the family moved to Detroit."

Nell said quietly. Silence surrounded them. Turning suddenly, Louise pointed in the direction of the patch of wildflowers again.

"You really can't see that patch of fieldstones out there in the pasture. Can you, huh?" She searched Nell's eyes, holding them.

"Sorry, but I can't see anything out there but the overgrowth of the weeds, and the yellow wildflowers you pointed out." Nell tried once again to scan the undergrowth for the image of fieldstones. "Sorry Louise, I can't see nothing."

"Oh hell', it ain't really, important, no more anyway. It's just a bad place, but not important. Not no more." Her attitude suddenly changed, as if she lost track of where and whom she was with. It was obvious to Nell she had suddenly lost awareness of her standing by her side. Blankly she stared at the ground as her thoughts intruded into her consciousness. Painful images of a young girl being chased across the fields by an enlarged shadow of a man, seemingly taller and whiter than her daddy.

"Daddy!" Louise uttered under her breath, just loud enough to be heard by Nell. The exclamation startled Nell who appraised Louise carefully. She had broken into a sweat. She rubbed at the perspiration running between her breasts, shaking slightly as if chilled. Her face flushed, and a well of tears inched down her cheeks. Steadying herself she took a deep breath through her nose. Holding it deep in her lungs, she exhaled it slowly through her mouth. It settled her. She wiped her face with the sleeve of her shirt, sighing deeply.

"Louise, you all right?" Nell came closer, concerned. Louise turned away from her, facing in the direction of the car. Finally, without looking up, Louise tugged softly at Nell's hand, and they walked silently hand in hand back to the car. After she settled herself, Louise retrieved a small half-pint bottle of whiskey from her purse. She wiped the mouth of the bottle with the tail of her shirt and offered it to Nell, who refused.

"You go ahead...I have to drive," she said starting the car. Louise looked frail sitting next to her, but took two large sips of the honey colored liquid, frowning as it passed her throat.

"Whew! Opens your eyes like nothing else I know." A tentative smile danced around her lips, and her blue eyes, still red from the tears struggled to dance happily again.

THAT AFTERNOON after Nell and Louise took down the old screened partitions on the sides and the front of the porch. They took extra care to leave the old screen door intact. Nell was pleasantly surprised at the strength of Louise. She handled the partitions easily, leaving the decisions on what to do next to Nell. She was a dedicated worker, and as Nell gauged their progress she was pleased Louise had asked her to help. They finished just as the sun was settling low in the sky, and the shadows were starting to stretch out across the backyard.

"Losing the light," Louise said wiping her face on her sleeve. Nell agreed.

"Let's just store these partitions on the side of the house. Tomorrow will be another good day," she said, as Eva watched from the door to the kitchen area.

"Y'all can wash up now...if you want, dinner won't be long." For dinner Eva fed them baked sweet potatoes, fried chicken wings, and a large helping of mixed mustard a turnip greens, raw onions and fresh tomatoes. Later they relaxed in the backyard. They sat in a circle on the old reclining chairs Eva kept stored on the back porch. Old citronella candles added an eerie feeling to the scene. Louise objected to the smell, but Eva insisted the candles would keep the mosquitoes away.

"You know Evie," Louise changed the subject. "This kind'a reminds me of the times we would sit on the woodpile when we were young." She drew deeply on a cigarette, exhaling it noisily before continuing.

"Kind'a." Eva turned to face Nell. "When Louise and me grew up, here in the Cove, we lived just a holler from each other." Eva pointed back toward the swamp in the distance.

"I remember the first time we met," Louise said flicking the ashes from her cigarette. "We couldn't been no more than five years old. Big Poppa brought you over to our place one day when he came to help Daddy put a fence around the hen house," she said looking at Eva, who smiled at the memory.

"We played together--at first kind'a circling each other," she said to Nell. "Mostly curious I think about our different color and hair. Oh, I'd seen coloreds since I wuz born...what with living at the plantation and all, but never a little colored girl my age up close I could play with. More than anything else I wuz mostly surprised at how soft Evie's hair was. It was supposed to be kinky...that's all I learned from my Mama 'bout coloreds. Ever since then we been the best of friends." As she spoke, Nell thought of the similarity of her own life. Images of meeting Jacob in the old church surfaced in her mind. Always taken to the little church by Mae--many times against her wishes, she was not happy about going until she met Jacob. Like Louise and Eva, she had been curious about him too, especially his brace, and the scars. She wondered would she and Jacob still be friends if he were still alive.

"See that big old oak tree spreading out every which way over yonder covered with moss?" The words scattered Nell's thoughts when Eva turned to see if Nell was following her outstretched hand. She pointed emphatically in the distance over her shoulder.

"Matter of fact is, that old oak tree used to be in the back of our place before my Mama died. Louise lived off to the left of us with a small group of white sharecroppers on the plantation...bout a quarter mile or so."

"You be talking about Shugababy...your Mama?"

"Shore was...yeah Shugababy! Big Poppa gave her that name. Said she had an affliction with sweets...that's why she loved him so! Mama, she was always hiding candy around the cabin so nobody but her could find it. I think when we wuz kids we ate more syrup and biscuits than anybody else in the whole wide world," Eva chuckled, "and she made the best blackberry cobbler in the world!" Louise sat up and leaned forward in her chair, looking across Eva.

"Evie and me, we would meet at that same ole tree on hot muggy days whenever we could sneak off from our chores. I'll always remember catch'n butterflies, and things. Sometime in the evening we would meet and catch fireflies...and talk about how we would get away from this place when we got grown up and all. If we could drive back up in there," she pointed again. "You could still see what's left of the old cabin where Evie grew up."

As she was speaking Nell thought of the times she, Jacob, and Uncle Charlie would lay in the hot sand near the old dock at Hobo Junction. She and Jacob also talked freely then about what they would do, and how they would live after they grew up. She didn't say anything, but she thought quietly about the similarity of relationships between friends while growing up. It seems it doesn't matter where they grow up. There is always one childhood friend with whom one always seems to build future dreams together, she thought. She found the two women unique. Even with all the troubles surrounding race and poverty in the south, they had managed to remain life-long friends. Eva grunted as she stretched reaching under the front of the porch to retrieve the half bottle of clear liquid. She silently handed it to Louise, who removed the cap, wiped the top of the bottle and handed it to Nell. She took a small swig and coughed in reaction to the liquid. It was very strong. It burned her throat as she swallowed it. She wiped her mouth looking at Louise.

"Strong!" The liquor burned a trail to her stomach and sat there radiating the discomfort into her lungs. "Whew, I thought you said that was vodka. Man, that's not vodka. That stuff can take your head off." Louise turned the bottle up for a healthy swig, and sighed.

"Better than vodka," she said smacking her lips, " pure corn liquor. The best I ever tasted too." She turned her chair and slouched down into the webbing, stretching her legs away from the small candle next to her. She laid her head back and closed her eyes. Eva got up moving one of the candles closer to Nell, before turning to Louise.

"This takes me back to the times when Shugababy would get all upset and put us out of the house. Only difference is ...all we had to do, in those days, was sit outside the cabin on the woodpile and, on them hot days, drink that sweet water from the rain barrel. Remember that beat-up tin cup?" She laughed at the thought. "It was so refreshin' on hot days."

"I really loved your mama, Evie," Louise said sleepily. "I will never forget how I felt when she passed on. Like one of God's angels goin' home...and, and just tore my heart out not knowing what was going to happen to you being left alone and all. Good thing Nappy stayed as long as he could." The hardness was creeping back into her voice, as she stifled a yawn.

"Louise, I think you better be getting on home...or better yet, maybe you stay over here tonight," Eva said sensing Louise, tired from the long day, might be feeling the effects of the alcohol. Nell sat up in her chair.

"Is something wrong; is she OK?"

"I think Louise had a little too much of her tonic. She might walk off into the swamp if we don't take her home. She be all right. It happened before." Eva nudged Louise awake and helped her find her way into the small cabin. Louise complaining loudly fell asleep quickly across Eva's bed.

"I got some old quilts. I just make me a pallet on the floor tonight," Eva said when she returned. Nell waited until she was comfortable again before she asked about Charlie and Shugababy.

"Nappy? Louise must'a told you 'bout that. Guess you call him Uncle Charlie. To me he was just like my brother. Didn't come but a few years to help with the plowin'...pickin' the cotton and such." Nell sat silent waiting for her to continue.

"Daddy named my Mama Shugababy cause, he said she wuz so sweet, not just cause she loved sugar." She laughed, looking at her hands. She rubbed them. Both sat silent, momentarily aware of the tension surrounding them. Nell noticed in the moonlight Eva's face. It had taken on a stony appearance. She sat stiffly in the chair staring trance-like away from Nell into the emptiness of the night. Her words were soft when she spoke again, and it was as if she was reliving the story as the words came from her lips. She knew Nell was there, because as she spoke she would, on occasion, look directly at her. She didn't respond to Nell's questions. She simply kept on talking, the words spilling out as from her unconscious.

"It's been a rough life down here for all us. It really wuz hard on Mama with Big Poppa leavin'...though soon's he could, he sent money back home. I remember Mama worried herself sick until she finally got word from Big Poppa. He was workin' the coalmines in West Virginia. Miz Pete brought it herself all the way from the highway so she could read it to mama. It had a postal money order for twelve dollars, first we'd ever seen. He promised to send more whenever he got paid. He wanted us to come there, soon as the baby was born. Mama just screamed and cried with happiness. She says we go and be with him again as soon as the baby comes, but the Lord, he took her away."

The old lady cleared her throat, before continuing.

"Thank goodness for Nappy, yore Uncle Charlie. He stayed wit us for a long time while Big Poppa be gone. Nappy, he really worked hard too, soon as sun up, and late into the night so we could get our fair share of the crops in 'fore the end of the plantin' season." Eva sighed deeply breathing loudly into a long silence. Nell had questions she wanted to ask the old woman, but held her patience watching her in the sliver of moonlight outlining her face. Eva blinked her eyes rapidly as awakening from sleep.

"But I never forget my Mama dying right there before my eyes," she said. "Sometimes late at night when I cain't sleep, I can still see that little place, as if it's happenin' all over again."

IT HAPPENED AT NIGHT, but the midwife had come earlier in the day, and was busy in the cabin. Sitting in the yard with Charlie, Eva stared into the darkness of the night. They could hear the voices of her mother and the midwife, against their wills, pushing into their minds. Eva flinched at the screams, and the sound of the words of concern coming from the midwife. Charlie walked away down closer to the pasture. But Eva could not pull away. It was like she was outside herself watching a senseless trauma unfold. She could see the entire scene as from above it, and she calmly watched herself, a frightened little girl covering her ears as an old woman ushered a small brown bundle from the thighs of a prostrate woman, who screamed into the night. She lay on her back, her legs spread wide, and bent at the knees seemingly frozen in an upright position. The old lady quickly cleaned the baby's mouth, and nose with her fingers, cradling it close to her breast. And suddenly its loud squall filled the air, as the woman's screams on the bed suddenly ceased.

"Healthy baby girl all right," the mid-wife said loudly examining the baby. "But Shugababy didn't make it. She's dead Eva!" There was a stern look in the old woman's gaze as she held tightly to the squirming infant; she looked sorrowfully across through the door at Eva, the young girl.

"Yore Mama's dead child...she must'a been through too much." The young Eva watched as the old middy woman, dressed in black turned slowly from her mother's body, laying quiet and stretched out on the rumpled bed in the small shack. Eva stepped into the cabin, looking down at the still form laid out before her. Shugababy's curly hair stood rigid around her. Her head was elevated on a pillow made of feathers and straw, eyes closed she seemed to be caught in a distorted state of pain. It was frozen on her face, and the blood on the makeshift mattress had spread out from her raised legs. The woman lowered her legs and pulled the sheet over her head. The old mid-wife slowly wiped her bloody hands on the edge of the sheet. She laid the child on the bed next to its mother, where the baby continued its lusty wail. She turned to the washbasin on the small stool near the foot of the bed.

"Evie... hand me some mo of that hot water."

Eva didn't answer, but with the shock of what she had just witnessed still in her eyes, went quickly to the fireplace to retrieve the container of hot water. After placing the water on the table, she moved quickly, going back outside. She wondered what she could have done to save her mother. Her mind was flooded with the things she had not done as quickly as Shugababy wanted her to do. Maybe God was punishing her for those things, and the times she had threatened to run away from home. She blamed herself for her mother's death, whimpering loudly. Suddenly she wanted her Big Poppa, and called his name repeatedly aloud.

The smell of the amniotic fluid and blood mingled with the smell of the hickory wood from the fireplace, and the combined odors gagged her. She coughed violently into her hand. The middy woman had picked the baby up and was at the small table cleaning the mucous from the baby's body.

"Y'all have to tell yore Pa," she said nodding at Eva, and Charlie who now stood hesitantly at the door of the cabin. "I spect he be comin' back now from the mines up north soon's he can... under the circumstances. I be over in Tuscaloosa then. Don't spect to be back this way before the harvestin' all done. All the while's I reckon I just better take this here child on along to Miz Mamie. She still got plenty milk, and I'm sure she won't mind nursin' another young'un for awhile." Eva finally turned away, and slowly walked out the open door toward Charlie. Her small body shook violently and she spoke haltingly between breaths.

"Mama's dead." Charlie came to her, a blank stare on his face. He tried to comfort her by circling her with his arms, but the impact of Shugababy's death welled in him and he also struggled to contain the sobs. They clung to each other staring through the open door at the covered body as if expecting Shugababy to rise-up, and call them to her. The old middy woman wrapped the baby in clean cloths, before approaching the children.

"Eva?" She took the little girl's hands. "You and Charlie go now. Go to the big house on the other side of the creek, and tell Miz Pete yore Ma just died birthin' the baby. Tell her the body still here in the cabin; she'll know what to do. You understand me?" The old lady drew Eva closer to her. "Tell her the baby's 'live, and I took her to Miz Mamie for wet nursin'." She shook Eva for a response.

"Yassum" The old woman turned away, but Eva, not moving, continued to stare at the covered body of her mother. The old woman turned back snatching Eva by her shoulder.

"You understand me child?" Her voice was stern. Eva nodded, but the old woman moved to Charlie. Her voice was still stern.

"Look at me," she insisted. "You help her get through this, you hear? You got to help each other out. I know you be just children...but you can do this together." After Charlie nodded, she was satisfied they understood what to do. She called to her mule that was grazing close by in the pasture. She tied the cloths into a makeshift cradle and secured it with the crying newborn to the saddle horn, walking silently off toward the dirt road on the other side of the distant fields. She didn't look back. The children watched her as she walked off into daybreak that was starting to creep above the horizon. Eva stifled a cry as she clung to Charlie's arm.

"Nappy, what we goin' do without mama? Eva was concerned he would leave her alone now that Shugababy was gone."I want Big Poppa!" She blurted the words at him.

"Hush Evie...we gonna' take care of each other now, just like Shugababy would want us to." He was more focused now, but he still struggled to control his emotions too. She knew it by the shakiness of his voice. He watched the old lady receding into the distance.

"Don't you worry none. This cryin' ain't gonna help none. Shugababy is gone now, and we got to do what's right. Big Poppa be dependin' on us." He took Eva's hand. "Come on, we got to go get Miz Pete. She'll know what to do."

Eva knew the way to the Pete's place. It was the

biggest house owned by coloreds in the area. It sat out nearest to the main road on the edge of the Cove. The main portion of the house was constructed from field-stone by Mr. Pete's grandfather after he was freed from slavery. Several other rooms had been added over the years, and it served as a place where the people of the Cove could meet and discuss problems affecting the area. They could also barter their produce, things they made and get other things done through Miz Pete. She always seemed to know what was important and how to solve problems.

Everybody in the Cove eventually showed up at the house because the mail was delivered there. The roads and trails inside the Cove were simply footpaths, and too rutted for the mail wagon. Once a month, the mail-man would stop at the Pete's house, where he would leave all the Cove mail in small boxes outside on the Pete's side porch.

When Big Poppa started sending the money back to Shugababy, Charlie would be workin' in the fields, so once a month Eva would run to pick up the mail, and the money from the postal orders Big Poppa sent. Shugababy always gave her a small brown cloth sack in which to bring the mail home. On those days before she left, her mother would take a dipper of cool water from the rain barrel, wet a clean cloth and wipe her small face, let-ting some of the water trickle into the little girl's hair. It dripped down across her shoulders wetting her dress, and cooling her from the morning sun.

"You go straight to Miz Pete's. She put the mail, and the money in this here sack, and you come straight back home, you hear? I mean don't you stop for nothin'." She stroked the little girl's face, handing her another dipper of the cool water. "I don't want to miss you; you hear?"

"Yassum."

Eva would take her time relishing the cool water

from the dipper, before jumping from the porch and running barefoot through the small yard. Shugababy's chickens scattered clucking under the cabin's rickety porch. She ran towards the dirt trail the cows and mules had worn onto the brush. It led to a small pond at the beginning of the swampy marsh. A wider trail skirted the edge of the pond, forking left away from the swamp up an incline and over a ridge lined with old pine and oak trees laden with Spanish moss. She would follow the tree line until she came to the fenced pasture off from Ole Marse's smokehouse.

Crawling under the fence, she would run across the pasture through the grazing cows while watching out for the lone bull that acted as if the place was his personal property. Breathing hard, on the other side of the pasture, she would run back toward the creek that ran through the property. She knew a place where a log had fallen across the creek. It was large enough to be used as a bridge to get to the other side. Watching for snakes and gators that came close to the creek bank to feed on the muskrats and frogs, she would slow her pace, in order to balance herself carefully on the slippery surface of the log. Sometimes she could see the ripples and hear the slurping of the water on the creek banks caused by the movement of the snakes and the gators in the water. Once across the creek, she could relax to more easily climb over the brush and up to the main road leading out to the interstate. Frequently she would run past the prisoners from the state penitentiary cutting back brush and grading the main road. All black, they were dressed in simple striped gray and green uniforms, and they could be seen stretching out along the road like a wavy ribbon. Shackles were on their legs, and a long chain was attached to the shackles in such a way so they were connected to each other. Some had shovels; others had picks, and hoes. Big Poppa had said the men worked all day in the hot sun, and in the rain, only breaking when the lunch wagon came. Sometimes they sang songs to help establish a work rhythm. Two white men on horseback guarded the prisoners. It seemed to her they always knew when she would be coming through to get the mail. One of them always hollered and waved his shotgun at her in a threatening manner as she ran past them heading for the Pete's house further down the road.

Usually Miz Pete and her son Lovie would see her before she got to the house. They would gladly greet her with the precious money from Big Poppa, a dipper of cool water and a sugar cookie. Miz Pete would insist the little girl come inside out of the sun to eat and rest briefly before making the trip back. This was the best part for Eva. She loved the spacious cleanliness of Miz Pete's house, and she also liked the attention she got from Lovie.

Even at her young age, she admired Miz Pete. She was so different from Shugababy and the other women at the Cove. She could read, and her letter writing was like a flowing picture. Eva loved the way she spoke; her hair was always combed, and she moved in a graceful manner as though her feet barely touched the floor. When she sat next to her, Eva thought, the air that moved around her smelled like fresh cut flowers.

"Evie, would you like another cookie?" Miz Pete moved closer to the young girl.

"Yassum." The woman held out the plate of brown cookies, and the little girl was careful only to touch the one she took. She dropped it into the mail sack. Miz Pete smiled and blinked at the act.

"What's the matter, saving it for later?"

"No'm. It's for my brother." She referred to Charlie.

"Oh I see...for Nappy," Miz Pete had come to understand Eva's relationship with Charlie, and she smiled knowingly.

"Yassum."

"You can take more, if you like," she said extending the plate again. Lovie hovered around the two of them excitedly laughing and grabbing another cookie off the plate for himself. The two of them ignored him as Miz Pete, still smiling, hugged the little girl. She put two more of the cookies into the sack and brushed the sweaty hair back out of the girl's face.

"You better be getting along now. Shugababy'll be missing you soon. She'll be worried."

"Yassum. Thank you, mam."

◆ ◆ ◆

MR. FRED SCRATCHING at the closed screen door suddenly broke the spell Eva's words had created in the room. Nell jumped at the sound. She had slipped deeply into the story. Nell looked at her watch, wondering how long Eva had been talking. The story about Shugababy for Nell had been so mesmerizing she had been brought into its center, watching Eva as it all happened. For Eva, it was the opening of a door to the past she had closed off for many years, and she was shocked, she was sharing it again. It was like walking backward in time to experience those same emotions she must have felt as that little girl. She finally reacted to Mr. Fred as arousing from a deep sleep.

"Can you let him in daughter?"

She realized as Nell walked past her toward the porch, she had taken some risks talking so much about her life. She questioned the wisdom of her actions and wondered who Nell really was, and even if she could be trusted. She pushed the thoughts away when Mr. Fred jumped into her lap, nuzzling his arched back against her breasts. Nell followed him slowly back to her chair, and exhaled loudly when she sat down. Eva calmly put the cat back on the floor.

"Miz Eva, what ever happened to the baby...your sister that the midwife took away?"

"Oh...she doing fine, livin' down in a little town in Florida. Miz Mamie named her 'Patience' and raised her till she could go live with Big Poppa. No way he could come back here to live," she sighed. The old lady struggled to get up from the chair.

"She usta' come see me every now and then, not so much lately. We all be too old now."

"...sometimes it causes me to tremble...tremble"

CHAPTER FIFTEEN

*T*HE NEXT MORNING NELL drove into town to check out of the hotel. While there she called Dean, and Mae. She became disturbed when both asked if she would be home for Thanksgiving. Mae became irritated, and insistent, when Nell said she was not sure about Thanksgiving. Mae was unhappy with the response. Her voice elevating, she yelled into the phone before hanging up.

"The past is over Nell. Just leave things alone down in Eden." Later Nell checked her E-Mail. She had a note from Hill. He had made some suggestions for the query, and wanted to see some sample photographs. She responded and promised to send him some digitals along with the modifications later that day. Afterwards she took the digital camera, attached a telephoto lens, and went to the little restaurant for breakfast. As she drove back to the cabin she took several exposures of the colored section of the town, concentrating primarily on activity around the restaurant, the cemetery, and the old church. On the trail, leading up to the Coot's place, from a distance she took more pictures of Eva's cabin, the surrounding marsh, and the remains of the old slave cabins. Back inside the cabin she made a pot of coffee and spent the remainder of the morning on the front porch in the cool shade working on the query modifications for Hill.

Occasionally when she looked up from the laptop her

eyes would drift to the freezer bag containing Charlie's ashes. It still lay on the table. She still wasn't sure know what to do with them. She forced the problem from her mind, by thinking about the serenity of Cove. She knew if she sat still long enough, the wildlife in the area would soon present itself in full view as they searched for food, or made their daily trips to the creek. She also knew if she could get some great shots of the wildlife, they would help to complete the pictorial representation for her query. She spent the next several hours sitting quietly photographing every animal, from butterflies to the swamp deer that passed within view of the lens she had on the digital camera.

Later in the day she went to Eva's. She and Louise had planned to take the heavy bag of concrete from the car, mix it, and pour it around the porch pilasters. When she got there Eva was standing in the front yard with a woman, several years younger than Nell. She had a bag of freshly cut cabbage, and tomatoes from Eva's garden. Another bag stuffed with collard greens and carrots had just fallen from her arms to the ground.

"No child, you cain't carry all that by yourself," Eva admonished her as Nell walked up. Embarrassed the woman looked shyly at Nell and turned to walk away in the direction of the old slave cabins.

"Wait child" Eva held her back. "I want you to meet Nell." She pointed at the bag on the ground. "She can help you carry this back up to your place." Eva looked sternly at Nell as the woman walked out the gate and past the parked car before stopping. Nell picked up the bag, before looking at the woman, who still stood a few paces away in Eva's front yard.

"Louise's daughter Angel," Eva said, as Nell instinctively appraised her. She noticed the woman was barefoot, and was concerned with her hair, trying to control it away from her face. It was reddish gray and stringy.

She tried to smooth it with her free hand, as her eyes met Nell's briefly.

"Pleased," she mumbled, nodding her head. Nell nodded back, still appraising her. She was a thin woman with luminous eyes much like Louise. Her skin was tan and freckled from the sun. The quality of her hair and full lips impressed upon Nell this is the little girl from Uncle Charlie's photographs. Nell reached out to shake her hand. It trembled and the skin on her palm was dry and hard in spots. Nell was impressed how she moved like a young woman, but suspected she was closer to her own age.

Angel mumbled her thanks to Eva for the food, as Nell, with the other bag silently followed her back up the trail toward the old slave shacks. The thoughts flooded her mind. What if this is Uncle Charlie's child? How is she related to me, to Mae? She sighed deeply again. Mae would be shocked. She couldn't wait to tell Dean, she thought as the slave cabins came into view up ahead of them. Angel stopped suddenly turning she adjusted her load and took the bag from Nell.

"I can make it from here," she said shyly. "Thank you for all your help." On the trail, back down to Eva's place Nell thought briefly of the old slave shack she had seen earlier that appeared occupied.

"Louise's daughter," Nell said as Eva met her at the cut-off. They turned and walked around the house into the back yard where Louise was working. Louise had already dug a hole around the rotted pilasters. She was trying to pull them out, but they had been set in creosote, and they were heavy.

"Fuckin' piece of shit!" She was cussing loudly to herself. She drank from a cold beer in her hand as she walked back and forth surveying the pilasters.

"Son of a bitch...got'a come out." She was exasperated.

"Don't fret so much Louise. Let Nell help with that." Eva approached her calmly. "She told you she would help with that. She's younger than us."

"Don't know about that," Nell laughed. "But it might be easier if we had some rope. Louise looked up.

"You know...Ole Coot's got some rope, chains too...and some other rusty tools in a box under his porch," she said, taking a healthy swig from the beer.

"If you give me one of those beers I'll go back and get the chains...maybe we can hook something on to the car and pull these out" Nell said pointing at the pilasters. "Then all we have to do is pour the ready mix. Right?"

"Right." Louise sat on the edge of the porch. "I'll wait right here for you."

Over the next several days, Louise and Nell finished restoring the porch back to a usable condition. Together they dug holes and mixed the Ready-Mix concrete to set the pilasters in to support the frame of the porch. They also replaced all the rotted wood with treated wood that was resistant to the termites and the humidity of the area. Between the two of them they finished close to a case of beer, but it provided the energy and kept them in good spirits to finish the job. Other than the times Nell and Louise went into town and brought back Chinese food, they worked through lunch, Eva insisted on them eating dinner each night. She cooked hardy meals of pinto beans, fried onions, ham hocks and corn bread slathered with margarine and large jars of Kool Aid.

As they drew closer to finishing the porch, Nell knew it would be difficult leaving the two old women. But she knew it was time for her to get back home. Mae and Dean both had pressed her to be back home for Thanksgiving. On the final day, when they finished the porch, she and Louise stood in the back yard proudly admiring their work. It stood straight, braced against the rear of the house. It was not as square and level as it could have been, but it was usable again, and all the screens were in place. Louise had put the folding chairs back on the porch, and had brought one of her small tables for Eva to use to hold an outside lamp as well. Louise sat in one of the chairs smoking as Nell swept the sawdust and other small trash from the porch. When she finished, she called Eva, and the two of them surveyed the completed porch from all angles. Eva stood close and hugged Nell's arm in gratitude.

"Lord! Bless you daughter. I just wish Lovie could see this place now. He just loved sittin' on this ole porch so much. He used to eat all his meals out here, and it's where he would doze off most nights before I had to roust him for bed." Nell could feel the perspiration on Eva's face as the old lady embraced her before walking slowly over to Louise.

"Now, we's done a good job Louise...you gota'help me get it painted to stand up to the hurricane season. Louise was quiet. She got up and went to the screen door to throw her cigarette butt outside before turning to face them.

"Can you tell me about Nappy?" She looked at Nell. "You gonn'a be gone soon...probably tomorrow. I just need to know how he died before you go. Did he suffer?" Nell was surprised Louise brought Uncle Charlie up again. She nodded in agreement.

"I understand," she said. Louise looked at Eva for support. Eva simply said, "Let's eat out on the porch this evening. It's so nice out here. Side's I still got some them collards, and a speck of that ham left over. Lovie would have liked that, us eatin' out here." She retreated into the small kitchen, as Louise pulled three of the chairs into a semi-circle next to each other. She sat in the center one, indicating Nell should sit to the right of her. They heard Eva moving in the kitchen.

"Y'all want another beer?" She yelled out to them. "We still got some left over from yesterday." Without answering Louise retreated inside and returned with two cold beers. The quiet look dominated her face, as she handed a beer to Nell. It was late afternoon, and the Cove was silent except for the rustling of the tree tops stirred by a slight breeze.

"Feels like a storm might blow in from the Gulf later." Nell said looking at the tops of the tall pines in the distance. Louise shuffled in her chair so she could look at Nell.

"Nappy came back here only one time after he left," she said. Her voice was mellow, but her words were slurred. She sounded tired. "He wrote and told me he wanted to come and see me after he finished basic training in Georgia. It was just before he was going to be shipped out". Her voice stumbled. "It's still hard to talk about, but you's family. You deserve to know bout what happened here." Nell sat up straight in her chair, leaning in toward Louise, as Eva came outside with a jar of Kool Aid. She sat silently in the other chair next to Louise, her eyes directed at the floor. Louise continued.

"He came like he wuz scared one night, leavin' just before dawn. Angel was little then. She only knew he wuz important to us, neva how he wuz important to us. After she went to sleep, we wuz just like animals all night," she paused, "won't never forget that night...I really loved Nappy," her voice fading.

"It's getting late," Eva interrupted. "The greens are hot; we can talk more after we eat." She and Nell headed for the kitchen. They brought out plates filled with hot collard greens and placed a platter of sliced ham sandwiches on the lamp table in the middle of the porch. Louise had sat quietly waiting for them to return. The images of Charlie still provided her mind with a comfort she had not known for years. She was also filled with questions about what had happened to him all these years, but she was patient. Nell had been sent to her for a reason, she thought. God would reveal himself to her.

They ate in silence. Dusk slowly settled across the sky, and the crickets began singing their constant song. Nell, between bites of food, studied the rising mist clouding the swamp and knew she would miss this place. It moved slowly in toward the little cabins surrounding them as in a cloud, punctuated by the light from their warm lamps. The scattered lamps flickered like large fireflies in the early evening, and the smell of cooking food, and burning hickory floated in the wind. Occasionally the sound of a woman singing or calling her child to come home could be heard in the distance.

"That was the last time we saw Nappy," Louise said finishing her sandwich. I knew that night I 'd never see him again, and I just clung to him tryin' to hang on." She paused looking at Nell with drowsy eyes. The heavy work on the porch, and the many beers she had consumed was telling in her speech.

"I guess me and him, we just couldn't be, least not down here in the Cove," she said quietly. "Any way we never seen him again after that. But he did send money back down here for Angel and me. Once a month, all the time up until the war ended." She closed her eyes, as her voice trailed off. Eva collected the dishes and took them back inside.

"Nappy wuz something special," Eva said when she returned. He owned up to that child...though I don't believe he's the daddy. He and Louise wuz in love all right, but she wuz too scared to go all the way with him back then. I know cuz me and Lovie would sneak around with them at that ole schoolhouse too. She and me, we always talked afterwards about what had happened. She and Nappy, they wuz really too-scared to do much more than, you know fumble around with each other and kiss with their mouths open. I know cuz that's what we mainly did as kids!" Nell had expected Louise to respond to

Eva's comments, but she had dozed off. Her head was slouched on her chest and a nearly empty beer bottle lay in her lap. Eva took the bottle from her hands, turned it up and drained it.

"Clay Cromwell...he be Angel's daddy, Eva said, "but that family had a way of denying their own. Louise refuse to accept it, but it's true. We all might as well face up to it. We too old now for it to matter no more any way." Nell sat forward to look across Louise at Eva. She flashed on LD telling her at the restaurant about Clay Cromwell and the Klan comin' after Big Poppa.

"She shouldve gone after his family for some support," Nell said. "Maybe Louise is too proud. LD told me she took a shot at Clay once when they were kids."

"He's right. She did shoot at him. I wish she had'a killed him. Nobody round here could stand Clay. She wouldn't want me tellin' you this, but that nasty bastard caught her coming back from meetin' Charlie at the school house one night." Eva sat up in her chair to look at Louise who still slept peacefully. She lightly brushed the hair back from Louis's face before continuing.

"Nappy had just come into the cabin when we heard Louise. We heard her long before we saw either one of them. She was yellin' at the top of her voice for her daddy to come help her. I could tell right away by the dirty blond hair of the thin man following her, it was Clay Cromwell. Even from a distance I knew him. He had been riding through the pasture as he often did after Big Poppa left. Miz Pete said the Klan probably thought Big Poppa would come back for me right after Shugababy died. Clay must'a saw Nappy and Louise huggin' on their way home. He must'a left his horse, and followed them on foot from a distance, until Louise left Nappy to cut across the pasture on her way home. When we saw them, he was chasing Louise through the back of the pasture heading up toward the slave quarters, and thats where he caught her. She struggle real hard, but he strained her down on the ground. ******

"Nappy and me, we watched it all from a distance scared to death till we couldn't stand it no more. We knew bout what the Klan did to coloreds, and scared we stayed out of sight of the window and the door at first.

"Louise finally broke away from him, and was running for our cabin as fast as her legs would carry her. She was only bout twelve years old, and you can tell not very big. She was crazy scared. I can still hear her calling for her daddy to come help her, but he wuzn't there. Then she called out for me, and Nappy. I wuz so scared I just covered my face and slid to the floor wondering what we should do if she got to the door. Nappy kept watchin', a stone look on his face, his chest rising and falling real quick like. I heard that ole son's a bitch amidst some scufflin' again. He had caught her again, and wuz callin' her a whole bunch of things, but I only remember the words 'little Nigga' lovin' whore'. I got up just in time to see, she must'a sinked her teeth into his lips as he tried to kiss her, cause his head jumped away real quick like. He swore again striking her hard in the chest with his fist. Knocked the wind out'a her...into the ground. She didn't move. I wuz scared he'd killed her!

"God dam...he just killed her!" Nappy's eyes were rollin' around in his head. "He killed Louise," he said looking at me. I could tell he wuz 'fraid, but I could also sense a rage buildin' in him. He started pacing around the cabin.

"The bastard," Nappy stood there, just a'shakin' as he glared at the scene out the window. Clay now stood over Louise breathing hard wiping the blood and tobacco spit from his beard. Picking her up he covered her mouth with one of his dirty hands and dragged her quickly away from near the cabin out toward the center of the pasture. He stopped, and we watched quickly lookin' at the dark cabins. Satisfied no one had seen him, he carried Louise out toward one the old oak trees goin' out away from the Sangster place. Standing in the depth of the cabin, Charlie and Eva watched intently now.

"After they faded out of sight in the darkness, Nappy ran to the woodpile, and took the biggest piece of hickory he could find. He followed them, crouching low in the tall weeds running along the creek. I followed him, picking up the largest piece of wood I could handle.

"My head barely stood above the weeds, but we found them from the sounds. They were in a clearing near the decaying remains of the first old plantation well, about fifty feet in front of us. There was some moonlight, but if it hadn't been for the sounds we would have stumbled right over them.

"The sight stopped us for a moment. He was on top of Louise in the brush hidden from sight by the side of old abandoned well. His coveralls were down, and he had raised her legs, straddled her on his knees between them. He was just'a grunting like a bull after a sow as he thrust himself hard into her spread legs. She struggled trying to get him off her, screaming from the pain of his penetratin' her." Eva stopped to swallow. She was breathing hard, reliving her story. "I'm sorry," she said. "I need a minute." Nell sat on the edge of her chair. She needed the old woman to continue, and she looked at Eva, her eyes begging her to finish the story. Finally, Eva continued.

"Louise just lay there in shock. He just had his way with her as she sobbed into her hand. He finally twitched collapsing on her with a shudder. Lying there breathless he was not aware, but Nappy stood up over them with the hickory raised. But he didn't hit Clay. He hesitated. I don't know why he didn't, but I just kept a'comin without hesitating. I had felt that pain he caused Louise with each thrust of his body, and the anger boiled overflowing inside me.

'Better not tell anybody either...you little Nigga'

lover,' he said loudly, 'or when we come back for that little coon boy friend of yours, I'll kill you.'   "He looked
down at Louise smiling as he started to rise-up from his
knees. Her blood had stained his crotch, and he casually
knelt back down to use the hem of her dress to wipe it
away. My heart beat like a drum in my chest, but finally
I was just behind him, the hickory log raised high over
my head...gathering my strength. Suddenly he sensed my
presence and raced to get up, but his coveralls were still
hanging around his knees. He stumbled just as I swung
the hickory. It caught him with a glancing blow on the
side of his right temple. Like a mad person, I took a better stance and swung again. This time it was a solid hit.
I could feel the weight of the hickory meetin' flesh. I hit
him again; he moaned and fell, leaning into the side of
the old well. Louise still in shock lay there taking in the
scene playing out before her.

"Finally, very deliberately she said, 'Hit him again
Evie, he's still breathing.' Fumbling to get his coveralls
up, he half crawled, stumbled off in the darkness to the
other side of the well. I could hear him knock some of
the crumbling fieldstones into the sour water. I put the
hickory down and went to Louise, but she pushed me
away. Snatching the hickory, she stumbled to him and
struck him again and again until his face was swollen
and bloody. With each thud of the hickory she cursed
him aloud. She finally stopped hitting him when he
crumpled into a heap across the opening of the well.
Louise also fell to the ground exhausted.

"Is he dead?" Nappy asked warily. He still held his
piece of hickory.

"Don't know," Louise whispered, her small hand
holding her stomach against the pain. Out of breath she
could barely speak, and she leaned against me when I
helped her to her feet. I could barely hold her and we
both eventually slid to the ground.

"He hurt me Evie," she said lying there on the warm grass. "It hurts Evie!" She struggled to her feet and picked up the wood again. Screaming in anger she flung herself against his still form, and on her knees at his side she repeatedly rained blows at his crotch, until she was unable to swing the wood anymore. We both sat on the ground leaning against each other, when he groaned and started to flinch. His hands moved against the field-stones, and he turned to look at us. Louise tried to pick up the piece of wood again, but her arms and legs were trembling and heavy as lead. I couldn't help either. I was dead tired as much from the emotion I was feeling as from beatin' him.

"She dropped it looking pleadingly up at Nappy. He still had his larger piece of hickory. We wuz just kids, and to this day I know without Nappy's help, we never would have survived that ordeal. Perhaps it wuz because he wuz a little older and stronger than us, or maybe it wuz because he had recently been whupped by the sheriff...don't know; but in a rage like I ain't never seen since, he killed Clay with that ole hickory branch. He hit him again and again until we heard his nose and cheekbone cracking. The piece of hickory looked like a bloody battering ram but Nappy, he wuz not even breathing hard. Clay's body lay on the ground at his side, with one arm caught on the top of the decaying fieldstones. A circle of blood surrounded his head like a halo of spilled wine. Louise and I, both in shock, sat there unable to move. 'We killed him.' My voice sounded like a stranger speaking to me.

'I don't care Evie...the bastard... he needs to die. He raped me.' Louise leaned forward and spit on Clay's body, her straggly hair slumped against her chest.

'He hurt me bad Evie...real bad.' The words were a whisper as her eyes welled into tears. Nappy didn't say anything, but, calmly he dropped the hickory branch down the shaft of the well. Moving quickly, he struggled to lift Clay's body into the mouth of the well. Louise and I helped him. After what seemed to be an eternity we finally got Clay's upper body over the mouth of the well. Nappy lifted his legs as we fed the rest of his body into the shaft. The sound of it hitting the stagnant water came back to us like an echo, and when the slurping and gurgling of the water quieted down I knew we had done the right thing. I threw the other piece of hickory wood down the shaft.

"Louise was bloody and dirty from the ordeal. The side of her face and neck wuz scratched, reddish and marked from his dirty fingers. Blood and other sticky fluids still trickled from her and were drying on the inside of her thighs, and there was blood splattered on all of us. With Charlie's urging, we stripped, and wrapping them in the fieldstones, threw our clothes down the well too.

"Afterward Nappy threw stones at Clay's big bay, chasing it back deeper into the Preservation.

"Just after we made it back to the cabin, the thunder started. It was as if God himself knew we needed his help...cause later that night the heavens opened-up, and it rained heavy for the next three days. It flooded the marsh all the way back up to the Pete's place. The thunder and lightning scared me to death, but when it finally stopped the rain had washed any traces of what happened that night. The rain even crumbled most of the old fieldstones into the well, practically sealin' it up.

"It was several days later, but the big bay finally found its way back to the mill. It caused quite a stir through the area when folks found out Clay Cromwell was missin'. For days, the sheriff and some of the mill hands searched the area, mainly the marsh lookin' for Clay, or his body without any success. Word around the Cove soon spread he was probably gotten by one of the larger gators down at the creek.

"Bout three weeks after that, Grady sent Nappy a train ticket, and he left the Cove. He was so-messed up...

he could not sleep, and was just scared of everybody. One day, without saying a word he just left. I heard he went up to Detroit. never came back I knew of. Things around here eventually settled back to normal." Eva cleared her throat, staring deep into Nell's eyes, and the two women, connected across the room through their silence. Off in the distance, the noise of scattering chickens, and the rustle of the wire of her chicken coop forced her to open the door. She yelled into the darkness, before turning on the light on the rear porch.

"Damn old fox! I guess I better kill him fore he gets in the coop," she said while standing in the doorway, before returning to a silent Nell.

"When Big Poppa got sick, I finally went to live with him in Virginia til he died. Louise stayed on, and she and I never talked about what happened at the well. And I never told anyone before now. She'd Anyway, for days after he raped her she was in a lot of pain, and had to struggle to hide her pain from her father. In our minds, we knew we should stay away from the old well, but you know at the same time we wanted to know if he ...his body was still there. I guess to be sure he was really-dead, more than anything else. That urge stayed with me for a long time, until some of the men from the plantation decided the partially closed well was a hazard, and one day filled it with dirt. Only a few of the larger fieldstone still mark its location.

"We been friends a long time...a mighty long time," she said. She sat back into her chair and sighed deeply. She looked lovingly at the sleeping Louise. "Just like sisters."

Nell stunned by what she had heard stared silently into the depth of the dark yard. It dawned on her that Charlie must have told Mae what had happened, cause Mae was too protective of him, she thought. They had kept this from her and Grady all this time. What a

powerful commitment on Mae's part, like a mother, she concluded
"Thank you, Miz Eva, although I still feel there is more to the story, I think I can go home now," she said. A single firefly sparkled off in the distance, and an occasional squawk of a small animal being caught by an owl rustled one of the trees.

Before Nell left the Cove that next afternoon, she walked with Louise and Eva through the scrub out to the area of the old well. Three large fieldstones marked the opening, and a few smaller ones lay scattered around in the dirt. They be angry if she knew I betrayed her trust, but you be family. You keep the secret, you hear me," the old lady voice pierced Nell's thoughts.

"I understand, it's safe with me," Nell assured the old lady. "I'll be leaving tomorrow evening," she said. "I have to go back, but tomorrow, perhaps we can find the proper spot for Uncle Charlie's ashes before I leave.

THE NEXT AFTERNOON the three women quietly walked up to the spring on the back side of the Coot's place. They stopped at the spot where the old tree roots splash into the spring. Louise led the way, carrying the bag of Charlie's ashes in her hand. When they approached just outside the Coot's place above the spring, she stopped.

"This be the place Nappy, and me, we loved best. This be where he wuz happiest when we swam in this warm water." Louise made the sign of the cross on her breast, and quietly uttered a short prayer.

"God bless you, Nappy...I never forget you and God knows I loved you." She held the open bag over the spring, "I'll always love you," she said louder as she sprinkled the ashes into the waters flowing away, and down into the creek. She folded the empty bag and put it in the pocket of her jeans. No sounds of animal life came back to greet them, but a lone butterfly flitted close, pausing momentarily at a patch of wildflowers. It soon captured a soft breeze and moved dramatically with the wind. Eva watched the lovely creature ride the wind delicate as a feather until she lost it in the blueness of the sky.

◆ ◆ ◆

THE AIRPORT IN MONTGOMERY was not crowded like the one in New Orleans had been. Nell sat alone at the counter in the small bar waiting for her flight. The only other customers were a young couple sitting at one of the tables near the window looking out on the tarmac. The television over the bar was on CNN and the commentator was speaking about America's war on terrorism. She didn't listen.

In her mind, the voice was the caller from the VA hospital awaking her from a deep sleep to tell her that Uncle Charlie had died, and how pained the words 'cremation' had left her. Then she remembered how peaceful she felt when Louise poured the last of Uncle Charlie's ashes into the spring, and they saw the butterfly. It was as if Uncle Charlie had been fulfilled, and he was finally at peace. She sighed as the images of his life paraded again through her mind. Each one seemed to stab at her heart with more force than the one preceding it. Finally, and without warning the tears came, flooding her eyes, and she publicly sobbed. The bartender came over to touch her shoulder and handed her a tissue.

"Everything alright?" He asked concerned.

"Yeah. Thanks...everything's alright." Leaving the bar, she pushed the thoughts of Charlie from her mind and called Dean.

"I'm coming home baby."

"You sound tired...I'm glad you're coming home. It must be over with Uncle Charlie. Hill called, he has a buyer for your query...needs the full story with copies of photographs for the client by the end of the month." Silence.

"Nell, did you hear me?"

"I can't deal with that right now for awhile...it'll have to wait, but there's not going to be no story," she said defiantly.

"You OK?" She could hear the concern in his voice. A silent smile crossed her face, as she blew her nose.

"...Oh...oh, sometimes it causes me to tremble!"

CHAPTER SIXTEEN

DETROIT, MICHIGAN, THANKSGIVING DAY, 2002

*T*HANKSGIVING DINNER WAS unusually strained and quiet. Nell was relieved when the day was coming to an end. For the first time, she could remember she felt awkward in her mother's presence. Dean had watched the tension between the two women most of the afternoon, and felt helpless and uncomfortable. He quickly excused himself after dinner, and retreated away to another part of the house to watch football games on television for the rest of the evening. Mae still sat at the table praising the meal, while Nell busied herself clearing the table and storing the leftover food in the refrigerator.

Each time she returned into the dining room from the kitchen, she carefully apprised her mother, who now sat quietly staring out the window. She has been avoiding me ever since I came back from the Cove, Nell thought to herself. I know she has...or perhaps, am I imagining things? Our telephone calls have been unusually short and constrained...almost meaningless. I know for sure she changes the subject whenever I mention anything about the Cove. Obviously, she doesn't want to talk about it.

Perhaps, Nell thought, it was her own guarded behavior that was making things difficult between them. She had only tried to talk in generalities about the beauty of the people she met in the Cove, intentionally staying away from the violence, and the Cromwell family. She had told Dean, but had awkwardly talked around it with Mae.

"Mother would you like a cup of tea? Dean has some good green tea." She carried a cup and pitcher of hot water. Mae sat absolutely-still at the table, as Nell stood across from her. She didn't respond, but quietly looked out the window. It was snowing, and she focused on the rose garden at the rear of the house. The last dried buds still on the vines looked like the heads of stick men against the background of the falling snow. She pushed the image aside and turned to face Nell.

"I'm sure they told you about what they did to Charlie, and the killing down there."

Mae's statement virtually exploded between them. To Nell, it felt as if all the air in the room was being sucked out. She didn't answer as she struggled to take a deep breath wanting to slow her beating heart. She didn't look at her mother, rather she stood where she was as glued to the spot, looking at the floor. Well, she thought I did want to talk about this, but is this a good time, she wondered. I really, just wanted to sit and have her tell me things about the history of the family that was never shared with me before she passes on.

"Oh mother," she finally stammered, before Mae cut

her off.

"Eva probably didn't want to hold it anymore after all these years. She always been basically a very religious person." Nell sat the cup, and the teapot on the table, while holding her mother's eyes

"What, how did you know Mother? Did Uncle Charlie tell you? Why didn't you tell me that you and daddy lived down there when all this happened?"

"Too painful I guess," Mae sighed, couldn't betray Charlie either. I was one of the teacher's helpers at that little schoolhouse out in them cotton fields. Knew each one of them little children. Smartest one was Eva...and another one called 'little David. It was me took that picture of the school children. I was shocked when I saw it in Charlie's old footlocker, but I couldn't tell you then.

"But mother, why didn't you? You didn't say anything, you was real guarded then."

"Wrong time Nell...too much going on in my head back then." She shuffled in her seat to face Nell more directly. "After you went to the Cove I figured we would have our time to talk, but don't know who took that other picture of Louise and her baby. Me and your Daddy had left by then." Shocked Nell sat down. It's finally out in the open, she thought, relieved. But the air in the room still felt heavy to her as her voice whispered into it.

"How did you find out about the killing, mother... did you know the Cromwell family, or the person they killed?"

"Your Uncle Charlie told me about the killing a long time ago. I was happy they killed that little bastard. Them Cromwell boys raped every black woman they could. Yes, I was happy Charlie told me. He told me right after he came to live with us, swore me to secrecy and I kept his secret all those years...didn't tell anybody, not even your father." Mae looked away through the window at the rose garden again. The snow was coming down heavier.

"I knew if you found Eva alive, and she found out who you were, she would eventually tell you. Eva was such a pretty little black child. I remember seeing her the last time before Grady and me, we was being taken to the train station. She was dumping the chamber pots for Shugababy off in the distance...just a pretty little barefoot child walking in the morning mist. Nell's mind spun around and around. So much she wanted to know about the Cromwell's, but instead asked about the note Charlie had left in the footlocker.

"So mother you knew what Uncle Charlie meant about taking his ashes back to the Cove where he became a man? You think it was because of the killing?"

"I knew what he meant child...all us that lived that life knew what Charlie meant. Taking a human life is the hardest thing a grown man can do...and Charlie's, he was just a boy. He be one of a precious few blacks got away killing a white man in this country."

"It wasn't just Uncle Charlie mother...Eva and Louise too. They all helped. Nobody will ever know who actually killed him. But I'm glad they killed him. He raped Louise." Nell was surprised at her words. They sounded angry and vindictive in the room. "She was just a child'" Nell whispered as to herself. "I'm glad they killed him," she said more resolved.

"Me too," Mae said taking Nell's hands across the table. "Its bad, not feeling safe when you're a child," Mae continued. "No black person, especially little girls. they were never safe down there...specially the colored ones. Soon as one started to come into womanhood, the men, you know... Unless she had a real protective father, the trashiest men you ever seen would be around her like bees after blossoms. Lot'a babies born that way, just messing up little girl's lives." She took her hand back from Nell's and brought them to her face as ashamed.

"Some them baby's the midwives gave the fever," her voice stumbled and she took a deep breath. Looking past Nell at the garden, her eyes settled on the dead rose buds. "Others, though they just took those babies into the families, no shame...maybe sometimes raised by a family member in another state, or something."

"Gave the fever? Mother what does that mean?" She reached for her mother's hand again as Mae's eye misted into tears.

"Mother...what are you talking about?" Mae's face was stern as she looked into Nell's eyes again.

"The old folks, specially the old women knew how...right after birth...the practice was passed down from the slave women. Many of them didn't want their children raised in slavery, or if their slave masters had raped them, right after the birth of the child, the midwife would push a dirty, rusty pin into the crown of the child's head, hiding it under the hair where it couldn't be seen." Nell sat shocked as her mother continued.

"The baby's crying couldn't be stopped; so the old folks, they knew to give the child a sugar tit laced with a little rum, or pergoric. Wouldn't be long before the fever came, and the child would soon pass. Nobody knew the wiser."

As if she read Nell's mind, Mae broke eye contact and looked down at the table, anxiously rubbing her hands. She finally shuffled her feet nervously under the table and stared out the window again. Nell, shaken and breathing hard followed her gaze, as an uncomfortable silence settled into the room. Outside a strong wind had started to blow and it rattled the windows in the old colonial. The snow was falling heavier and swirling into drifts. They sat, not speaking, each frozen into their own thoughts for a long time. Off in the distance the roar of the crowd could be heard from the television. Still staring out the window, Mae finally broke the silence.

"Looks like traveling going to get pretty bad out there. You reckon I can get Dean away from them games long enough to drive me home?"

"I'll take you home mother when you're ready to go."

"I'm ready...if you are, and I'm glad you finally know everything", she said reaching for her purse. "The old folks told me long ago most folks have secrets they never share with anyone. Cause when they do they betray a trust. As much as I wanted to tell Grady and you, I couldn't betray Charlie; and he also never betrayed me." Mae wiped at the tears. A stern look crossed her face, as she quietly followed Nell toward the door.

"We can talk more tomorrow, better days are coming," she said closing the door behind her.

"...Tremble, tremble...tremble."